TED TAYLER

# PRESSURE POINT

## By Ted Tayler

**The Freeman Files**

*Fatal Decision*

*Last Orders*

*Pressure Point*

*Deadly Formula*

*Final Deal*

*Barking Mad*

*Creature Discomforts*

*Silent Terror*

*Night Train*

*All Things Bright*

*Buried Secrets*

*A Genuine Mistake*

*Strange Beginnings*

*Dead Reckoning*

*A Normal November*

*Into the Sunlight*

*Tame the Storm*

*One True Friend*

*Whispered Truths*

*A Morning Murder*

*Quick to Anger*

*Red Herring Season*

*Gathering Clouds*

*Still Standing*

Vinci Books

vinci-books.com

Published by Vinci Books Ltd in 2025

1


This work is a work of fiction. Names, characters, places and incidents are the product of the author's imagination or are used fictitiously. Any resemblance to actual persons, living or dead, places and incidents is entirely coincidental.

A CIP catalogue record for this book is available from the British Library.
Paperback ISBN: 9781036704896

# Chapter One

***Sunday, 12 June 2011***

LAURA MALLINDER PREPARED to leave for work at half-past five in the evening.

Only a three-hour stint tonight. A typical Sunday. She had her regular clients to see to and perhaps a phone enquiry. With luck, she could earn one hundred pounds. Not a bad rate of pay for three hours. Twice the national average for women.

When she left Bedminster Down Secondary School in 2000 with seven GCSEs, she had no burning ambition to continue studying. University wasn't for the likes of her and other family members. Her Dad worked in a factory, her Mum served dinners at her old school, and her two older brothers worked in the building trade.

Laura wanted something different. Her best friends Mo and JoJo enrolled at the City of Bristol College to gain hair-dressing and beauty therapy qualifications. She followed in their wake as she wasn't ready to commit to a full-time job.

Instead, she studied Business and Professional Services. That seemed ironic now.

When she left the College in the summer of 2002, she landed a job in a solicitor's office. Laura found it boring. She hated seeing the same people every single day.

At her first firm, the partners were all men. A couple had wandering hands. They seemed to think the office junior was there to give them a cheap thrill. Laura complained to one of the older secretaries.

"We've had to put up with that too, Laura. It goes with the territory. Why complain?"

"It's not right," said Laura.

"The partners will be here long after you've gone. So bite your tongue and hope they take on a new girl in a month or two. They're like children with a shiny new toy."

Laura stayed until the end of the month. There was no sign of a new arrival to disrupt the constant harassment. So she signed on at a secretarial agency, and the work took her to dozens of different working environments across Bristol for over three years. Large office blocks with open-plan layouts and hundreds of employees. Offices with plenty of banter to fill the empty gaps in her working day. There were smaller firms too, where she had a room to herself and a boss who rarely visited the office. The work was still dull, but it brought in a living wage.

That was part of the problem. Times were tough for a young girl wanting to leave home and strike out on her own. So, when Mo and JoJo suggested they rent a place together, she jumped at the chance. All three were single. There were plenty of boys in the pubs and clubs they frequented. Times had changed from Mum's day when she met Laura's Dad at the youth club at fourteen and walked up the aisle a virgin at nineteen.

The rented house wasn't a palace; it stood on a large housing estate with its share of social problems. The parties they held were wild. Laura lost track of the number of men who stayed over. Mo and JoJo proved more interested in the late nights, the drinking, dancing and recreational drugs than dealing with the housekeeping. Laura enjoyed the drinking and dancing, but the novelty wore off after three years. The temporary work from the agency was still well-paid and consistent, even if it bored her to tears. How could she break this vicious circle?

Laura recalled the night her life changed as she smoothed her short skirt and checked her stockings were pristine before she began the fifteen-minute walk to work. She had just ended a relationship with a twenty-two-year-old guy from Bradley Stoke. They met in a nightclub and saw one another for several months.

Not long after they broke up, he moved to the Midlands. It was a relief. Laura had wondered whether he was the one for a while, but he got too clingy. Plenty of other fish in the sea.

Her friends had arranged to visit a new wine bar that had opened in Redcliffe. Laura had nothing better to do, so she tagged along. While Mo and JoJo bought the drinks, she guarded a corner table as best she could. Unfortunately, the place was filling up, and soon it would be standing-room-only.

"Laura? Is that you?"

A slim, dark-haired girl had leaned towards her, gripping a large glass of white wine.

"Blimey, Carol Gullis? I haven't seen you since we sat our Geography GCSE."

"I know, what a bleeding disaster. Answer one question from Sections A, B and C. What did we do? Answered both questions in section A and the first in Section B. We couldn't fathom how we only found time to do three of the six questions. Silly mares."

"Are you with someone?" Laura asked.

"No, are you? Can I take the weight off and sit for a while?"

"My housemates are at the bar getting drinks. Please, sit here; it's not a problem. You look great."

She did; Carol's clothes looked to bear designer labels and her hair, which at school had been in bunches secured by elastic bands, now fell over her shoulders.

"You look good yourself. What are you doing these days?" asked Carol.

"I've been with a secretarial agency for just over three years. There is plenty of variety in my place of work when I'm temping around the city, but it's boring as hell. Where did you go after school? The Civil Service, wasn't it?"

"Yeah," Carol sighed, "the treadmill. Nine to five. Week after bloody week in offices out at Filton.

At that moment, her friends returned carrying two rounds of drinks.

"We thought it saved time," said Mo.

"It's heaving in here. So who's this then?" said JoJo.

Laura had made the introductions. Mo and JoJo were on a mission. They wanted to get their drinks down their necks and move on to a nightclub. So they begged Laura and Carol to drink up and accompany them.

"You go, Laura," said Carol, "time for me to get my beauty sleep. Here's my card; slip it in your purse. Call me if you're interested. Maybe we can meet up another time?"

"I'd like that," Laura had replied, taking the card and slipping it into her purse without a second glance. Mo and JoJo stood by the bar door beckoning for her to hurry. The night was a blur now as Laura stood thinking back five years. Too much to drink, a dodgy kebab and a sick day were as much as she could remember.

Laura had found the card in her purse later that week and given Carol a call.

"Cleo's, Amber speaking. How can I help you?"

Laura didn't know what to say. It sounded like her school friend's voice if she was trying to sound sexy. Was she messing around?

"Carol? It's Laura; we bumped into one another the other night in the wine bar. I thought this was your mobile number. Who's Amber?"

"Oh, hi Laura," giggled Carol, "this is what I do now. It pays a helluva lot better than the Civil Service."

"Where are you?" asked Laura.

"Cleopatra's, it's a massage parlour," replied Carol.

"That's gross, Carol," said Laura, "and dangerous, surely? There are many stories about those places being raided by the police because of what goes on."

"I work for a lady called Maggie Monk. She runs a chain of shops across the West. They're not brothels. We give a sensual massage, and there's a price list for extras. Intercourse is forbidden. If you get caught with condoms in your handbag, Maggie will sack you on the spot."

"How can you stand it? I don't know if I could do that," said Laura.

"How many hours a week do you work?" asked Carol. "Thirty-six? What do you take home? Three hundred quid a week? I work twenty-four hours in total over seven days. Depending on the extras my customers want, I can earn six to eight hundred pounds."

"You make it sound so easy," Laura had said.

"It's the same as everything else, sweetheart," Carol replied, "once you get over the first time, it's a breeze."

Laura promised to think about it. Carol begged her to keep in touch even if she turned down the chance to work as a masseuse.

That had been five years ago.

Mo gave Laura the push she needed. Another month had arrived when her friend's housekeeping money was late or non-existent. Laura had found another pile of dirty laundry to clear before she started her own. It was Monday, and the weekend had seen another succession of late nights and partying. Something had to give. She'd kept quiet for long enough.

"I know what you're going to say," sighed Mo when Laura said they needed to talk. Her mate flopped onto the sofa and burst into tears. JoJo wandered through from the kitchen with a coffee. She had just surfaced, too and looked like death.

"Why did you have to upset her?" she moaned, "she's up the duff and can't remember who she was with when it happened."

"Well, things would have had to change," Laura replied, "I can't go on carrying the extra load. I keep making up the housekeeping because you've maxed out your credit cards on clothes, drink and dope. Nothing ever gets done around here unless I do it. So I'm moving back in with my parents until I can find somewhere else to live on my own."

Laura left JoJo comforting Mo on the sofa and went upstairs to pack. Those two deserved one another. Whether they could sort out a future for themselves wasn't clear. Laura doubted it. She'd tried to make it work, but some people think they can keep taking and never give a thing in return — time to move on.

"There's always a place for you here, sweetheart, you know that," her Mum said when Laura rang to check if moving back to her old bedroom was okay. They welcomed her home with open arms.

"Are you still working at the solicitor's office?" her Dad had asked as he carried a case upstairs to her room.

"I've been temping, Dad, but I'm looking for a more permanent position."

"Good. We'd love to see you settled. You're still young, but flitting from job to job doesn't help in the long run."

"You think Mr Right will be more likely to find me if I stay in the same place for forty years like you, eh Dad?"

Her Dad laughed.

"I hope he wouldn't take that long, darling. You're as pretty as a picture. You're always smiling and have a bubbly, outgoing character. Just like your mother did when I met her at the youth club. Love at first sight."

Fate lent a hand two months later. Laura had been temping in Brislington for several months, covering maternity leave. When the boss called her into the office, she had expected it to be news of the date the other girl returned to work. It was far worse. The secretarial agency was bankrupt, and everyone on their books was now a free agent.

Then the boss added that the girl Laura covered for was indeed returning to work next month. Laura was distraught. The firm paid the agency, and she received her salary cheque direct into her bank account on the first Monday of each month. It was unlikely that she would get paid for what she'd worked so far this month. The boss could tell she was upset. He agreed to pay her until the end of the month. Two weeks at the rate he paid the other secretary. Less than the agency charged him, but it was something. Laura told her parents when she got home.

"It may prove to be a blessing," her Dad had said, "this might be your chance to find that more permanent position you spoke of when you moved back home."

"Don't worry about the money, sweetheart," her Mum said, "we can look after you until you find a job. There are a healthy number of vacancies at the moment. So it shouldn't take you long."

Laura had finished the temporary assignment in Brislington. She looked at the parlous state of her bank account and searched through her purse for that business card Carol had given her. She called from home after her parents had left for work.

"Cleo's, Ebony speaking. How can I help you?"

"Is Carol there? Sorry, is Amber working today?"

"Please hold,"

Laura soon realised the girl had her hand over the mouthpiece. The conversation became muffled, but she picked up the gist of it.

"Hey, Amber. It's a woman on the phone asking for you. Do you see female punters?"

"Hello?" Carol replied.

"It's me," said Laura, "and no offence, I don't want to book you. I'm out of work. I need money. Is there any chance of getting an interview with this Maggie Monk?"

"Oh, Laura, I'm so sorry to hear that. Unfortunately, Maggie's not here at present. We've got branches in Bath, Devizes and Swindon that she's visiting today. I'll leave a message for her. Can she call you on this number?"

"God, no, this is my parent's home phone. They can never find out I'm even considering working there. I'll give you my mobile number."

When she ended the call, Laura sat on the hall carpet and wondered what the hell she had just done. It was one thing finding the nerve to make a call to her school friend; how on earth could she steel herself to do the same job as Carol?

She considered the facts; it had been three months since that chance meeting in the wine bar. Carol was working at the same parlour. The place kept busy enough for more than one girl on each shift. The money must still be good. Money was what she needed. What did she have to lose? It was only an interview at this stage.

Maggie Monk called the following day.

"Is that Gem? Amber gave me your number. So I understand you're looking for a job?"

Carol had given her boss a false name. That was quick thinking. If she got cold feet and couldn't go through with it, Maggie Monk would be none the wiser.

"Yes, I'm Gem. I told Amber I needed a change of scene."

"Age?"

"Two months older than Amber,"

"Have you done this line of work before?"

"Never,"

"That's okay. We can train you on the job. Has Amber told you the rules? There's no funny business in any of my places. I intend to keep the doors open. I don't want the law sniffing around every waking hour."

"We know one another well. Amber talked me through the procedures. She thought I could be an asset to your business."

"I'll need to meet you to check if that's true. Amber said that you're a good-looking girl. Can you come to Cleopatra's in Knowle tomorrow morning at ten o'clock?"

Here goes nothing, Laura thought.

Laura found herself in a lounge area as she stepped off

Green Lane and made her way through the black entrance doors. The walls and floor were crimson, and the lighting was harsh and bright. The four-seater black leather sofas on either side of the room looked comfortable and welcoming. There were glass-topped coffee tables, potted plants and magazine racks by each sofa. High on the wall above each sofa hung a large TV screen showing daytime TV. She checked her watch — two minutes to ten.

Just as well, she had worn her watch today; there were no clocks in sight. At the Reception desk stood three women of similar height and build. Laura imagined Ebony was the dusky beauty beaming a smile her way. The two white girls beside her differed in age by at least ten years, maybe more. All three wore crisp white blouses, and as Laura neared the counter, she saw that a black miniskirt completed the branch's outfit. There was no sign of Carol. Maybe this was one of her days off.

"You must be Gem," said Ebony, "Maggie told us you were coming in today. Would you like a coffee?"

"Thanks, that would be great. Is Maggie here yet?"

"She's running late," said Ebony. The other two women giggled.

Laura wondered if that meant it was a regular occurrence.

"I'm supposed to give you the grand tour," the young girl continued. She led Laura along the corridor off the Reception area and into the first room.

"This is where the staff amenities are. Lockers for your belongings during a shift. Tea and coffee-making facilities. How do you take your coffee?"

"White, no sugar, thanks," Laura replied.

While they drank their coffees, Ebony asked if Laura had always lived in Bristol and what she did with her spare time. Ebony's family arrived in St Paul's in the early Sixties from Jamaica. It appeared she was a keen sports fan and watched football, rugby and ice hockey when not working.

As they made their way into the corridor again, Laura noticed mirrors and lights everywhere. It made the place seem far more extensive, and the decorations added to the ambience. But, if she forgot what went on behind each of the five doors, it felt like a pleasant working environment. It was classier than a few offices they had lumbered her with while temping.

"I'm sure Maggie will be here in a few minutes," said Ebony, "we'd better get back to Reception. You can see that none of the five doors is open now. We're open from ten in the morning to ten at night. Janina and Kathy, who you saw earlier, were waiting for their first clients. The other girls were still getting their rooms ready when you arrived."

Ebony had offered to show Laura how to answer the phone and book in the clients. Each girl who worked at the parlour had a card detailing the extras price list. If they hadn't committed the details to memory and destroyed it, that card was the first thing they grabbed in a police raid. They were to collect that before they picked up discarded items of clothing.

"The booking form is basic," Ebony had explained. "The guy's name, the time he arrived, the girl he went with, and the straight massage cost. It's always cash, which goes into the money box here at Reception."

That part seemed straightforward enough, Laura thought.

Ebony continued with the tour.

"Maggie charges us for sundries such as oils, tissues, tea, coffee and milk. That's a standard sum per shift. It varies from parlour to parlour."

"When I answer the phone, what do I say?"

"The name of the parlour, and can I help you? Don't say more than you have to, in case it's a reporter or the law. Just quote the opening times and the cost of a massage. If they ask, tell them who's working today. It's on a list at Reception. When it's a regular calling, they see the girl they ask for unless she's unavailable. After that, we take our turns in alphabetical order. So, I pick up a client before you if you want to use your name."

"I don't suppose Ebony is your real name?"

"Of course not. I ain't telling you what it is either,"

Laura smiled. If Ebony showed caution about revealing too much, then she could follow suit. Carol had kept her real identity secret so far. Why change things?

"I think I'll stick with Gem. I can't risk anyone learning I work here."

"Gem's a cool name. I still earn money before you, though," Ebony grinned.

The telephone rang, and Ebony swung into action. Laura heard footsteps outside the main door. High heels. The middle-aged woman who entered was short, stocky and smartly dressed. She looked every inch a businesswoman. Her hair may have been fair when younger, but it was cut short today, and the ash-blonde colouring gave her a sophisticated look. No way would anyone ever say Maggie Monk was mutton dressed as lamb.

"Are you Amber's friend?" she asked, offering a manicured hand towards Laura. "Has Ebony looked after you? I'm sorry that I'm late. It's my fault for being successful. I won't be in a rush to open another branch for a while."

"You need a massage," said Laura, shaking her hand and smiling. "You've come to the right place if you need to relax."

Ebony had entered the latest customer's details into the book and overheard the comment. This new girl knew how to sweet-talk the boss. They needed to watch Gem. She would steal their regulars if they weren't careful. The girl looked pretty and confident with it.

"I can offer you three shifts to begin with," said Maggie. "Monday, Wednesday and Friday. When can you start?"

"Next Monday," Laura had replied.

"We'll train you here first, then the following week, you'll work at the branch in Bath. I'll study the rotas over there when I visit next week. I'll guarantee there will be the same number of hours total, but the days and the shifts might vary. How does that sound?"

Laura heard herself reply, "It sounds fine," but she felt anything but fine inside. She was as nervous as hell.

LAURA MALLINDER CLOSED the door of the two-bedroomed terraced house she called home and walked briskly towards the main road. It was a pleasant evening. The afternoon showers had disappeared; tonight promised to be rewarding at Gentle Touch.

She had long since given up on her dream of finding something different to fill her working day. Her life as a masseuse was no different to the treadmill Carol Gullis felt she was on in the Civil Service. The upside was this particular treadmill paid well.

Over the past five years, Laura met men of all ages from all walks of life. That surprised her in the beginning. She had an image in her head of the sad individual forced to pay for any sexual experience. However, her time working for Maggie Monk showed her that it took all sorts, like everything in life.

Maggie had kept her promise. Janina and Kathy helped her with training in how speed, pressure, and contact were crucial elements in enhancing the customer experience. They also advised her to avoid the pimps that lay in wait to exploit vulnerable girls. Laura followed their tips and tricks to become skilled in her role and avoid the pitfalls. Maggie soon added Gem's name to the list at Cleopatra's in Bath.

Laura moved out of her parent's home within the first year. She bought a modest one-bedroomed flat in Kingswood and worked in the Bath and Bristol parlours. When the Gentle Touch brand name was added to her growing chain of premises at the end of 2007, Maggie asked Laura if she was interested in moving to Swindon. She wanted someone experienced to run the business in Broadgreen day-to-day.

"I want to be less hands-on with these new parlours," she told Laura.

Don't we all, Laura thought, but the money on offer would be better. If she lived in Swindon, she would save the travelling costs backwards and forwards from Kingswood on the bus to the two parlours where she worked.

She sold her flat while the market was high, and although prices plummeted because of the ensuing financial crisis, Laura came through unscathed. Some businesses suffered a recession, but theirs carried on as if nothing had happened.

Broadgreen was a district frequented by streetwalkers when she moved there. There was less evidence of girls loitering on Manchester Road these days. Why kerb crawl when there were the internet and smartphones? The girls did most of their business indoors, not in a car or a back alley.

Laura had never been propositioned on the streets,

walking to and from the parlour. She took care to cover the provocative nature of her work clothes as she made frequent visits. Swindon had several volunteer organisations attempting to clean up the streets. They weren't happy about Gentle Touch being in the Broadgreen district, but they had softer targets to strike.

Gentle Touch had never had a raid. There were never any lousy reviews on Trip Advisor, and Maggie's books passed an auditor's scrutiny every April. He was a regular customer in the Knowle parlour, but he was a straight arrow as an accountant.

Laura had arrived at the entrance to the alleyway. The Turkish barber's on the ground floor were closed until tomorrow morning. Maggie had leased the shop to the guy eighteen months ago. Before that, it had been a record shop. Laura unlocked the door halfway along the alleyway and climbed the stairs. Camille would be there soon. Time to get the rooms ready for their first customer.

After Laura had stocked each room with fresh towels, she heard the click-clack of Camille's high heels on the stairs. The Thai woman arrived in the UK twenty years ago. She was married with three children. Laura was unsure how old she was but based on the age of her eldest son; it was unlikely she would see forty again.

The other girls had asked Camille why she worked at the parlour. The tiny woman shrugged and said it was necessary for her and her husband to earn as much as possible. They had a family at home who needed their support. She had no qualifications. A cleaning job only brought in enough to feed her children.

Laura knew her colleague never wasted time on idle chat. Camille turned up for her shift, did what was required and then went home. She found her in the small staff room, checking her hair and make-up in the mirror.

"You look great, Camille,"

Camille nodded and gave Laura a brief smile. Then she rubbed cream into her hands and walked through Reception to await her six o'clock appointment. Laura did the same. Just another Sunday evening.

At half-past seven, both girls took a break. They recorded the details of three satisfied customers for each masseuse and put the cash in the money box. Camille brought two coffees through to Reception. Laura was waiting for Jeff Naylor, one of her regulars, to arrive. Camille was waiting for her last customer this evening.

"Is Maggie coming, Gem?" asked Camille.

"Don't worry. She rang to confirm she would step in to cover for you," said Laura.

"Good. I must get home. My husband is not well. I'm sorry."

"You can't help that, Camille."

Laura had called Maggie to warn her she would be alone when Camille left. Laura worked until nine. Maggie had a strict rule that there were always at least two girls in the parlour on any shift. Although this never became an issue on a weekday, most parlours had five or six girls available throughout the twelve hours opening time.

On a shorter Sunday evening shift, the two girls on duty accepted the odd phone booking. It filled the gaps between their regulars and boosted their earnings. If nobody called, they used their spare time at the end of the shift to get the used towels into the washing machine and give the parlour a general clean.

Laura hoped Maggie didn't mind giving her a helping hand later. An early night would be welcome.

Maggie Monk was running late. That was nothing new. When Gem called to warn of the lack of cover, Maggie had rung several girls to see if they could dash over to help. She couldn't believe how many had their phones switched off — what a bloody nuisance.

Gem caused no bother, though, and the parlour was one of the better-performing businesses in her portfolio. So Maggie could stand the hassle this one time, as long as Gem didn't make a habit of it.

Maggie was far later than intended when she parked outside the barber's shop. She hurried into the alleyway; the door was open. That was odd. Camille would have left ages ago. If Gem booked in a late caller, she should have locked up after he arrived. They didn't encourage walk-ins. They tended to be riff-raff, and Maggie wasn't in business to cater to the likes of them.

The lights were on in Reception and along the corridor; the cash box was in the drawer. Gem and Camille appeared to have been busy tonight.

It was silent now. Maggie checked the rooms; someone was in Room One.

"Gem?" she called. There was no reply.

Maggie couldn't hear a thing. She eased open the door.

Gem lay sprawled, fully clothed, face down on the floor. The room was a mess, with blood everywhere. There must have been a mighty struggle. Maggie closed the door and staggered back to Reception.

What a mess. Why would anyone want to stab Gem to death like that?

# Chapter Two

***Tuesday, 24 April 2018***

"ANOTHER DAY, ANOTHER COLLAR, GUV," said Neil Davis when Gus Freeman exited the lift in the CRT office. It was ten to nine on the second day of a new week for the Crime Review Team housed in the Old Police Station. The team knew that last week had been full of incidents.

Frank North, the older man with the adjoining allotment to Gus, had been murdered. Gus had escaped an attempt on his life as he drove to work. Those responsible for the violent attacks and operating a cannabis farm behind Cambrai Terrace in the village of Urchfont were either dead or in custody.

On Saturday afternoon, Gus exposed Krystal Warner as the killer of her best friend Trudi Villiers in 2003.

Yesterday, while the team attended a safeguarding briefing at the Police HQ, Gus had retrieved his beloved Ford Focus from the garage. As a result, his ten-year-old car now possessed a new windscreen and driver's headrest.

WHEN GUS RETURNED to work as a civilian consultant, the Krystal Warner item was the only one that should have registered. ACC Kenneth Truelove had convinced the retired detective his old-style methods were just what was needed to solve a series of stubborn cold cases. Gus wondered if he had been wise to accept the challenge. His team wondered how they would keep up their rapid success rate.

"I see you're up to speed, Neil," Gus replied without smiling.

"Sorry, guv," said Lydia, "I resisted the temptation to ring them over the weekend. That was hard enough. I blurted out the news as soon as they arrived yesterday morning."

"Neil and I were sorry to miss the fun, guv," said Alex Hardy, "but it was a team effort. I'm sure you'll pass that on to the top brass in Devizes when you report to them."

"Never fear, Alex. I'm a strong believer in giving credit where it's due. So before I get summoned to attend London Road, I suggest we get everything up to date on the Freeman file. Once that's achieved, we can forward a copy to DS Geoff Mercer."

"He'll still be busy with the Rexha gang and the fallout from their arrest," said Neil. "We may have a few days before we learn what's next on our agenda."

"There was me thinking you arrived early this morning because you were eager to get cracking on another puzzle, not looking for a holiday," said Gus as he looked up from his computer screen.

He could only see the top of three heads beavering away on the task he had just set them. He smiled. There might be an odd bump in the road, but his team was shaping up well. He glanced at a blank space on the far wall. He needed to check the translation.

*Torquem alius, alium diem* could become their Latin motto. Admittedly, it was a bit presumptuous on the back of only two wins; but if they didn't blow their own trumpet, no other bugger would.

THE MORNING PASSED QUICKLY as the team removed the Villiers case debris.

Wallboards and flip charts were cleaned or replaced. Paperwork got added to the physical files forwarded to them only a week ago. The Freeman file looked in pristine condition. Every interview was presented in full. No discrepancies in the reports were provided by whichever two officers attended. They had followed every clue or potential lead they unearthed. The conclusions drawn by Gus Freeman from the details gathered by himself and his team could get scrutinised with no doubts harboured of their integrity. The computer file didn't have a padlock, but the case was watertight.

Lydia looked at the only item they hadn't removed. The map of the town. Should it stay in place? Alex saw her hand hover over the first pin.

"Take it down, Lydia. I don't remember another murder in this town in the years I've been a copper. We're off to pastures new, I reckon."

"Variety is the spice of life," said Neil.

The phone rang at one-forty-five pm. Gus guessed who was calling.

"Good afternoon, Sir," he said.

"Sorry? Freeman, is that you? It's Truelove here. Can you drive over for a chat?"

"Certainly, Sir," replied Gus, "do you know what Kassie Trotter has been baking over the weekend?"

"You'll have to wait and see, Freeman. I had to attend meetings this morning with the new Chief Constable. She's eager to meet you."

"Another female in your life, Sir? Where did the Police and Crime Commissioner find this one?"

"In the Midlands, Freeman. Look, this phone conversation is preventing you from reaching my office. Please tell me you're on your way?"

"I apologise, Sir. I hoped to avoid negotiating the heavy traffic on London Road for as long as possible at this time of the afternoon. I'm running to the lift now."

Gus slammed the phone on his desk.

"We'll see you in the morning then, I assume?" said Lydia.

"When you'll be carrying folders with details of our new case," said Neil, rubbing his hands.

"Don't count your chickens, Neil. The PCC has appointed a female Chief Constable. Let's wait until we learn her approach to this team."

Gus had been right about the congested roads. The temporary traffic lights slowed progress to a crawl. If there had been a posse of workmen in sight as he threaded his way through the centre of Devizes, it would have been excusable. The only advantage of not arriving at Wiltshire Police HQ before ten to three was the prospect of teatime.

He was a familiar face in Reception now, and the officer on the desk recognised him. Police officers are another breed of animal that rarely forgets. The young man looked him in the eye as he nodded a silent greeting. Then his gaze descended as he checked for gardening trousers and dirty shoes.

"You're out of luck today," said Gus, resplendent in a short-sleeved blue shirt, black trousers and shiny shoes. He'd stuffed his tie in his pocket, deference to the warm day.

He took the stairs two at a time. The administration area was a hive of activity. Vera Jennings prepared to deliver refreshments to the ACC's office. The delicate bone china cups and saucers he recalled from his first visit were back in service. That meant only one thing. The new Chief Constable really couldn't wait to meet him.

"Good afternoon, Gus," said Vera, "we had almost given up on you. The ACC has been like a cat on hot bricks. When I entered his office earlier, he stood by the window, checking the car park for your arrival."

Gus didn't see why that felt out of the ordinary. Truelove spent most of his working day standing by that window. His executive chair would be in demand when he retired next year. 'As new. One careful owner.'

The Gothic vision that was Kassie Trotter emerged from the dark recesses of the passageway leading to Geoff Mercer's office. The top shelf of her tea trolley lay bare.

"No opportunity for baking this weekend, Kassie?" asked Gus, a trifle concerned.

Kassie nodded towards the ACC's door.

"Blame her," she replied, "her Ladyship's not a fan."

"Vera can slip me a custard cream to satisfy my cravings."

Kassie tapped the side of her nose.

"All is not lost, Mr Freeman. I'm hiding my Chelsea buns under a cloth on the bottom shelf. It will be business as usual when she's not in his room. Today, if you want to sink your teeth into my buns, I can put them in a doggy bag for you when you leave."

"Now there's an offer that's impossible to resist," said

Gus, heading for the ACC's office before things became more surreal. He tapped on the door.

"Enter," came the reply.

Gus crossed the threshold. Vera followed right behind him with the tray.

The ACC sat at his desk. A short, stern-looking woman stood by the window.

"Come along, Freeman," said Truelove, "we haven't got all afternoon. Thank you, Vera. A cup of tea will be most welcome."

Gus remained standing. He knew his place.

Vera was already leaving. The new Chief Constable spoke as soon as the door closed behind her.

"Good afternoon, Mr Freeman. My name is Sandra Plunkett. You're with us on a temporary assignment, I understand?"

"That's correct, Ma'am."

"The Crime Review Team was my initiative," explained the ACC, "we couldn't have hoped for a better start. Two cold cases have been solved since the ninth of the month. I knew Gus Freeman was the best detective for the job."

"I'm not a fan of parachuting retired officers into the workplace. There's usually a good reason for them being retired. It doesn't send the right message to rank-and-file officers struggling to make their way up the chain of command."

Gus picked up his cup and saucer. He didn't feel the need to comment. If this new broom wanted him to scuttle off to his retirement home and the allotment, fine by him, he would miss it now that he was back in the swing of things, but he'd never stay where he wasn't wanted.

"I'm sure we agree that while the CRT produces positive results, we should support them as much as we can," said the ACC. The sweat on his brow owed little to his tea cup's warmth.

"There are various aspects of policing in the county to be reviewed," Sandra Plunkett continued. "Some aspects will require a complete overhaul. Others will disappear. The vision for 2025 sees us move even further away from the service you provided during your time with us, Freeman. Things move far quicker these days."

The bloody traffic through the town centre doesn't, Gus thought.

"Am I to understand my team is under review, Ma'am?" he asked.

"I haven't been in post for enough time to have a timetable yet, Freeman. Let's say; I'll be watching you. Good afternoon."

Sandra Plunkett strutted from the room.

Kenneth Truelove stood and walked to the window; normal service could resume.

"Bloody hell, Freeman. I could have done without that woman becoming my new boss. After last week's coup, I hoped for a honeymoon period, followed by fourteen months of calm waters until my retirement. So sit, man; you're making the place untidy."

"I didn't want to claim the high ground, Sir. Sandra Plunkett and Geoff Mercer could model for the weather house couple."

"From memory, that weather house lady came out when it was sunny and warm. The man's appearance signalled bad weather. I think the roles would reverse if Mercer and Plunkett ever got involved. Our new Chief Constable signals dark clouds ahead. On the other hand, Geoff Mercer seems to be in far better humour since you've been with us."

"I try my best," said Gus.

The ACC was right. Geoff sat firmly in the CRT corner if push came to shove. Provided the ACC kept the Police and Crime Commissioner happy, his team could complete the programme that had tempted him to return.

"What did you want to talk to me about, Sir? Before Ms Plunkett hijacked this meeting. I take it she's not married."

"There's a press release in a file on my desk somewhere. I'll find it before you leave. What I want to discuss is last week's amazing turnaround. When Brendan Curran was here on Wednesday, you were light-years from solving the Villiers case. I have no idea how you kept your cool after the incident the next morning and then came up with the answers. That was awesome."

"Awesome? I'm surprised to hear you use that American term,"

"Blame my grandchildren, Freeman, and the youngsters my wife and I run into at our meeting house. Somehow, on this occasion, it felt the right expression."

"Thank you, Sir. A team effort, as I'm sure you realise. Despite the obvious reservations of the Chief Constable, Wiltshire Police will benefit significantly from my sojourn. However brief that may be. Davis and Hardy will be better detectives, and young Lydia will outshine the lot of us given the right opportunities."

"You lead by example, Freeman. That's good enough for me. The more knowledge you can pass on to those three, the better. All good things must end, though. I keep harping on about my retirement next year, but I anticipated the CRT still being in place when I left. I dreamed of you training a second or even third batch of likely lads and lasses before you finally retired. Sandra Plunkett might put the skids under that."

"Let's not get ahead of ourselves," cautioned Gus, "we've been very fortunate with our first two cold cases. Unfortunately, they remained unsolved because simple questions didn't get asked at the time. We can appreciate the reasons for that. However, things might have been different if the force had the right resources and adopted a more robust approach to serious crime."

"I think someone has expressed this opinion, Freeman. Unfortunately, we have to operate with the system we have, no matter how much we wish it operated otherwise. Things will never return to before 1965."

"Don't worry, Sir. Nobody outside these four walls will hear that comment. I think the new breed of copper would have a touch of the vapours just reading an account of a hanging, let alone attending one. The black cap had been consigned to history a decade before I joined the force. Several old hands in Salisbury worked on cases where a killer received the death sentence. One of my Sergeants said we would rue the day they withdrew the option. He said no matter how brutal the process appears to the public; they would lobby to reverse the decision in a heartbeat if they saw the horrors carried out in killings he witnessed. Far worse murders get committed today than that old Sergeant could ever imagine. There's no going back, as you say, but will society ever move forward while evil exists among us until it dies a natural death?"

"You're a deep thinker, Freeman. No wonder you get a handle on these cold cases. I imagine you would enjoy a change of scene. What do you know about Swindon?"

"I've spent many wasted hours at Crown Court there, Sir. Other than that, they've got an average football team and a Magic Roundabout. Nothing significant comes to mind from the last hundred-odd years. The town's railway history is a distant memory these days. Is that where our next murder occurred?"

"The victim was Laura Mallinder, a twenty-seven-year-old sex worker. Her employer found her body at nine thirty-five on the evening of Sunday, the twelfth of June 2011. The details are in this folder; if I can find them. So here we are, right next to Sandra Plunkett's life story. Get yourself back to the CRT office and have a read of both files. I haven't discussed this latest case with Geoff Mercer yet, but we'll set up the necessary contacts for you to access the proper personnel at Gablecross. The detectives who investigated the murder are still there. You can use interview rooms, have someone accompany you with a warrant card and so forth. I see no reason you can't continue using the Old Police station as your base. Ask Geoff Mercer for help if that proves an obstacle. I encourage you to continue to use the Hub's research facilities."

"I don't know how we'd cope without it, Sir," replied Gus, tongue firmly in his cheek.

Gus took the two files from the ACC.

"Are any of the serving officers likely to cause us a problem, Sir?" he asked.

"It might be best to consult DS Hardy on that matter, Freeman. He will know the lie of the land. Even though he's been on the sidelines for the past eighteen months, his insight will be better than any gossip I've gleaned. Will there be anything else?"

"I realise you have your hands full with the new Chief Constable and last week's organised crime caper. But I want you to press for a response from OCTF over Frank North's murder. His funeral is next Monday afternoon. Two o'clock at the West Wilts Crematorium."

"I'm not sure I can make it, Freeman. However, I'll

ensure a message reaches Mercer and Ferris that suggests they drum up a few officers to attend. We owe the poor chap that much. As for Brendan Curran and his cronies, I can only promise to do my best. But, rest assured, I've not forgotten the matter."

"Thank you, Sir," said Gus. Time to head home. The school run was over; office workers still had an hour to suffer.

There was nothing to gain from rushing. The Mallinder girl had waited seven years for someone to find her killer. Gus hoped she'd forgive him for not getting his team on her case until the morning.

ONCE BACK INSIDE HIS BUNGALOW, Gus organised a schedule for the days ahead. They would spend the remainder of this working week in preparation for this Mallinder case. If he could get to his allotment over the weekend, it would be a chance to get to grips with the chores May might present. Next Monday afternoon was set aside for Frank's funeral. As for the following Friday, the camera installers had left a message yesterday to say they would arrive at nine am. Gus wondered how long it would take him to learn how to access the feed on his smartphone. Progress can be slow for a sixty-one-year-old when technology is involved. Safety was a priority, though; it would be time well spent.

Thoughts of time spent in Swindon during the next few weeks prompted a quick check of his provisions. He mustn't let this increased activity associated with the consultancy role lead him into bad habits. That's why the allotment had become so important. He had to keep that going to provide his fresh fruit and vegetables. He made a note to visit the supermarket one evening after work to stock up on items he couldn't grow himself.

As he knocked up a mushroom omelette for his evening meal, he decided to call Vera Jennings later. He owed her a night out. Vera had played the role of a stood-up date last Thursday evening. The ploy was to convince anyone associated with the Rexha gang that Gus had died in that morning's assassination attempt. That move had bought the Organised Crime Task Force precious hours as it prepared for its widespread dawn strike on Friday morning. But, unfortunately, the gang were none the wiser until too late.

DI Suzie Ferris had helped with that misdirection. She had arranged for Gus to hide on her father's farm for ten hours. He owed Suzie something too, but how to repay that debt was another matter. The younger woman had made clear her feelings toward him.

Gus tried to put those thoughts out of his head as he ate his meal. The background music didn't help. He had chosen an album at random. Eva Cassidy was easy listening on a warm Spring evening, but Suzie had also picked it when she visited him the other day. Eva was another piece of common ground they shared. He dispensed with the musical accompaniment and concentrated on the Sandra Plunkett file.

Gus poured a glass of white wine and sat in his favourite chair in the lounge. With the ACC's file on his lap, he placed his drink on the table next to him. Under the coaster lay a scrap of paper. He didn't need to rescue it to know what it said. It was a quote that touched his heart after Tess's sudden death. The ACC said earlier today he reckoned he was a deep thinker. He had always thought long and hard about the cases he'd handled. Only after his wife's death did he consider other matters to the same degree.

*'One must first learn to know himself before knowing anything else. Not until a man has inwardly understood himself and then sees the course he is to take does his life gain peace and meaning.'*

He brushed a finger around the coaster and thought of Tess as he sipped his wine.

What would she make of him today? Time to delve into the madcap world of the stern-looking weather house lady.

'SANDRA PLUNKETT WAS BORN in Rugeley, Staffordshire, in 1970. She attended the Abbotts Bromley School, where she developed a passion for the creative and performing arts. After graduating with a degree in Film Studies and Media from Keele University, she joined the Staffordshire Police force as a Constable and worked in Cannock. Sandra got promoted to Sergeant in 1993, Inspector in 1997 and Chief Inspector in 2000. She attended the accelerated promotion course at Bramshill Police College in Hampshire and transferred to West Mercia Police as a Superintendent in 2003. She got promoted to Chief Superintendent in 2005 and was head of Professional Standards at Hindlip Park on the outskirts of Worcester. In 2009 she completed the Strategic Command Course. In June 2011, she returned to Staffordshire as an Assistant Chief Constable in charge of the counter-terrorism unit. She was appointed Chief Constable in September 2014 for the West Midlands. Sandra was awarded the Queen's Police Medal for Distinguished Service in the 2015 New Year Honours. Sandra has lived with her partner, Naomi, in a small village near Lichfield since 1998.'

So that was who they were up against, thought Gus. A

formidable woman on every level. Sandra had ticked the right boxes as far as her superiors were concerned. However, he had never flown high enough to be pointed towards the SCC, policing's most senior leadership development programme. It prepared police officers and staff for promotion to the highest ranks in the service. The course was open to Superintendent and Chief Superintendent ranks and staff at equivalent grades from all UK forces who had shown the potential to progress further in their careers. It was a statutory requirement for officers seeking promotion to Assistant Chief Constable and above in UK forces.

The course aimed to develop senior leaders in law enforcement to lead policing operations and organisations locally, regionally and nationally. It offered a unique opportunity to engage in a challenging leadership development programme, which benefitted from the broad range of experience and perspectives shared by others within policing and partner organisations, nationally and internationally.

Gus had never needed a personal development plan to support his continuing professional development. He had reached his limit and was happy with his lot. The problem with these biographies generated by the force's publicity machine was that they remained exclusively positive. He needed to dig deeper for reports on cases screwed on Sandra's watch, even deeper to discover any dirt. Perhaps it wouldn't be necessary. But, if he kept solving these cases, the new Chief Constable would find it hard to prevent the CRT from becoming a permanent fixture.

Gus decided on a change of pace and called Vera Jennings.

"Hello there," she replied, "you left in such a rush this afternoon. Kassie was distraught."

"Yes, I forgot to grab her buns. Can you apologise to her in the morning? So, my highbrow friend was distraught. I take it you weren't that bothered?"

"That would be telling. Anyway, I hoped you would ring tonight."

"Does the FEW have a social outing planned this week?"

"No, my diary is a wasteland. If we plan something, can I be sure you'll turn up this time?"

"I should hope to get shot at proves a once-in-a-lifetime experience. I have every intention of being wherever we agree to meet."

"OK, Friday suits me best. We could eat at the Waggon & Horses. I'll drop by and pick you up around half-past eight. How does that sound?"

"It sounds terrific. Book a table. We know from our last visit it will be lively. If we fancy a boogie after our meal, no doubt, there'll be live music again?"

"Get you," laughed Vera, "don't let Kassie hear you say 'boogie', though. I don't think anyone under seventy uses that term."

"Ouch," said Gus, "it's been so long."

"Until Friday then," said Vera. "Goodnight and…

"Sweet dreams," replied Gus.

***Wednesday, 25 April 2018***

AS GUS DROVE through Devizes on his way to work, he thought about the second file he had read through last night. The murder files on the young woman they were to reopen hadn't received national coverage. Laura Mallinder's chosen profession prevented her from receiving the sympathy other victims could expect.

How often had he read reports of sudden death where the victim's family and friends declared they were saints? Yet, whether they died in an accident or got murdered, it never changed the dialogue. Nobody was ever a waste of space, a liar and cheat, someone you crossed the street to avoid.

Yet when a sex worker was involved, the crime drew far less attention. Regardless of the service they provided, they were still human beings. Their family deserved the same closure as any other that lost a son or daughter. Gus hoped the Crime Review Team could find answers the original inquiry failed to uncover.

Gus noticed a flurry of activity on the High Street as he turned into Church Street. The Food Bank had opened for business, and the Cancer Charities staff unloaded furniture items from a van parked outside. The ground floor of the Old Police Station showed no sign of recession.

In his rear-view mirror, he saw the boarded-up windows of the Ring O'Bells. Sadly, the pub Krystal Warner had managed until last weekend got mothballed. The landlords had erred on the side of caution and protected it against vandalism. When it might reopen was anyone's guess. Gus patted his car on the roof as he left it in his parking space at the rear of the Old Police Station. He had no intention of mothballing his old friend. A glance along the line confirmed he was last to arrive — ten minutes to nine. The team had gotten the message. He let them know he had arrived as soon as he exited the lift.

"Right, this is our new task. We'll be knee-deep in the seamier side of Swindon for the foreseeable future."

Three eager faces looked up as Gus breezed into the office.

"Our victim was Laura Mallinder, stabbed to death on the evening of the twelfth of June 2011. Laura worked in a massage parlour in the Broadgreen area of the town. She worked a three-hour shift on Sundays from six until nine. Her body was found just after half past nine by the owner, Maggie Monk. Our twenty-seven-year-old victim sustained fatal stab wounds to her back. When the original investigation was closed, there were no known suspects."

"I don't remember much about this one, guv," said Alex Hardy, "my guess is DI Theo Hickerton handled it."

"What was he like as a copper?" asked Neil Davis.

"Keen enough," replied Alex, "but under pressure to get a result or move on to the next case on the books."

"Was that due to the sheer volume of cases or the fact it was a sex worker?" asked Lydia Logan Barre.

"The former, Theo, would have asked the right questions," said Alex. "He did things by the book when I knew him. With this killing, it's tough to get people to talk. Which business are we talking about, guv? There are so many these days."

"They weren't shy of advertising what was available on the premises," said Gus, "it closed within weeks of the murder. It traded under Gentle Touch, and Maggie Monk had run it since early 2008 without getting raided."

"Was it above a shop or in a private home?" asked Lydia, "I wouldn't know the first thing to look for."

"Maggie Monk owned the property," said Gus. "A Turkish barber leased the ground floor. The massage parlour on the first floor was accessed through a separate entrance halfway along an alleyway between two adjoining units on the quiet side street."

"If you lived next door, you would soon spot the steady number of male visitors," said Neil. "When it's a holistic spa on the High Street, it resembles any other hairdressing or beauty parlour. Lots of chrome, bright lights and a recognisable price list you can compare with the competition. Businesses such as Gentle Touch have subdued lighting and basic fittings."

"How far did the initial investigation get?" asked Lydia.

"I've had a brief look through the murder file," said Gus. "Despite the detectives' best efforts and numerous appeals to the public for help, nothing concrete surfaced regarding motive. However, the post-mortem examination indicated Laura had been stabbed to death by an unknown attacker as she worked alone."

"It sounds like they've landed us with a locked room mystery to solve, guv,"

"Nobody said all these cold cases would be easy, Neil," said Gus.

## Chapter Three

"WHERE ON EARTH do we start, guv?" asked Lydia.

"Get the murder scene photos onto the whiteboards. Find a street map for the area surrounding Old Town and Broadgreen. For starters, something covering a two- to three-mile radius of the football ground will do. We can change things up if necessary."

"Are we moving to the Gablecross building on Shrivenham Road, guv?" asked Neil, "it gives us easy access to anyone who worked on the case still stationed there."

"The option exists to use facilities there temporarily, Neil, but I don't want us to become part of the furniture. I want to keep them at arm's length. We need to find our witnesses, our clues, if possible. The cursory glance I made last night suggested despite hundreds of interviews in the weeks that followed, nothing came from them to throw up the name of a suspect."

"This doesn't feel like the first two cases we investigated, guv," sighed Neil.

"No matter how different it may appear, nothing

changes in our approach, Neil," said Gus. "We take it one day at a time and keep turning over pieces of the puzzle until something fits."

"I'll get the original investigation details into the Freeman file, guv," said Alex. "The sooner we can produce a list of people to interview, the better. What about the Hub? Did you think of anything we need to give them to do?"

"The attack was frenzied," said Gus, leafing through the file to refresh his memory. "There was no weapon left at the scene. Forensics recovered several complete and partial fingerprints from the room, but they never matched anyone. Wiltshire Police have appealed for new information every year on the anniversary of Laura's death. They receive a few calls, but no forensic evidence has ever surfaced which might offer a new lead."

"How often have the fingerprints been checked against those stored around the country?" asked Alex, "we should get them interrogated by the Hub. Can you sort that out, Neil?"

"Will do, mate. Isn't it unusual for a girl to work alone, guv?"

"It's not common. On this occasion, Maggie Monk was late," replied Gus, "she was due to arrive by half-past eight to stand in for a member of staff who left early. One point worth remembering. Those prints haven't matched in seven years. If it was someone targeting working girls, that's far less likely to be the case. They would have slipped up somewhere in that time. So, we're probably looking for someone Laura knew. It could be a punter with a grudge or even a co-worker who argued with her. We need the names of girls this Monk woman employed and their whereabouts."

"We know from our recent case that stabbing a person

to death can be someone's first and only crime," said Alex, "especially if it's a crime of passion."

"Do many tourists visit Swindon?" asked Lydia, "could it be someone who visited from abroad, and that's why his print had never matched?"

"It wasn't a football supporter from overseas," scoffed Neil, "Swindon haven't had a European match in decades."

These casual comments accompanied the work on the whiteboards and the computer file. The team were becoming more comfortable in their roles within the CRT. Gus let them consider various lines of inquiry. Some would prove invaluable. Others would get discarded. He didn't know at this stage whether either of the younger members thrown into the mix would end up in the invaluable camp.

Neil was next to think of something.

"Did you ever hear a rumour other coppers used Gentle Touch, Alex?"

"What, you think Laura was killed by one of our own, and they covered it up? Not a chance, mate."

"One angle we need to consider," said Gus, "did Laura have regular clients? One of them might have developed a one-sided attachment. If he became obsessed with her and couldn't stand the thought of her pleasuring other men, he could have returned that Sunday evening and killed her."

DS Alex Hardy made a note to follow up on that angle.

Gus paced across the room, firing thoughts at them while raising his left hand one finger at a time.

"Did they know who was there that night? Who paid for these appointments? Were they for thirty minutes or an hour? We need more information about these places. Do they keep proper records? Would it be possible for someone to enter the premises before or after nine? The door is down an alleyway, so it's unlikely anyone saw an intruder. If other men visited the parlour that didn't come forward seven years ago, how do we trace them?"

Alex grabbed the second sheet of paper. There were plenty of questions. How long before they headed to Swindon to hunt for answers?

***Thursday, 26 April 2018***

IT WAS the morning after the night before. Of course, that meant different things to different members of the team.

Neil was suffering the impact of Melody's crazy combination of hormones, plus her understandable excitement and concern at the prospect of motherhood. It wasn't just his wife that felt emotional and stressed this morning. He favoured her sharing her feelings with their family and friends, but he needed rest. He'd had less than four hours of sleep a night since last Friday, and they were only six weeks into her pregnancy if Melody had her dates right.

Neil liked a drink. Not when inappropriate. He took a taxi or got Melody to pick him up when he had a night out. He was careful not to drink if he was due to drive first thing the following morning.

Melody announced last night that she was now teetotal. Fair enough, but why did she insist he gave up too? Apart from sex, five pints on a night out with his mates was the best way to relieve stress. The first would be less frequent as the months progressed, meaning the second was vital to keep him from blowing a fuse.

Neil was not alone. Gus Freeman had his troubles. He'd driven to the supermarket in Devizes for the supplies he'd listed on Tuesday evening. As he transferred his bags from the trolley into the boot of his car, he spotted a familiar figure. Suzie Ferris strode across the car park towards the town centre, arm in arm with a tall, dark, probably handsome man.

Gus couldn't see her companion's face, but his movement marked him as an athlete. Broad shoulders, narrow hips and a full head of hair. He was twenty years from fretting over bushy eyebrows and nasal hair. Gus hated him on sight.

Whether Suzie noticed him and steered her new beau away to avoid an uncomfortable moment, Gus couldn't tell. So why did it bother him so much? He was seeing Vera on Friday night. So it shouldn't have been an issue. Nevertheless, Gus ignored his good intentions and took a Chinese takeaway.

He devoured that within minutes of reaching home. It made sense. He had far more time for a drink to drown his sorrows while he listened to Simon and Garfunkel's 'Wednesday Morning 3 AM.' It might have been ten to nine when he arrived in the car park at the rear of the Old Police Station building, but it was still three in the morning in his head.

At least someone in the office looked happy.

Alex and Lydia had visited the Imperial Dragon last night. Jason Li and his staff had looked after them superbly. There was no sign of his parents. The food was spectacular, and the wine helped the conversation flow.

As they settled the bill, fifty-fifty as agreed, Lydia asked after Steve and Mary Li. Jason told them they had left on Sunday for a cruise around the Mediterranean.

"Only fourteen nights," he'd told them, "they sailed from Southampton, and my father has called three times a day to check everything's okay. He'll never retire."

Jason smiled ruefully as he held the door open for Lydia to push Alex's chair onto the High Street.

"Come and see us again," he said.

"I'm sure we will," said Alex.

As they waited for the traffic lights to change at the zebra crossing, Lydia asked: -

"Why don't you follow me to mine for coffee to complete a lovely evening?"

The lights changed, and Lydia watched Alex propel himself across the road and head towards their workplace parking bays off Church Street. She had to quicken her pace to catch him.

"I'll get off home if that's okay," said Alex. "Tonight has been great, Lydia. I meant what I told Jason Li. We will go back there, but I'll walk through the door with you next time."

Lydia could tell Alex was trying to keep things light-hearted. He had been in relationships before his accident, so it wasn't a fear of the unknown. She may have only asked him for coffee, but he would have guessed that she hoped he would stay. It was only natural to be reticent. Lydia resolved she would be the one to heal those post-injury doubts.

"You're on," she said, grabbing the back of his chair, "but you're not leaving without a goodnight kiss."

As they sat in the office the following morning, trying to avoid looking at one another, they could see Gus and Neil were out of sorts. Ah, well, time enough for big, cheesy grins along the line. After all, last night, it was only a kiss.

"Where are we with that list, Alex," asked Gus.

"Maggie Monk should be our first interviewee, guv, don't you agree?"

"Maggie's our best bet for the names of her staff, potential customers and the general running of her parlours," said Neil.

"Have we traced her latest address?" asked Gus.

"She's still in the same place, guv. Although the Swindon premises closed after Laura Mallinder's death, her empire has continued to grow. There are parlours in Marlborough and Cirencester now. The larger towns have a branch of both Cleopatra's and Gentle Touch."

"Get her on the phone and make an appointment to meet her, Alex. Then, Neil and I will interview her at home. Where is that, by the way?"

"Castle Combe, guv. It's a village in the heart of the country fifteen miles from Bath."

"I know where Castle Combe is, Alex," said Gus, "and my sat nav will get us there in due course. Who's next?"

"DI Theo Hickerton and DS Jake Latimer are at Gablecross. Both worked on the Mallinder case. The police surgeon who dealt with Laura's body was Stuart Fitzwalter. He may have something to offer that's not in the original file.

"This list is like a bloody catwalk model. It's painfully thin," said Gus.

"Maggie Monk will add the more significant names to our list, guv," said Lydia, "that's where we'll find our leads hidden. Hickerton and the others will only provide background data."

"Lydia's learning fast, lads," said Gus, "you had better watch out. You'll be saluting her in years to come. What about Laura's family, Alex?"

"Mrs Mallinder died of breast cancer aged sixty-three in 2016," said Alex. "Laura's father is still alive. Sam Mallinder's retired, aged sixty-seven, and he lives in Bristol."

"It appears Mrs Mallinder knew of her daughter's chosen profession, guv," said Neil. "In her statement at the time, she insisted that Laura was still her daughter, and it didn't matter what she did for a living."

"Did any other family members know what she did for a living?" asked Gus.

"The father never mentioned it in his statement. Laura had two older brothers; both are married and work in the building trade. Whether they knew or not isn't recorded. Laura's sister-in-law Emma seemed to be closer to Mrs Mallinder. Jake Latimer noted that Emma mentioned that Laura had been involved with a lad once when she was out of her teens. However, she didn't have a partner at the time of her death. Emma didn't recall Laura dating much after she ended that relationship."

"Why did the relationship end, do you know?"

"No idea."

"Did Emma Mallinder remember the chap's name?"

"Hewson, Ian Hewson; he was with the football academy at Bristol City. Good-looking and as fit as a flea, according to Emma. I checked that out. I don't think they kept him on their books. A high percentage look good at junior level, then don't kick on to make it as a professional."

"We had better keep his name on the list for now. It should be straightforward enough if we need to find out where he went after Bristol City. Does the name ring a bell, Neil?"

"I've never heard of an Ian Hewson in the Premiership, guv. If he were one of the many that fail to kick on after early promise, he would be playing non-league football somewhere. It will be tougher to find him then, but not impossible. Did this sister-in-law know where he went after

City let him go? Did he stay local, for instance, or might we have to start looking country-wide?"

"There's another question to add to that list you're compiling, Alex," said Gus. "We would benefit from that conversation with Theo Hickerton as soon as possible. I need to learn who identified the body. Which family member had that sad task? What was their reaction? Did anyone else ask to view the body?"

"Or did DI Hickerton make a note of anyone who expressly declined the invitation?" added Lydia.

"We mustn't jump to conclusions," Gus cautioned, "there could be a perfectly rational explanation for a loved one not wishing to see the body. However, Laura had three male family members with a possible motive and opportunity. We must check what Hickerton and his team found during their investigation. Neither man became a viable suspect, so their alibis must have been sound. Our task will be to test the strength of those alibis before we look for further suspects."

"So, you're sticking to the belief that it's more likely to be someone close to the victim than a random attack by a stranger, guv?" asked Neil.

"You've read the file, Neil. I don't see a long list of potential killers despite the hours the Gablecross detectives spent on the case. If we can, it makes sense to discount the father and two sons first. In due course, we'll source former clients to interview or hand this file back to Geoff Mercer without getting a result."

There was a sombre mood in the CRT office for the first time since they had worked together. All four knew the solution to this cold case wouldn't fall into their lap. The graft continued throughout the morning at a steady pace. The conversation was at a premium. Finally, Alex

Hardy broke the silence just after one o'clock in the afternoon.

"DI Hickerton is available tomorrow morning, guv. Ten o'clock at Gablecross."

"Excellent," said Gus, "you can come with me. I'm sure you will enjoy catching up with your old mates."

"You'll have to take Neil with you, guv. My physio appointment is at noon tomorrow. It's on the Freeman File calendar. We may struggle to get back in time."

"Gotcha," said Gus, checking his copy of the file. "I spotted it the other day, but it didn't register in the excitement of having a meeting to look forward to. This is an important appointment, isn't it?"

"The final hurdle, guv. If I get the green light, I'll hop in here on Monday morning with my crutches."

"I'm sure we wish you all the best, Alex. Right then, Neil, you and me tomorrow morning. Pick me up at nine o'clock, please."

"No problem, guv," said Neil, hoping he got a good night's sleep tonight. It wouldn't do to fall asleep at the wheel.

"I'll try Maggie Monk again later, guv," said Alex. "While you're in Swindon tomorrow, perhaps Neil can fix up meetings with Hickerton's DS, Jake Latimer and the Police Surgeon, Stuart Fitzwalter. Both should be on the premises during the day."

"I doubt we'll be lucky enough to get access to everyone tomorrow," Gus said. "Try to avoid Monday morning for appointments unless they can visit us here. We must leave the office in plenty of time to reach the crematorium."

"I'll schedule the Maggie Monk interview for Tuesday morning if I can, guv," said Alex.

"Don't stand any nonsense from her, Alex. We need her

cooperation in a murder enquiry; you dictate the terms, not her. We'll drive over to Castle Combe first thing Tuesday morning. Mrs Monk will be there when we arrive; is that understood?"

"Yes, guv," Alex replied.

Gus knew his reaction was excessive. But, he was frustrated with the absolute lack of a feel for this latest case.

They had worked on it since mid-morning yesterday, and nothing had emerged that might unlock a single thread that could lead them to a vital clue.

"Sorry, Alex, I didn't mean to snap. I can well imagine Theo Hickerton will tell me tomorrow that the Mallinder case was his version of the one every detective dreads. The case which keeps you awake at night, sifting through the sparse details you've uncovered, trying to determine what you've missed. I've known blokes go to their graves still wracking their brains over an unsolved murder that occurred forty years ago."

"It's early days yet, guv," said Alex, "we'll get a break, eventually,"

As he drove home through Devizes that evening, Gus hadn't seen any bright, shining light emerge from their efforts after Alex's hopeful comment. Neil's comment about a locked room mystery stubbornly refused to fade from memory. He decided to spend time on the allotment after his evening meal. Tomorrow was another day.

As he strolled along the lane towards the village church, he spotted Bert Penman ahead. Bert ambled, along with his usual considered pace. Gus lengthened his stride and caught the older man before they reached the allotment gateway.

"Ah, Mr Freeman. You've taken a break from your sleuthing to tend to your babies."

"I wish I had more time, Bert. I needed a break from

work to think this evening; this spot is the best place on earth. You've performed miracles while I've been absent. But, first, what progress have you made with arrangements for next Monday afternoon?"

"I got together with the other allotment holders. We're each of us encouraging our friends and neighbours to be there. Transport might be an issue, but we're meeting tomorrow night in the pub to discuss matters."

Gus smiled. After finishing gardening, Bert never missed an opportunity to visit the Lamb.

"I can't offer any help with transport, I'm afraid. My colleagues and I will go straight to the crematorium from work. I won't be back in the village until six o'clock."

"I can't see Irene North organising much of a wake," said Bert, "but a few of us will have a drink for Frank in the Lamb. The village would appreciate you calling in if you can spare a half-hour."

"How could I refuse?" said Gus.

"You said, first, Mr Freeman, for the funeral arrangements. Was there something else?"

"Another month is almost over, Bert. Can I look forward to a quiet May?"

"Gardeners always look forward to May, Mr Freeman," said Bert Penman. "It's the first month of Summer, but it marks the end of Spring. We can get caught out by mini droughts and heatwaves. The biggest threat is to those young plants we recently transplanted into open ground, and your freshly emerging seedlings. We must keep them well-watered and provide shade protection from a hot sun or drying winds."

"There's so much to learn, Bert," said Gus, blowing out his cheeks, "this climate change issue is proving a nightmare, isn't it?"

"Don't run away with the idea that it's all about the Earth warming up, Mr Freeman. May can still bring damaging frosts, cold winds, heavy rain and hail. So you need to be on your toes every one of the thirty-one days."

"Why didn't I take up stamp collecting as a hobby?" moaned Gus.

"You can't eat stamps," laughed Bert as he hobbled over to his shed to start his evening's work.

Gus fetched his trusty chair from his shed and sat.

Bert knew better than to interrupt. Mr Freeman was a deep thinker. His young seedlings weren't what was giving him that furrowed brow.

### ***Friday, 27 April 2018***

NEIL ARRIVED outside the bungalow by five to nine. Gus was soon through the front door and into the passenger seat.

"Off we go then, Neil," he said.

"Someone's brighter this morning," said Neil, feeling anything but after another night of broken sleep.

"I spent a valuable hour on my allotment last night," said Gus, "I didn't get any gardening done, but I convinced myself today would be educational. The better we understand the background of this business, the more we'll understand who might have committed the murder and their motivation."

It took Neil forty-five minutes to reach the Gablecross Police Station. They suffered the now-standard hiccup in Reception as they persuaded a youthful counter clerk they were genuine visitors with an appointment with DI Hickerton. Once attached to their Visitor's badges, they finally made their way through the modern rabbit warren to his office.

Theo Hickerton stood well over six feet tall. He was in his late forties and balding. What little fair hair was left at the sides was flecked with grey. He looked harassed.

"Gus Freeman, I presume?"

"That's right," said Gus, "may I introduce one of my Crime Review Team? DS Neil Davis."

The men shook hands, and Theo Hickerton invited Gus and Neil to sit.

"You've got Alex Hardy with your team, too, I understand? How's he coming to terms with life after his accident?"

"He's not coming to terms with anything," Gus replied. "He's fighting tooth and nail to get back to full fitness. Alex would have been with me today, but he's hoping his physio will get him out of his chair and onto crutches with effect from Monday."

"Good Lord, I never believed that possible. I attended the scene of the accident, Gus. I didn't think he'd make it out alive at that stage. He must have a will of iron. I'll pass the news on to the lads with whom he worked. Tell him to take care, though. Those injuries were so severe. It would be tragic if he overstretched himself in a rush to prove he's back."

"He's a team player," said Neil, "he knows we'll support him every step of the way."

"I spoke to your ACC at the weekend, Gus. He gave me a head's up that you were looking into the Laura Mallinder case with a fresh set of eyes. Your new team has already had success with other cases. Have you uncovered something we missed at the time?"

"Early days yet, Theo," said Gus, "I imagine the code of silence these businesses encourage proved a major stumbling block? We can tell from the murder file you looked for the usual means, motive and opportunity. You found various fingerprints at the scene, too, I see?"

"We could never match them with anything, though," sighed the Detective Inspector, "as for narrowing it down to a possible suspect, that was impossible. We keep having another look on the anniversary of her murder. You know the score. We don't have the resources to commit officers full-time to a case not leading anywhere. If they can't solve it in seventy-two hours, the attention switches to a new case, and resources diminish and eventually die altogether. It's a source of frustration for each one of us."

"Is Jake Latimer in the building, do you know?" asked Gus, "Neil wants to meet with him and run through the aspects of the case he handled."

"Jake's in court this week. We make real progress now and then when the CPS pull its finger out. However, his team can let Neil know when you can set up a line of communication. The two of them can meet here; Jake can visit your office, or if it helps, they can meet in Old Town and tour the patch. Things have moved on in seven years. Jake can give Neil a better appreciation of what things were like on the ground seven years ago."

"We prefer that approach, Theo," said Gus. "I suggest we do something similar today if that's OK? Then, Neil can follow up on Jake, and we also need to interview Stuart Fitzwalter."

"Stuart was the Police Surgeon on that case. Yes, I remember. He was new at the game back then. I believe he hadn't long transferred in from a country office. The Lake District, if memory serves. The rural cases he dealt with in the early years after he qualified varied somewhat from the horrors he faced. Nevertheless, the crime scene left a lasting impression on many of us that night."

"It was a savage attack based on the photos we've viewed," said Neil.

"Everything pointed to the crime being an act of passion," said Theo Hickerton. "Nothing suggested a robbery. The cashbox was untouched. According to the owner, there was little in the way of easily portable equipment in the parlour; but nothing was missing. There was no apparent sexual motive, despite the business's dubious nature."

"If Laura had a customer who wanted something extra to the activities Mrs Monk sanctioned, that could have led to violence, though, couldn't it?" asked Neil.

"Yes, but he would have had to have carried the weapon with him to the parlour," said Theo. "Mrs Monk stressed to her girls that sharps of any kind were banned. So the girls didn't need knives, needles or scissors during a shift. It was a sensible precaution to protect her girls from being harmed by a drunken or belligerent client."

"So, the killer brought the murder weapon to do Laura harm. Was that your theory?" asked Gus. "Where did that lead?"

"We worked on the premise that it was an act of passion. Our first thought was a family member. More often than not, someone close, a loved one, is responsible. We looked at the father and then the two brothers. Jake investigated the regular clients of Laura's we managed to identify. We shook the tree, but nothing came loose. Everyone had strong alibis for the time of the murder. It was a small window of opportunity. The two girls on duty had a brief break between clients at half-past seven. Laura's colleague then left at around half-past eight. Their final booked sessions overlapped. When her last client left, Laura was alone. That hadn't been the plan. Mrs Monk had agreed to arrive in time to cover for Camille, the other girl on shift. Maggie Monk was there merely for security; she arrived an hour late. Someone entered the massage parlour between eight forty-five and nine-thirty. A person we could never get a lead on."

"You never established whether Laura received a phone call to book a later session?" asked Gus.

"There were no incoming calls on the landline," said Theo, "and nothing on Laura's mobile."

"Would she have entertained someone off the books?" asked Neil.

"I don't imagine Maggie Monk expected every booking to be traceable via the call listing from BT. We understood regulars made appointments as they left the parlour after a visit — same time next Friday sort of thing. Then there were the walk-ins. At this particular parlour, walk-ins weren't encouraged because of the sheltered access to the premises. The girls escorted clients to the door and ensured it closed behind them when they left."

"Maggie Monk found the door open when she arrived. Is that correct?" asked Gus.

"Yes, but we don't know whether Laura failed to lock the door after her final client or if someone rang the bell and wanted to pay for a thirty-minute session."

"Did you identify the men who had booked sessions that evening?" asked Gus.

"Jeff Naylor was the last person to leave. He was a regular. He always asked for Laura, well Gem, as she was known to her clients. The other girl's real name wasn't Camille either, but they switch names regularly in these places to avoid the taxman. We never traced her. Maggie Monk thought Camille and her husband might have returned to their native Thailand. Once news of the murder broke, the place remained closed, and girls were re-assigned by Mrs Monk to her other parlours."

"That sounds heartless in hindsight but understandable given the circumstances, I guess," said Gus. "The girls go into this business to make good money. They have commitments, the same as the rest of us. Do you believe this Camille returned home?"

"She could be working in another parlour in Swindon under a new name. Who knows? We raid the dodgy ones when we get a tip-off that it's operating as a brothel. We've never found a Camille anywhere. Apart from a vague description from clients and Mrs Monk, we wouldn't have proof if someone lied to us and hid their connection to Gentle Touch."

"I don't suppose they post pictures of the girls available on the walls of the parlour," said Neil, "and their adverts stress that discretion is their motto. The whole business aims to make it hard for the police to identify the girls and their clients."

"You've hit the nail on the head," agreed Theo Hickerton. "I wish you luck solving this one. It did my head in at the time, and every year that failure against my name rubs my nose in it as we take another pointless look."

Gus had heard enough negativity. He needed to shake those trees again.

"Neil, why don't you chase up Jake Latimer and the Police Surgeon?" said Gus,

"Will do, guv," said Neil, "what time do you want to head back to the office?"

"No later than three o'clock. If you speak with Stuart

Fitzwalter, ask about the murder weapon. God knows how many blade varieties exist out there now, but let's try to narrow the search. We know the killer brought it with him. If we can determine what it looked like, that might suggest who had a reason for owning it."

Neil left the DI's office in search of the detective squad. His first task was to find Jake Latimer.

Neil was no nearer seeing a way through the gloom of this case.

They were chasing shadows.

# Chapter Four

"I'LL TAKE you to the murder site, Gus," said Theo Hickerton after Neil had left. "We can't see the parlour, of course. It's all changed out there now. After Mrs Monk closed the business, the Turkish barber moved upstairs and completely refurbished the ground floor. He opened a nail bar and re-jigged the staircases to access the barbershop through the nail bar. They removed the side door in the alleyway."

"The Turkish guy leases the whole building from Maggie Monk, does he?" asked Gus.

Hickerton nodded. "It's a thriving business. Mrs Monk gets a good return on her investment. I suppose she thought the stigma of the murder would never leave the massage parlour. It was easier to find alternative premises elsewhere in the town. Her empire has expanded despite the tragic murder."

"So we understand, New places in Marlborough and Cirencester. She has a branch of both Cleopatra's and

Gentle Touch in Swindon too, so where are they? Do any of her previous staff work there?"

"Maggie has one on Cricklade Road, and the other is near the Designer Outlet. Several of her younger girls are still working for her. The older ones may have retired."

The two men walked outside the busy station and into the warm sunshine. Hickerton drove a Wiltshire Police Ford Kuga. The livery wouldn't have suited Gus Freeman's needs these days, but as they motored through traffic towards Broadgreen, he could appreciate its advantages over his old Focus. They parked across the road from the building where Laura Mallinder was stabbed twenty minutes later.

Gus guessed the building was from the first quarter of the twentieth century. The brickwork above the first-floor windows showed signs of wear and tear. They had replaced the original sash windows. Modern fixtures and fittings gave these places a cosmetic overhaul that suited their business aspirations. Still, the buildings rarely had any attention paid to structural damage caused by the passing years.

"It's hard to imagine what happened here seven years ago, isn't it?" said Theo, "the world moves on. There's no trace of how the place looked."

"Laura wasn't a girl to get a blue plaque on the wall to remind the locals how and when she died," said Gus.

"You're not old enough to remember Eddie Cochran, are you? My late father was a fan. They've got a memorial for him in Chippenham, near a railway bridge. He died, aged twenty-one, after a road accident while travelling to London in a taxi during his British tour in April 1960. He'd just performed at Bristol's Hippodrome theatre. Gene Vincent, another American rock and roll star, was injured. So whenever I drive past that shrine, I remember my Dad.

Once his generation is gone, it won't be long before nobody knows why it was there."

"I remember Buddy Holly, Eddie Cochran and the rest of those music stars that died over the decades. You could almost always explain those deaths. They were accidental or self-inflicted through drink or drugs; very few were murdered. Maggie Monk may have eradicated the visual record of the murder site, but I intend to discover who was responsible. Laura deserves no less."

Theo Hickerton didn't comment. Gus wondered whether he cared one way or another.

"Laura bought a house a fifteen-minute walk from here, I believe. Which route did she take? Can we drive there, please?"

Theo Hickerton drove Gus past Laura's home. There was no car on the drive, the garden looked well-kept, and there were flowers in a vase in the large front window.

"Any idea who lives here now?" Gus asked.

"Not a clue," Theo replied, "Laura hadn't made a will. Her parents would have had to wait while they sought other claimants, but she had never married, she wasn't in a relationship, and this property was something she'd financed alone. Once they cleared all the hurdles, they would have received the contents of her estate. Unfortunately, there was an outstanding mortgage. My guess is the family sold the place, cleared the mortgage and added any profits to the modest sum she had in the bank."

"Would the sums involved have been enough to give her father a motive for murder?"

"If you were desperate for money, any sum might be big enough. Laura's father couldn't have been in Swindon that night, so you can rule that theory out."

"Theo, we've just solved an ancient case where the passage of time was a huge factor in providing us with clues they missed in the initial investigation. Laura's mother died of breast cancer in 2016. When was she diagnosed? Was there any point when traditional treatments deemed to have run their course and a more speculative, expensive option dangled before the Mallinder's? Something for which they needed a large amount of cash and quick?"

"The time frame doesn't fit, Gus. Laura died in 2011. Even if she had willed her estate to her parents, it would have taken a year for any monies to materialise. Solicitors move at a snail's pace. Once intestacy rules came into play, it could have easily doubled the time involved. I doubt the family received a penny of her estate before the middle of 2013. Laura's murder was never a fast track to the cash they might have needed for a miracle cure. They had access to the money during the last three years of the poor woman's life. That's when desperate measures are the only options."

"You're probably right, Theo. I'm just testing theories. Moving the pieces of the jigsaw around the board."

"We pray that we get a cluster of pieces to fit together early in an investigation, don't we? When they don't, it can be a bugger. I wish you luck, Gus. No matter how often we looked at the pieces, we could never find facts that fit."

"My team don't have fresh ideas on tackling this case," admitted Gus, "we've handed the full and partial fingerprints you gathered to the Hub at London Road. They're checking them against everything recorded around the country in the intervening period. Maybe that will throw up something. I'll talk to Maggie Monk before I do anything else. I don't buy that she doesn't know where Camille went. All this subterfuge with exotic names is a smokescreen. We'll apply gentle pressure and squeeze some cooperation out of her. If her girls have relocated, they could be engaged in the murkier end of the business. I might need to send Neil undercover. We won't progress unless we find the girls and get them to name their clients."

"It might be a slow process," said Theo, turning the car around and heading back towards Shrivenham and Gablecross.

"Agreed, but maybe Stuart Fitzwalter will offer a different angle for us to pursue. I want his in-depth analysis of the wounds and what could have made them.

"After seven years, you're unlikely to unearth the murder weapon," said Theo.

"Stranger things have happened," said Gus, "this wasn't an opportunistic attack. On the contrary, someone planned it with military precision. They knew what Laura did for a living. They knew she was working a short Sunday evening shift and somehow learned she would be alone once Camille left. So why was Maggie Monk an hour late?"

"A witness we interviewed told us that was Maggie all over. She was always busy, rushing from appointment to appointment. I cannot see how someone could have known she'd be late."

"We can't answer that question yet, but let's assume they knew they had a thirty-minute window. How did the killer reach the massage parlour in the first place? Did they follow Laura on foot, then wait outside until Camille was out of sight? How did they know they could gain access? Perhaps our killer was a frequent visitor. Someone who knew that if the door was locked, Laura only opened it for a familiar face if someone arrived without a phone booking."

"If she recognised them and let them in, then they could have attacked her when they reached the door to the room upstairs," said Theo. "As soon as they were confined, the killer could carry out the brutal attack. It makes sense. It was personal, as we believed at the outset. The problem was everyone close to Laura in her personal life, and Gem in her working life had an alibi."

"One more thing, Theo, if it was a client, he had to pay cash at the Reception desk before entering the room. No pay, no play. Did the money in the cashbox tally with the clients they saw?"

Theo had nothing to say.

"Nobody thought to check, did they?"

"I don't recall whether we had paperwork to check it against, Gus. Mrs Monk didn't visit her parlours every day to collect the takings. The parlours may have maintained a level of petty cash for essentials. The girls took their share of the extras they provided and stowed the balance in the cashbox. Maggie Monk told us nothing was missing."

"Maggie was unlikely to tell you any more than she had to, Theo. It's a cash business and, therefore, flexible and prone to manipulation. She would go to great lengths to hide her real income and that of her staff."

As they turned into the car park at Gablecross, Gus spotted Neil Davis leaving with a passenger.

"Was that Jake Latimer with Neil?" he asked.

"Jake must have returned from the court earlier than planned. I hope that doesn't mean there's a problem."

"Neil won't be back for an hour or two," said Gus, "I'll let you get on with your day, Theo. Many thanks for the additional background and for letting me ramble through my various theories. We'll keep you in the loop with our progress, or lack thereof. I plan to visit your local eating places to see if Egon Ronay is still flipping burgers."

"Bon appetit. Keep in touch, Gus."

"One more thing, Theo. Were there any CCTV

cameras in the area that might have captured the killer as they arrived at Gentle Touch or as they left after the murder?"

"If there wasn't a record of it in the murder file, then we didn't find any," said Theo.

Gus Freeman wondered how hard he and Jake Latimer had looked. A missing child would have merited a massive fingertip search for days. However, Laura Mallinder didn't warrant too much effort.

Theo Hickerton went inside and climbed the stairs to his office floor, and Gus followed the signs towards the Greenbridge Retail Park; the walk would do him good. He only needed a snack; he was eating out in style tonight. Until Neil was back from his trip around the hot spots, he could use the time working on the identity of the mystery visitor.

"THAT WAS YOUR BOSS, wasn't it?" Neil Davis asked DS Jake Latimer.

"Thank goodness we missed them," said Jake, "he will want to know why I'm not still in court. But, unfortunately, our main witness was a no-show."

"Dodgy tummy or intimidation?" asked Neil.

"The latter, I shouldn't wonder. No doubt your guvnor goes on about the old days when the criminals were just local blokes who had gone off the rails. The bad apples didn't fall very far from the tree back then. Organised crime is just that. Bloody, well-organised with a command structure that's nationwide. We're fighting a losing battle, mate."

"Maybe, but we're still fighting," said Neil.

DI Hickerton and his Sergeant appeared to be paid-up members of the Browbeaten Brigade.

"Where are you taking me on this Magical Mystery Tour, Jake?"

"The railway station on the right was at the heart of old Swindon," Jake told him as they passed by, "the original red-light district area was here around Station Road. The road layout has changed since then, and when that happened, the girls moved up to Manchester Road. A decade ago, we had forty-odd prostitutes here, and we made great efforts to take them off the streets and offer them treatment for addictions to hard drugs."

"Was that successful?" asked Neil, looking for signs of activity on the street.

"You might find a few on the streets at night. For the past ten years, the area has had its fair share of criminal problems that have nothing to do with the sex trade. But, until recently, it hasn't been a priority."

"Is it on the increase again?"

"In Broadgreen, yeah, but it's not disproportionate to areas in other parts of the county or compared to other force areas of a similar size. We do what we can; teams venture out weekly with outreach workers from a local charitable trust. Women can access a sexual health clinic, get food, clothes and emergency alarms. Street sex workers are at constant risk. Women like Laura Mallinder and the others who work in massage parlours can be in danger, but it depends on the extras they provide. For every parlour such as those owned by Maggie Monk, half a dozen exist where anything goes."

"I'm concerned that several of Maggie Monk's girls have gone that route," said Neil, "I haven't mentioned it to Gus Freeman yet. What we've learned of Laura Mallinder suggests she stayed clean throughout her involvement with the parlours. No drugs, nothing more than the specified menu and no pimps. She was one of the lucky ones. Many more have been exploited and encouraged to numb the pain with drugs. Once they're addicted, the pimps turn them out for all types of deviant nonsense. The girls with the clues we need that lead us to Laura's killer could be dead if they've spent several of the past seven years on the wild side."

"I wouldn't call Laura lucky, but you might have a point, Neil. Up to thirty pop-up brothels are being opened each week in Swindon," Jake Latimer said. "In any one week, fifty sex workers market their services in properties for a few days before moving on. Most are Eastern European, and the brothels link to criminal gangs that traffic women from Poland and Romania. Swindon is just one of dozens of locations nationwide targeted by gangs running these brothels. Many of these women move between addresses within the town and outside it. Of these fifty sex workers, we estimate they populate twenty to thirty brothels in short-term to medium-term rental properties."

"Catch me if you can, Jake," said Neil. "It must be a bugger to be a client shopping around. You could end up with the same girl in a dozen houses."

"My missus reckoned we needed more variety in our sex life before she left me," said Jake. "I don't think she meant sex with the same bloke in a dozen locations. She just wanted it with someone other than me."

Neil sympathised but decided not to rub Jake's nose in it by telling him he and Melody were happily married and expecting their first child. Jake had already moved on with his whistle-stop tour of the red-light district.

"Officers look to intervene, offer to safeguard, and check if organised crime is involved as often as possible. The number of reported suspected brothels in Swindon doubled over the past three years. We're currently monitoring one hundred and eighty women involved in sex work, predominantly in Swindon. Owners are often unaware that their rental or investment properties are used this way. They are alerted when neighbours report unusual behaviour to us. These brothels get set up quickly, booked online, and their services are advertised online. You wouldn't see adverts in the local papers, nor do you catch women touting for business in the street. It's web-based. The human traffickers also use hotels and guesthouses in the countryside near Swindon."

"The current scene feels a far cry from what you faced when Laura was alive," said Neil, "yet you never made significant progress in uncovering any suspects."

"I know what you're thinking. You reckon Theo and I didn't try hard enough because of what the victim was doing. That wasn't the case as far as I was concerned. We got dragged off the case to clamp down on young people carrying knives in Swindon. That weekend, two sixteen-year-olds were arrested on Thames Avenue for possessing knives and drugs. The pair were spotted outside Morrison's supermarket at around half-past eight on Friday night and stopped by uniforms twenty minutes later. They got released on bail until the middle of July. That was concerning offences of possession of an offensive weapon, possession of class C drugs and, for one, possession with intent to sell drugs. That incident was the last straw. It was the latest high-profile incident involving knives and young people. It was only a matter of time before one resulted in death or serious injury. We changed the policy. Young people aged sixteen or under found carrying a bladed article faced the certainty of being charged and brought before the courts. That crackdown was in line with government guidelines.

There was a hardcore of young people carrying knives, and we adopted a robust approach. We worked with schools and youth organisations to get across our message. That's why Laura's case didn't get the attention it warranted."

"A knee-jerk reaction, as usual," said Neil. He knew what Jake Latimer meant.

"The spotlight gets shone on a hot issue, and everything else slips into the shadows."

"Exactly. If we had the right level of resources, it wouldn't happen. Back then, knife crime represented only one per cent of criminal activity in the town. For two months, it got out total attention."

"Look what good it did," said Neil, "knife crime's a damn sight worse today."

"If you've spoken with Theo Hickerton this morning, he will have told you we did a cursory annual review on the Mallinder case. We remain committed to finding the person responsible. We need the public's help to bring Laura's killer to justice. Each year we urge anyone with information to come forward. Theo reckoned it had to be a close relative, a neighbour or a friend who had committed this murder. They may have been a client or perhaps worked at the massage parlour. Yet, seven years on, nobody still feels able to contact us in confidence."

"Gus Freeman has a knack of getting facts from the public they haven't voiced in the past," said Neil. "I wouldn't bet against him unearthing a vital clue once we trace our missing witnesses. So, apart from calling on the public for help, what else did you try during these cursory annual reviews?"

"We used the latest advances in DNA testing each year when we re-examined various exhibits removed from the scene," said Jake Latimer. "We hoped they would offer us a lead to Laura's killer. But, once again, it was always a dead-end."

"The Hub is processing the fingerprints at present. Their expanded search could offer us a lead. If it had been a random attack by a criminal with no link to the victim, our potential suspects would grow off the chart. I prefer they told us the prints didn't match anything they have on file. It narrows the field of suspects to family, friends, colleagues and clients."

"Didn't have much luck with that lot in the past. I wish you luck, Neil."

"We need to head back to the office," said Neil, looking at his watch. "The boss wants us to leave Swindon at three o'clock. Thanks for the tour. I've got a far better grasp of the area's layout and issues. We'll be back over the coming days, and maybe weeks, as we delve deeper into the case."

"I'm sure we'll meet again soon. Call me if you need someone to keep you safe on trips to our local massage parlours. The wife left a while ago."

Neil dropped Jake outside the Gablecross building and watched as he immediately drove away in his car. It surprised Neil he hadn't reported to his office. However, it wasn't his problem. He heard a shout from the other side of the road; Gus Freeman waved a thumb in the air. He needed a lift. Neil picked him up, and they headed for Devizes.

"Did you get the guided tour too, guv?" asked Neil.

"Yes, very informative. What did you get from the Police Surgeon?"

"I found Jake Latimer first, guv. He was back from the County Court sooner than planned. I'll call Fitzwalter to set up a meeting."

"It can't be helped. Ring Fitzwalter and invite him into the office on Monday morning."

"Got it, guv," said Neil.

"Keep driving," said Gus as they passed the London Road HQ, "we need to update our files with what we've learned today. Also, I want to see how Alex got on with his physio appointment. Once we're up to date, I hope to produce a complete schedule of our activities for next week and assign team members to them."

Once inside the CRT office, Gus sat and winced at the meagre amounts of new data Alex and Lydia could offer him. Then, while Neil updated the Freeman File with his contributions from Gablecross and Broadgreen, he listened in.

"We have to up our game next week," Gus said, leaning back in his chair after the updates had been exhausted. "The ACC will have our new Chief Constable on his shoulder, demanding results."

Gus swung his chair around and began updating his computer file. Neil looked at Alex. He could tell his colleague was itching to say something.

"Er, did you forget something, guv?" he asked.

Gus had a big grin on his face when he turned.

"Never play poker, Alex," he said, "ever since we arrived, you've been bursting to give us the news. It's written on your face in big letters. Lydia's just as bad. She kept glancing your way, urging you to say something. Finally, the physio gave you the green light; I take it?"

"Yes, guv. I've been ordered not to overdo it, but I can reduce my use of the wheelchair daily. The physio wants to check me over in two weeks."

"That's great news, Alex. DI Hickerton asked me to pass on your old team's congratulations on the progress you've made so far. Theo agreed with your physio. Take it steady. One day at a time."

The mood in the office had lifted. It was the first lighter moment since the Laura Mallinder murder file had arrived.

"I suggest you three get off home. Make sure you have a restful weekend. I'll finish my file updates and won't be far behind you."

Neil Davis made one final attempt to trace Stuart Fitzwalter. In the end, he left a message inviting him to call the Old Police Station first thing on Monday morning. Alex and Lydia didn't need asking twice. They were in the lift and gone from the car park when Neil finally made his way outside.

Fifteen minutes later, Gus made his way home from the office. He couldn't imagine many light-hearted moments over the next few days. But, at least, he had the prospect of an evening meal at the Waggon & Horses with Vera Jennings to brighten the cloudy horizon.

Gus parked the car and threw his keys into the tray by the door; there would be no driving for him tonight. He showered and wandered into his bedroom. As he scoured his wardrobe for something to wear, his hand hovered over a light sweater that hadn't seen the light of day since Tess had died.

This last week of April had been less warm. It was much more comfortable to work in than the heatwave that preceded it. Did it warrant something warmer for a Spring evening? How late might they be, anyway?

Gus learned it was National Gardening Week next week when he had leafed through a Sunday supplement. Perhaps he should use this sweater when walking to and from his allotment. If it wasn't an immediate choice for a night out, it might be the only way to get any use from one of the last items of clothing Tess bought him.

He opted for his leather jacket over a casual short-sleeved shirt. The mirror check confirmed his thoughts; he looked good enough, considering his age. Tess wouldn't have tutted and suggested he change before he left the house. If only his hair grew quicker. He was still wetting his fingers to persuade odd strands to lay flat on his head.

The front doorbell interrupted his reverie. Surely, that wasn't Vera? Eight o'clock. She must be keen. He opened the door.

Gus was happy that he'd attempted to make a silk purse out of a sow's ear. His dinner date looked stunning. He remembered Vera's appearance that first afternoon when he visited London Road to listen to what Kenneth Truelove wanted to say.

Tall, slim, and elegant with green eyes that could only belong to something feline. Tonight was something else. Vera's mane of dark hair tumbled across bare shoulders, and the sequin top with a long sweeping skirt made Gus swallow hard.

"Wow, you look great," he said.

Vera stepped inside and kissed him.

"You say all the right things, Gus," she said, "good, you're not still pampering yourself. The Waggon & Horses couldn't accommodate us as late as we wished. I booked a table for eight-fifteen. If we leave now, we'll make it in time."

Gus checked his pockets.

"I've got everything I need," he said, "let's go."

The lane near the pub was as busy as it had been the last time they visited. Vera swept into the car park and eased her Spider into the only vacant spot as one of the bar staff removed its no-parking sign.

"How do you do that?" asked Gus.

"I blame my father," said Vera, "the clout his family name carries around here hasn't diminished despite my unhappy marriage. There are dozens of places in the vicinity that bend over backwards to encourage our patronage."

"So, you call them to book a table, and they keep you a parking space. Nice one."

"It makes sense. If you were passing a pub with top-of-the-range cars outside in full view, doesn't it suggest it's a great place to eat? Everybody wins."

"If I drove into this car park in my ageing Focus, that young barman would scamper out with traffic cones to keep the riff-raff at bay."

Vera laughed. Gus thought it was a lovely sound; he couldn't wait to get inside the old pub and spend a few hours in her company.

They walked into the restaurant to be met by the manager.

"Mrs Jennings, how lovely to see you again. We have seated you and your guest here by the window. Is that acceptable?"

"It will be perfect," said Gus, "I can keep an eye on the car."

Vera elbowed him in the ribs as she passed. The manager left them to settle and found something urgent to attend to on the other side of the large dining room.

"You're incorrigible," said Vera.

"I try my best. The manager looks to be recovering his poise. He's pointed a waitress in our direction. We should soon get offered drinks while we peruse the menu. He might be a pompous prat, but I bet he won't forget we're against the clock."

Gus chose a pint of cider. With Vera as his designated driver, there was no point rubbing her nose in it by guzzling a bottle of red wine with his roast lamb.

"You raised the subject of your marriage first," said Gus, "so I feel able to ask, how is Monty faring?"

"The authorities appear satisfied he was ignorant of what the Rexha brothers were doing with the land and building Monty leased them. It doesn't surprise me. If someone offered him a twenty per cent rent over the going rate, he wouldn't automatically think there was something fishy. Monty would bank it for as long as he could, thinking they were mugs for not knowing better. It's only a matter of time before the creditors are banging at his door, anyway."

"Because your father was wise to him before the wedding, you won't suffer any backlash when that happens, I take it?"

"My share of the family money was never part of the marriage's assets. The family solicitor assures us that Monty cannot force us to bail him out. After all, while we've been married, the money I've earned has helped keep him afloat for far longer than if he'd been single. I've been bailing him out for over two decades."

Their food arrived, and the conversation switched. Gus could see from empty plates on nearby tables that nobody was going home hungry tonight.

"This tastes great," said Gus, "you can't beat fresh vegetables."

"I don't suppose you have enough time to spend on your allotment these days?" said Vera, "May is a busy time for gardeners, isn't it?"

"The more time I spend with old-timers such as Bert

Penman, the more I reckon there isn't a time when it's not busy. There's always something that needs attention."

"I've arranged to have time off work on Monday," said Vera. "Kassie has agreed to stay at London Road to look after those bigwigs that aren't attending Frank North's funeral."

"I hope there will be a good-sized congregation," said Gus, "Irene has enough family members barely to fill a pew. Bert will do his best to get the villagers there, which will help."

"Can I sit with you?"

"Of course. I imagined you would sit with Geoff, Suzie and anyone else they press-ganged into going from HQ."

"I'm sure they won't be far away from us. It's not a joyous occasion, but it will be nice to meet up with Alex, Neil and Lydia again."

"Oh, they've had their cards marked. They know they need to be there suited and booted. The way this Swindon murder is shaping up, we'll be glad of a distraction."

"Are you finding it tricky to get a handle on?"

"The length of time since it happened isn't helping. The victim's nature of business brings new problems. Everyone has an opinion on how to deal with the situation, but those at the heart of it are unwilling to speak out."

"I can well imagine. The local councillors and residents don't want it in their backyard. The more enlightened ones want it legalised. A few extremists want the girls burnt at the stake. As for the girls themselves and their clients, they prefer to keep calm and carry on."

"We won't solve that conundrum this evening," sighed Gus, "do you fancy a coffee?"

Vera looked at her watch.

"It might be best to drive back to your place," she said.

"That meal was excellent. It would be shameful to spoil it by rushing a hot coffee because they needed the table."

Gus watched the manager. He was weaving between tables, heading for the door as he and Vera settled the bill.

"Thank you so much for coming. I hope you enjoyed your meal."

"It was lovely, thank you," said Vera.

"Do we leave the parking space vacant for your next customer?" asked Gus. "I could save your legs and drop a traffic cone in plain sight if you wish?"

"That won't be necessary, Sir," the manager replied, still forcing a smile as he closed the door behind them.

"If you keep this up, there won't be many places we can get a meal," said Vera, slipping her arm through his as they walked to her car.

"I can always cook for you," said Gus.

"I'll hold you to that."

The roads were quiet, and Vera soon parked her Alfa Romeo next to the Ford Focus. Then, as they walked towards the bungalow, she turned and looked back.

"They look an unlikely pair, don't they?"

"Is that what people say about us?"

"Not to my face. They wouldn't dare."

Gus opened the front door, and they went inside. He headed straight for the kitchen and started fetching cups from the cupboard ready for the coffee. Vera laid a hand on his arm as he went to switch on the kettle.

"I'm sure you would prefer a drink," she said, "you nursed that pint of cider through a starter, main course and dessert. You love a good single malt, and so do I. So pour me a glass."

Gus did as Vera asked. Then, in the lounge, they sat together on the sofa.

“Does this suggest the first meal I cook for you will be breakfast?” he asked.

“Tomorrow’s Saturday. There’s no rush. We might make it brunch or even a late lunch if things go well. Who knows?”

Gus wished he’d had time to turn over Tess’s photos. Unfortunately, he wouldn’t have time to ask her if she approved.

# Chapter Five

***Monday, 30 April 2018***

THE WEATHER FORECAST promised to be cool, partly sunny and with a light breeze. Gus sat in his old Ford Focus and thought of the numerous funerals he had attended over the years. Heavy rain or biting northerly winds had accompanied the vast majority.

Sometimes, the UK's fickle climate had delivered both, while dark skies lowered to the rooftops. When Tess died, he travelled alone in this car behind the hearse as it headed for the West Wiltshire Crematorium.

A light drizzle had started as soon as he stepped outside the front door. Then, as the procession travelled through Seend, the heavens opened. Neither had a family to justify the expense of a funeral car; hers was one of the first budget funerals. Gus had followed Tess's instructions to the letter. Twenty or thirty years earlier than she had hoped, she had never wanted the service to include hymns or prayers.

Eva Cassidy featured on the playlist, and someone read a Joyce Grenfell poem Tess had liked. The humanist celebrant couldn't help looking like a snake oil sales associate, but he did as instructed. Tess's colleagues from Salisbury College and teachers from various schools where she taught sat on one side. His fellow officers and a handful of neighbours from their previous home in Downton occupied three rows of pews on the other.

When he stood outside afterwards, receiving the line of people, the sun inexplicably deigned to burst through the receding clouds. He felt wretched, yet everyone else seemed brighter merely because the sun shone. Although, of course, they might have been glad to escape the confines of the room and the nondescript service.

Gus couldn't have cared less. He was alone for the first time in his life.

In the days and weeks following that sad occasion, he had alternated between throwing himself into work and drinking copious amounts of malt whisky. But, unfortunately, neither did much to make him feel any less alone.

Somehow he dragged himself back from the edge. It would have been simple to give up the allotment and stop decorating the bungalow to concentrate on drinking. But, instead, for the next two years, he had muddled along, making the best of his lot. Any thoughts of sharing things with anyone couldn't have been further from his mind.

In the blink of an eye, that changed.

He had stepped inside the London Road HQ for that first meeting with Kenneth Truelove, and Vera Jennings had escorted him to the ACC's office.

Last Friday evening had been their first actual date. Before that, they chatted and flirted on several occasions at work. He had bumped into her on his trip to the Bear to have a drink with Geoff Mercer. Gus had planned to meet Vera for a quiet drink and invited his team to join them to celebrate their first successful cold case. Then after a dramatic morning in which he narrowly escaped death, Vera came here with her distant cousin Suzie Ferris to ensure he was back in bed the same evening. That was the sum of their relationship until Friday night.

Did what happened after they returned here mean he was no longer alone? Was that what he wanted? Or had he subconsciously found a busy office or encouraged others to join him on earlier occasions to provide a security shield? Was he ready for what might follow? Would Vera be content to keep things low-key? After all, her divorce would get finalised in early May. This needed time for reflection.

Gus had never slept with anyone other than Tess. Then, on Saturday morning, he opened his eyes to the bright light of day. Gus was immediately aware that he had a companion and that she was naked. He stared at the ceiling in shock for a few seconds as his fuzzy brain tried to decipher what had happened.

When fully awake, he remembered everything that had occurred in the last ten hours. He lay there, not daring to breathe and luxuriated in enjoying his first sex since Tess's death. Then the guilt washed over him.

Gus left Vera sleeping. He showered and dressed. As he sat in the kitchen with a mug of strong black coffee, he heard movement in the bedroom.

"I slept well," said Vera as she came to stand by the kitchen door. She wore the shirt he'd worn last night. It looked good on her. Gus remained seated. Vera came over and wrapped her arms around his neck, and kissed his cheek.

"Last night was wonderful," she said.

"I feel guilty for enjoying it so much," Gus said.

"You shouldn't," she said, "look, I'll get in the shower. Can you do me a favour? My car keys are in the lounge by my purse. Pop to the car; I've got a bag in the boot with a few casual clothes to wear today. Once I'm ready to face the day, we'll have that breakfast you promised, and then we'll talk."

The awkwardness he'd anticipated melted away as the morning progressed. Gus cooked, they ate and then sat in the lounge with fresh coffee. He talked to Vera about Tess, and she spoke of her years with Monty, the good and the bad.

"Ever since we met, I've wanted last night to happen," said Vera. "I hope that doesn't make me sound a man-eater. I'm far from that, I promise."

"Geoff Mercer encouraged me to ask you out. Geoff suggested I ask anyone out to jump-start my social life. The truth is, Tess and I had very little in the way of social life. We took an annual holiday together and enjoyed weekend trips to National Trust properties. Other than that, our careers kept us apart for long stretches. Neither of us played a sport or joined clubs or societies; the thought of either activity had us breaking out in a rash. We preferred to spend those rare moments of calm by ourselves. It was always just the two of us against the world."

"That was the marriage I craved," sighed Vera, "of course, we had the children who change your outlook. If we hadn't had the kids, Monty would have carried on wining and dining, burning the candle at both ends. Life had to be one long party in his world. We needed to entertain the businesspeople he was schmoozing for his next big deal one weekend. Then the next, we drove upcountry to celebrate a potential client's birthday, anniversary or promotion. He needed to get seen in the right places. When the kids came along, I elected to stay at home. After caring for them throughout the week, I was tired and fed up with the merry-go-round. Monty travelled to functions alone. We still entertained clients at home, but when the kids lay awake half the night, or God forbid one of them fell ill, it drove him mad. In the end, he splashed out huge sums of money for caterers. He told me I could avoid lifting a finger, even if it meant saving his business. As if it was my fault those get-rich-quick schemes of his fell flat."

"I'm surprised you two lasted as long as you did," said Gus.

"I wanted to make sure the kids were grown-up and independent. So once I was happy they would survive without the bank of Mum and Dad, I left him. I don't think he noticed for a while."

"What are your plans for later?" asked Gus.

"If you mean, after my divorce, the first thing is to sort out where I live. I'm renting a tiny cottage from my father at present. Monty has dozens in his portfolio, but I could not move into one of those. So I'll have to see if I can find something a little bigger, close to work that doesn't break the bank."

"I meant later today," said Gus, "do you want to do something together this afternoon? Or will you be driving back to your cottage for the rest of the weekend?"

Vera stood up, walked across to his chair and took Gus by the hand.

"Come on, let's go back to bed. We've waited long enough to break the ice. We could drive into the country for a drink and a meal early this evening. Then I'll get off home to my bed. This is still new. I'm enjoying it too much to want to risk spoiling it. A little and often might be best."

"I could have left those spare clothes in the car," said Gus as they reached the bedroom door.

"I hope that trip to my car and back didn't exhaust you," said Vera, "anyway, I'll need something to wear tonight."

GUS REALISED TIME WAS TICKING. He should quit daydreaming and drive to the Old Police Station. The team had a morning's work on the Mallinder case to get through first. Then this afternoon, they would say goodbye to Frank North.

Cool, partly cloudy and a light breeze. What did Frank do to deserve this weather?

Gus's drive through Devizes was pleasant this morning for a change. The traffic flowed better than it had since he had started work again. Was this the Vera effect, or was he wearing rose-coloured spectacles?

Gus couldn't help recalling the events of Saturday afternoon and the cosy meal in a restaurant beside a canal afterwards. Everything had been perfect. Friday night's urgency was in the past. A leisurely pursuit for mutual satisfaction took its place.

Vera had dropped him at the bungalow and then driven to her home on the other side of Devizes. They agreed to take things easy; they would both be busy in the coming weeks. Gus spent Sunday alone. He visited his allotment, and after an hour's gardening, he sat and read. When he returned to the bungalow, he considered the photographs dotted around. He didn't want Tess hidden from view. She retained pride of place in the lounge and the hallway. He apologised to her, removed her photo from their bedroom, and placed it in the spare room. The guilt was still present, but it weighed less now.

When Gus reached the Old Police Station, he found the rest of the team had reached the office ahead of him. They knew the score for today. Their outfits were in tune with the sombre occasion this afternoon. What Stuart Fitzwalter might make of it was irrelevant.

"Good weekend, guv?" asked Neil.

"Quiet," Gus replied, "what time was the Police Surgeon expected?"

"If you recall, I had to leave a message, guv. So I invited Fitwalter to attend first thing."

"We must hope that for Fitzwalter, first thing isn't late morning,"

Gus spotted the crutches lying on the floor beside Alex's desk.

"Have you been practising over the weekend?" he asked.

"A little and often, guv," Alex replied.

"Good," said Gus, "my sentiments exactly."

"I believe that's our guest that I can see on the CCTV, guv. Shall I go down in the lift and escort him up," said Lydia.

"Perfect, now perhaps we can make progress," said Gus.

Stuart Fitzwalter entered the CRT office and took in his surroundings. He was in his early fifties, sandy-haired and wore rimless spectacles. His clothes reminded Lydia of the care-worn lecturers from her student days.

They were just the right side of scruffy to pass for academic chic. Stuart's brown eyes flicked from person to person. Lydia realised he must have been born within a few miles of her foster home in Dundee when he spoke.

"You asked me to pop in for a chat," he said, "so here I

am. This place knocks spots off anywhere I've worked before. As for my appearance, I can only apologise. The invitation didn't mention wearing my best bib and tucker."

"Don't fret, Stuart," said Gus, offering his hand. "We have a funeral to attend after lunch. The office, on the other hand, looks this good every day. I'm Gus Freeman. I was a DI before I retired, and I'm now a consultant leading this Crime Review Team. We need your input on the Laura Mallinder murder from June 2011. So grab a chair, and let's chat."

"Laura Mallinder, yes, what a dreadful business. I hadn't had to deal with anything like it. I thought I knew what I was letting myself in for when I switched from a country practice to assisting the police. In my ignorance, I believed that a largely rural county such as Wiltshire suffered its share of accidental deaths on its roads and in various factories and farms. Statistically, brutal stabbings of young women were supposed to be a once-in-a-career occurrence in the county. Instead, Laura died within ten days of my move to Gablecross."

"We've read the murder file and the autopsy reports, Stuart and sent the whole and partial fingerprints for further analysis. We're checking whether there's a match somewhere around the UK that indicates her killer has struck again in the past decade. I have questions that need you to relive those first moments in the massage parlour. I make no apologies. Her killer is still at large. I intend to keep the success rate for this team at the level we have achieved to date. The devil is always in the detail. Leave nothing out. Most of all, try to tell us what you felt as much as what you observed."

Stuart Fitzwalter sat back in his chair and relaxed for the first time since he arrived.

"I was at home; it was a quiet Sunday evening watching TV with my wife. She tutted when the phone rang. It was Gablecross. Hickerton and his team had responded to a 999 call from a distressed woman at the parlour in Broadgreen who reported a murder. They asked me to attend. I drove there, pulling up outside at ten minutes past ten. A uniformed officer checked my credentials before notifying Hickerton by radio that I had arrived. As soon as I climbed the stairs, I could smell death. There were forensic people in Reception and the other rooms. DS Latimer passed me in a rush without a word. He looked as white as a sheet. He made it outside before being sick. At least there was no evidence in the stairwell when I left. I steeled myself for what lay ahead."

"Were there any signs of a struggle other than that you saw in the room?" asked Gus.

"None. The attack was confined to the room where I found DI Hickerton and a forensic officer. I'm not sure of the correct terminology, but the treatment table was on its side. It was narrower than I imagined. A wall mirror had cracks, and shards of glass littered the wooden shelf beneath. Towels and various plastic bottles got swept from the table where they were stored and scattered over the carpet. There was blood everywhere. The victim was face down. She was fully clothed. Blouse. Short skirt. Stockings and suspenders. If you've got the murder file, you know there were eleven stab wounds. The wounds varied in depth. The killer lashed out time after time at her back as she tried to get away."

"You found no wounds or abrasions on any other part of her body?"

"None. If Laura turned to face her attacker, they did not attempt to strike at her face, arms or torso. Not with their fists or the knife. I couldn't determine the order in which the blows occurred. The killer launched their surprise attack from behind, and Laura sustained eleven wounds in quick succession."

"What did that suggest to you?"

"She knew her attacker."

"Why, because she felt safe enough to walk into the room first? How many visits have you made to massage parlours?"

"None," said Stuart Fitzwalter. "But I would have thought the owners would train staff to lead customers to the room, go inside first and invite them to walk through to the shower area. It gives them control of the centre of the room. They can observe the client's actions and prepare for what comes next without exposing themselves to danger. Then, if a customer tried it on, they could summon assistance from Reception or the other rooms."

"Laura couldn't do that, though, could she? She was alone that night."

"All the more reason to be careful, surely, if it was a stranger. No, I believe she knew her killer."

"Hickerton says the attack was passionate and personal. How do you react to that statement?"

Stuart Fitzwalter considered this for a while.

"Impassioned, as in filled with emotion, yes, I can go along with that. Which emotion was the attacker experiencing, though? Was it anger, fear, disgust, love or hate? That I can't tell you. If you can determine that, you narrow your search for the killer. You asked me to tell you what I felt as well as what I saw. It was the ferocity of the attack that left the deepest impression. I wondered what this attractive young woman had done to deserve such treatment. That stayed with me for many weeks. It pained me that Hickerton and his team never turned up a suspect. I needed to see what person could inflict terror on another human being. Death from stabbing is rarely instantaneous. Laura Mallinder knew she would die as soon as she received the first blow."

"Is there any way of telling how much time elapsed between the first and last blows?"

"Come now, Mr Freeman. I used the word 'second' for a good reason. The window of opportunity for the murderer was small. It wasn't a scene played out over an hour or even thirty minutes. No, I consider the gap between the first and last stab wound between forty and sixty seconds. In cases of violent death, we focus on whether an injury occurred while the individual was alive or during the agonal or post-mortem period. We need to determine how long the victim survived after the wound got inflicted. A series of vital reactions, such as haemorrhaging and inflammation, are considered to get convincing proof of ante-mortem injury. The vitality of the wound relates to whether the victim was alive at the time of the trauma and how long before death someone inflicted that trauma. In my report, you will find that I believed the final three blows were delivered post-mortem."

"Fair enough, Stuart," said Gus, "we can agree the attack was savage. The killer didn't stop striking at Laura despite her having stopped breathing. Did you come to any firm conclusions as to the weapon used?"

"The blade was five to six inches in length and one-and-a-quarter inches at its widest point."

"Any suggestions who might have easy access to a knife of that nature?"

"I think we both know the answer to that one. Knives are far too accessible, whether designed for a specific profession, a trade, the military, or a more sinister application. Nothing about the wounds pointed to a knife custom-built for a particular function. It was most likely a kitchen knife. The blade width may have been slightly lower than I expected, but…."

"You're saying it could have been an old knife with a blade that had been sharpened over the years, reducing its original profile?"

"Without seeing the murder weapon, I couldn't confirm that, but it's possible."

"Who identified the body?"

"Laura's two brothers. Their names escape me now."

"The father didn't attend?"

"No, but it isn't necessary for a parent to attend. We dissuade family members from viewing the body when the injuries are severe. If the body were that of a soldier blown to pieces by an IED or a victim of a blazing inferno, it wouldn't be possible. In Laura's case, we didn't have those problems. Her face was completely untouched."

"The sons never explained why their father didn't come with them?"

"I never asked, I'm afraid."

"How did they react to seeing their sister's body?"

"Much as you would expect. The brothers were nervous before entering the room. Neither man cried as I recall. The elder son was the only one to speak."

"What did he say, exactly?"

"Yes, that's our Laura. He added nothing further."

"I'm sure you observed their body language, Stuart. It becomes second nature. We both wish it weren't so. But in a long career, we endure this scenario many times."

"I suppose I did. I didn't note it at the time, which suggests nothing unusual occurred. Going over it again with you today hasn't triggered a forgotten impression. Both men were grieving the death of their loved ones, as one would expect. I certainly didn't wonder whether one of them was the killer."

"As far as Theo Hickerton was concerned, their alibis were watertight. They were never in the frame for her murder. However, I wanted to double-check with you. In case you caught an odd vibe from someone coming face-to-face with their victim and seeing the full import of their actions."

"I got nothing of that nature from either man, Freeman. I'm sorry."

"Is it possible to commit a frenzied attack but not remember it?"

"Dissociative amnesia, you mean? I heard you were old-school, a detective who was dogged rather than one who indulged in psychogenic arguments. Although dissociative amnesia in defendants is relevant to both competency to stand trial and criminal responsibility in principle, courts remain sceptical of such claims in practice. Forensic psychiatrists often get asked to provide expert testimony regarding amnesia in defendants. Diagnosis presents a challenge as claims of amnesia may stem from several sources. I wouldn't presume to tell you how to do your job, Mr Freeman, but I would exhaust every other possibility before pursuing that one. A dissociative or fugue state, as it used to get called, is extremely rare. It's frequently temporary, and memory of the event returns intact in time. If your killer wiped the horror of what they did from their mind immediately after the event, it's more likely than not they will have relived it in glorious technicolour. I suggest you watch and wait while following your other leads."

Gus didn't think there was anything useful Stuart Fitzwalter could add to what they had learned this morning. It was as they had suspected. Laura's case was cold for an excellent reason. Every angle they had tried so far had produced the same negative result.

"Many thanks for dropping in to see us, Stuart," he said, shaking the Police Surgeon by the hand, "you've been most helpful."

Stuart Fitzwalter was surprised at that response.

"I didn't think I'd offered any significant help," he said.

"It never hurts to have people on your list of possible suspects ridiculed by an expert. We've crossed two names from our list if we can look past the sons for our killer. Every little helps. One final question before you leave. Would you think a woman capable of the murder, given the savagery of the attack?"

"I couldn't discount it," replied Fitzwalter, "the blade was thin and sharp. A strong and determined female could be responsible. If a colleague rang the bell after the final customer, that would explain Laura's willingness to open the door."

"If indeed it was locked," mused Gus.

"We may never know the answer to that," replied Fitzwalter.

With that, he left the CRT office.

"Impressions?" asked Gus as the lift descended to the ground floor.

"He's increased our number of potential suspects," said Neil.

"If he believes a common kitchen knife made the wounds," said Alex, "the killer could be male or female, young or old. The only positive thing I got was that the killer was someone known to Laura Mallinder."

"That's a positive enough starting point, surely?" asked Lydia. "We need to determine how many people Laura knew were in Swindon that evening. The number can't be that high."

"Anything else?" asked Gus.

His three team members were silent. Had Gus noticed something they had missed?

"Roll on tomorrow morning when we visit Maggie Monk," said Gus, "we can add names to that list of yours, Lydia. I also want to confirm the description of the feel of the murder scene provided by Stuart Fitzwalter."

"What's next, guv?" asked Neil.

"Lunch. We may not receive an invitation to the wake for Frank North. Bert Penman was vague about getting anything organised. Let's update our computer files with our report on this morning's meeting. Remember what I told the Police Surgeon? Feelings and facts in equal measure. The answer will be in these interviews somewhere."

ALEX AND LYDIA travelled together to the West Wiltshire Crematorium. Neil and Gus took their cars, and Alex and Lydia would return to the Old Police station car park after the funeral service before driving to their respective homes.

Neil and Gus had elected to be available for a trip into Urchfont if Irene North asked them to attend the wake in the Lamb. Gus suggested to Neil that he could park outside the bungalow, and they walked to the pub. Neil told him he wouldn't be drinking. Melody was adamant that Neil was on the wagon until after the baby was born.

The long, sweeping approach to the crematorium was visible from the main road. When Gus arrived at ten minutes to two o'clock, the hearse was waiting on a slip road to the left of the building. A succession of vehicles queued to exit the car park as they arrived. The number of occupied spaces was dwindling. Whoever they'd just cremated had a big family and many friends or acquaintances.

"We didn't struggle to find a place to park," said Neil, as they waited for Alex and Lydia to reach them, "that's a bonus. I came here last year for a young mother who died of breast cancer. There were cars parked on the grass under the trees from here to the entrance. When they built this place, they thought the main service would always be in a church or chapel, and only close family would come here for the final reckoning. These days the vast majority come straight here and get it done in whatever way seems appropriate."

"Tess and I were never religious, Neil. She wanted a basic humanist service. No frills."

"Sorry, guv, I forgot. I didn't mean to suggest one method was superior to another. I'd draw the line at having 'Bob the Builder' belting out if I was in the building trade and had laid my last brick. But some of those hymns were too morbid for my taste. I can't hear 'Abide With Me' without thinking of the FA Cup Final."

"I reckon Irene North will be more of a traditionalist, Neil."

"Come on, Alex, I thought you practised with those crutches over the weekend?" said Neil.

Lydia and Alex had parked closer to the exit. The uneven grass and gravel surfaces had slowed the motorcycle pursuit rider's progress.

"I did, but even though I've done months of physio, my stamina isn't at the level it was before the accident. So Lydia suggested I take the opportunity to walk the furthest distances possible."

"Well, you'll both benefit from that, I suppose," said Neil with a grin.

Gus's face wore a puzzled look.

The hearse had moved silently to a halt in front of the entrance door. Irene North appeared from inside the building.

"She must have arrived with family members and waited in that anteroom on the right-hand side," said Neil, "there's not many with her, are there?"

Gus noted the time. Two o'clock. Vera must have got delayed, or something came up at HQ.

The coffin was removed from the back of the hearse and rested on the bier. Irene and a few elderly relatives followed the coffin as it wheeled up the central aisle. Then, as the meagre congregation filed in behind them, the bearers lifted Frank North onto the raised platform between the blue velvet curtains.

A mournful dirge filled the room via the PA system. Gus could hear movement behind them as people took their seats on the right-hand side. Irene North and her family barely filled the front pew to his left.

"What do they call that thing?" asked Neil.

"What, where Frank's casket is resting? Not a clue," said Gus.

"A catafalque," Lydia whispered.

"Blimey," said Neil, "one new fact every day my old teacher used to say…."

"Was the high road to success," said Gus, "yes, Neil, we remember."

Everyone who was attending the funeral of Frank North was in the building. The doors closed. The mournful dirge faded.

Gus picked up the leaflet containing the Order of Service.

He'd been wrong. Irene North wasn't the traditionalist he had imagined.

# Chapter Six

ELVIS PRESLEY WAS in the building, and 'Hound Dog' opened the show.

The Order of Service followed a more normal pattern after Elvis left.

Gus thought whoever was in charge of the PA system had turned the volume up a notch. The joint was rocking.

He risked a look behind him. Vera Jennings and Suzie Ferris smiled in his direction as they took their seats. They did make it. Good. The rest of the pew was filled with police officers in uniform. Geoff Mercer had rallied the troops and come up trumps.

On the other side, he spotted Bert Penman, his walking stick hanging on the end of the pew. Gus didn't recognise many of the villagers Bert had with him. However, the woman who came in from next door to sit with Irene to share a bottle of sherry after he'd notified her of Frank's death was there. Gus didn't look any further; he didn't want to draw attention to himself more than he already had.

The celebrant ended the introduction with a short

prayer and then introduced the first two hymns. Finally, a proper hymn thought Gus. I remember singing this at school.

'Oh God, our help in ages past, our shelter from the storm,'

There weren't many singers in the congregation, but the female with the dog collar knew the words by heart and fair belted them out. Stirring stuff. Gus tried to remember the name of the TV show. The Vicar of somewhere. Not the actress herself, but her body double. If that wasn't sacrilegious.

Gus watched as a young girl, no older than twelve, walked to the podium to read a poem. The youngster was unaccustomed to public speaking, and Gus only caught the last verse when the PA system operator risked feedback by increasing the volume.

"A golden heart stopped beating, hard-working hands at rest. God broke our hearts to prove to us; he only takes the best."

Ah, the innocence of youth. Time for another prayer, and then the young, rotund celebrant delivered the sermon. She also told them about Frank's early life and his happy marriage. Neil wiped a tear from his eye as the inevitable 'Abide With Me' ended the audience participation part of the service. A final round of prayers and commendation followed, and Frank's casket disappeared behind the blue velvet curtains.

Buddy Holly soon reminded everyone what a 'Brown-Eyed Handsome Man' Frank North had been in his youth. There was a hum of conversation as Irene North walked to the exit door to thank the woman for a lovely service. Irene's relatives ushered her outside into the cool, partly cloudy afternoon. The light breeze wouldn't trouble her, despite the thin black cardigan she wore over a maroon blouse. Irene's black trousers flapped at her ankles. Perhaps flares were coming back; Gus didn't know.

"Do we queue up with the rest?" asked Neil.

"We won't cause Irene much grief, Neil, even if she's never met the three of you. It's these characters behind us with Geoff Mercer that might put the wind up her. It will remind her of the number of occasions uniforms visited the house to arrest Frank. If Geoff's got any sense, he'll shove Vera and Suzie in front of Irene first and let the others escape while they're chatting."

"Thanks for coming, Mr Freeman," Irene said when Gus reached her, "you brought your colleagues with you, I see. It means a lot. I hope you can make it to the Lamb?"

"Two of us will be there, Irene. See you later."

Geoff Mercer was next to speak with Irene. Suzie Ferris waited her turn, and Vera walked across to where Gus and Neil stood.

"Sorry we were late, Gus," she said, "the Chief Constable delayed our departure. She queried why we were deploying so many vital staff for the funeral of a convicted criminal. She told Geoff it sent the wrong message,"

"Geoff didn't back down, though, did he?" said Gus.

"The ACC told her it was his decision. He reminded her that the Rexha brothers and their colleagues would still be distributing drugs across vast swathes of the West Country without Frank North's sharp eyes. If we want the public to help us fight crime, he told her, we need to show our support when someone who helps us gets shot in the head for his troubles."

"Good for him. He might get that retirement earlier than he'd planned, though."

"I'll call you later tonight," whispered Vera as Suzie

stepped forward to chat with Irene North. Vera joined her. Gus and Neil made their way to their cars.

When Gus passed them on the exit road, Alex and Lydia were halfway to his car. He slowed and called out of the window that he'd see them at work in the morning. Then, Gus headed towards Seend and onward to Devizes. He pulled into the gateway of his bungalow thirty minutes later; Neil sat outside in his car waiting.

"Bloody school run traffic," Neil said as he got out, "doesn't anybody walk to school anymore?"

"Let's get to the Lamb, have a drink and a curled-up sandwich, then you can make your way home," said Gus. So they walked along the lane, and Gus noticed the car park was almost empty. This wouldn't take long.

As soon as he opened the door, Gus realised the villagers had forgiven Frank for his previous misdemeanours. They may not have travelled to the crematorium in significant numbers, but the bar was as full as on a New Year's Eve. Moreover, the villagers were here for the duration, so they had sensibly left their cars at home.

Bert Penman sat on a stool at the bar. He was in his element, chatting with all and sundry, a pint of cider in his hand.

Gus nodded to Bert.

"You've worked miracles, Bert. Well done," he called above the general hubbub.

"We're a tight-knit community out here in the country, Mr Freeman. Townsfolk such as you don't understand."

"Sorry, you're not drinking, Neil," said Gus, "I'll have a large scotch and water, please."

Neil ordered himself a slimline tonic. He gazed at the plates of food on the side tables and reckoned he could reconcile missing out on a couple of pints if there was that much free grub on offer.

Irene North and her family arrived to find the wake in full swing. She stopped briefly at the bar to collect a large sherry, then went across to where Gus stood.

"I never expected this," she sighed, "I'm glad only a few of them came to the service. You can't blame the vicar, poor girl. They're so busy up there."

Gus wondered what she meant.

Irene took a generous sip of her sherry.

"Clemency, her name was," Irene continued, "she visited me last week to jot down Frank's details; when he was born, which school he attended, where he worked and how we met. The usual bits and pieces they cobble together. But, of course, it's not for the family's benefit because it's something they know as well as they know their name. It's news to a few of their friends and colleagues, though, I suppose."

Gus couldn't admit to Irene he hadn't been concentrating. Instead, he had been reminiscing about the few occasions he spoke with Frank and how those conversations had resulted in his murder.

Irene had finished her glass. She waved it expectantly. Neil took it from her and eased through the crowd to the bar.

"Clemency got the pieces of paper she'd collected on her travels mixed up," Irene continued, "Frank never went to grammar school. He certainly never played cricket for the county. We were married for years, but we were half-happy at best. The rest of the time, he was in prison."

"Irene, I'm so sorry. That must have been awful for you," said Gus.

Neil returned with a fresh schooner of sherry. Irene grabbed it and laughed.

"I'll get over it," she said, "but wouldn't you like to be there when Clemency reads Frank's real life story to another poor widow and the congregation? That's who you should feel sorry for."

Gus had to smile.

"You appear to be bearing up well in the circumstances, Irene. The villagers rallied around. Are you sure you'll be able to manage?"

"I had a visitor this morning, Mr Freeman. He was at the crematorium, sitting at the back. He told me Frank was entitled to a Crimestoppers reward for giving you the tip-off that led to the arrest of those criminals."

Gus knew the amounts involved weren't huge. It might help Irene cover the costs of Frank's funeral, but little more.

"I didn't notice anyone," said Gus.

"He said he had to slip away before the very end," said Irene, "he needed to return to London."

"Brendan Curran," said Gus.

"That was his name," said Irene, "a well-dressed chap. He spoke like a gentleman."

The crafty bastard, Gus thought.

"Twenty-five grand will make a big difference, Mr Freeman. I couldn't believe it when he handed me the cheque."

"Did he say anything else, Irene?" Gus asked.

"He apologised for Frank getting caught up in their operation. His people realised they couldn't regard it as a complete success when a member of the public lost his life. Lessons learned, he said. I'd better get back to keep an eye on Frank's sister. She's not used to drinking in the afternoons."

With that, Irene North made her way through the

crowded bar and disappeared from view. Neil appeared beside Gus with a plateful of food.

"It makes sense to get it in one visit, I suppose, Neil," said Gus, "to save battling through the crowd for second helpings. So I think I'll follow your lead."

"Never gave that a thought, guv. There's a huge choice of sandwiches and savouries. I just grabbed one of everything I liked. I can try a few new things later when I pick up my desserts. There's plenty to go around."

"I'll get us another round of drinks, Neil. You'll need something to wash down that lot."

"Cheers, guv. How was Mrs North?"

"Irene landed on her feet. Frank gave her plenty of sleepless nights over the years. They never had two halfpennies to rub together at times. Brendan Curran and OCTF salved their conscience over his murder by wangling a payout under the Crimestoppers banner. You might be interested to learn the authorities reckon twenty-five grand equates to the loss of Frank's life at the hands of Eron Dushka. OCTF had the decency to deliver an apology in person."

"I reckon that brings the episode to a close then, guv," said Neil, "apart from learning the sentences handed to the gang members when it finally gets the court."

"Curran told Irene North that they learned a harsh lesson. I'll pass that information on to Geoff Mercer and the ACC. It will probably come as news to them. We can only wait to see whether OCTF keep our people in the loop when another operation creeps across the county's borders. Frank would never have died if they had done that at the outset."

"Your Mrs Jennings came to the funeral from London Road with the others, I noticed," said Neil.

Gus wondered whether Neil had overheard Vera say she was calling him this evening.

"Vera's a friend, Neil. We visited the Waggon & Horses on Friday evening for a meal," said Gus.

He didn't give Neil a chance to follow up with further questions. Instead, he made his way to the bar for drinks. Neil was still munching his way through the pile of food on his paper plate when he returned. Gus pointed to the tables where the food was laid out and headed in that direction.

Neil was right. Bert and the landlord had provided a superb spread. It would kill conversation for a while. Fingers crossed, telling Neil he and Vera had merely enjoyed a quiet meal together would satisfy his curiosity. He could always encourage Neil to ensure he didn't miss out on the trifle and the banoffee pie. They were both disappearing fast.

"Have you got anything else planned this week?" asked Neil.

The next sandwich was poised, ready to be devoured. Again, a typical copper, not easily thrown off the scent.

"My security cameras are being installed on Friday, Neil. I'll be able to shout at intruders when my smartphone warns me someone is invading my privacy."

Neil smiled. Gus knew the message had hit home. He and Vera wouldn't be able to keep it a secret forever, but what happened at the weekend was nobody's business but their own. Gus remembered something Neil had said earlier.

"What did you mean when you mentioned the benefits of Alex improving his stamina?"

"Those two went on a date the other night, guv. They visited the Imperial Dragon. They've been getting closer since day one. Don't tell me you hadn't noticed?"

"I hope they realise the problem it causes for the CRT if

it becomes serious. I don't want the team split up just when we've started. It might be time to have a word with Alex. I'm sure he knows the score, but a quiet word now might save a shitstorm in a few months."

"Blimey, it's six o'clock, guv. Melody will wonder where I've got to," said Neil.

"Yes, I reckon I'd better make a move soon. Another large scotch, and I'll be asleep in the chair before long."

"Are you going to pick up more grub on the way to the door, guv?"

"I hadn't planned to, Neil."

"If I gave you a plate…."

"I always thought it was the expectant mother who was said to be eating for two, Neil?"

"The food is free, guv, and it will only go to waste if we don't eat it."

They escaped from the Lamb with two platefuls of sweet and savoury items. Then, as they walked up the lane to Gus's bungalow, the sounds of muted merriment inside the pub faded away.

Frank North's wake had a while to run yet.

Once Neil was safely in his car with his extra portions and on his way to join his beloved Melody, Gus made himself a strong coffee. What a strange day it had been. First, he had met with Stuart Fitzwalter and confirmed how tricky it would be to solve the Laura Mallinder case. Then, he attended Frank's funeral and learned that the small village where he and Tess had planned to spend their twilight years had more community spirit than they could have imagined.

The phone rang at half-past seven.

"Dorothy's friend, it's been far too long," he said before picking up the phone.

It was Vera. The strong coffee had helped, but he still felt a trifle skittish.

"Hello, Vera. Have you called to apologise for not sitting beside me this afternoon?"

"I thought I would have arrived earlier, but our new leader had other ideas. It would have been more natural if we'd met outside and five of us had gone inside together. I didn't want to make things awkward with your team by moving one of them along to make room for me. We were so late the only sensible option was to keep the London Road contingent intact. Suzie said to say hello."

"The wake at the Lamb proved to be far better than I imagined. The place was still heaving when Neil and I left at six. Irene North was in good form too. Bert Penman and his cronies will keep an eye on her over the coming months. I think she'll be OK."

"Did you spot Brendan Curran there today?"

"No, but Irene told me he'd been to see her this morning with an apology and a cheque."

"Only proper. Curran hasn't been near HQ since you threatened to thump him. Perhaps, he'll feel it's safe to drop in to see the ACC again now. Did you make any progress on the new case today?"

"Nothing significant. We're interviewing the massage parlour owner in the morning."

"Have you ever had a massage?"

"Not in one of those places," said Gus, "well, never now you mention it."

"Well, that's something to look forward to."

"Mrs Monk doesn't provide those services herself."

"Who mentioned Mrs Monk? Well, you've got a busy day tomorrow. I'd better let you go. I doubt if you've eaten yet. Goodnight, Gus. Maybe, we can arrange something for the weekend. Call me."

Vera had gone. Gus hadn't had time to tell her he couldn't eat anything tonight. He sat in the chair and went through the questions they needed Maggie Monk to answer in the morning. As darkness fell, so did his eyelids. Midnight had come and gone before he awoke.

Gus stretched as he got up from his chair and felt a twinge in his shoulder. He had stayed in the same position for too long. A massage might be the answer. He hoped this slight niggle wouldn't wear off before the weekend.

## *Tuesday, 1 May 2018*

GUS LEFT for the office at his usual time. He had showered and dressed before noticing the twinge in his shoulder had disappeared. So typical. One consolation was that he could expect to experience more creaking joints at sixty-one as he grew older. So far, with his regular workout on the allotment, he was keeping those terrors at bay.

Gus parked the Ford Focus and went to the lift. How would Alex be this morning, he wondered? If he felt the effects of his first full day with his crutches, he might take Neil to interview Maggie Monk.

He would have to wait a while. He was the first to arrive.

Gus spent the next few minutes staring at the whiteboards. The photos of the murder scene suggested nothing new to him. If the murder weapon was a bog-standard kitchen knife, it was unlikely they would ever find it now. He tried to imagine a weapon a woman might carry if she planned to murder someone.

There had been a dramatic rise in the number of women caught carrying knives in recent years. Statistics showed that this was mainly for self-defence against an attack by a male. Domestic violence was also seeing a steep increase. It was still rare, however, for a woman to stab another woman. However, they had to pursue the possibility based on Stuart Fitzwalter's analysis.

His three team members arrived in the lift together. Alex was swinging along smoothly this morning. Lydia kept pace with him. Neil brought up the rear; he looked tired.

"Alex, you seem in fine form. Fancy a trip to Castle Combe?"

"Sure, guv. Give me five minutes, and we can get moving."

"Neil, did you get enough sleep last night? You look shattered."

"My eyes were bigger than my stomach, guv. Melody wasn't keen on a cold collation in case it upset her. That meant muggins had to eat the lot. I've been suffering from broken sleep for a week or two. It's catching up with me."

"You've reminded me of something my old Sergeant told me in Downton," said Gus, "his wife was pregnant, and he suffered from morning sickness. She sailed through without problems, and he had a dodgy tummy for two months. When he went to the doctor, the GP laughed and told him he was lucky. Two years earlier, he'd had a couple in his surgery and was pleased to tell them the wife was expecting their first child after trying for twelve years. The husband was over the moon, as you might expect. The next patient the GP saw was the lodger. His stomach was playing him up. So, count your blessings."

"I'm ready, guv," said Alex, "I wanted to check for any messages from the Hub. Unfortunately, the results are back on the fingerprints. I'm afraid they found no matches on the system anywhere in the country."

"I expected as much," said Gus, "come on then, let's give Mrs Monk the third degree."

Alex stashed his crutches on the back seat of the Ford Focus and eased himself into the passenger seat.

"Steady as she goes, Alex," said Gus, "remember what Theo Hickerton said, don't overdo it. We won't think any worse of you if you spend the odd day in your chair until you are fully fit."

"I've advertised it already, guv, and the flat. My family thought it was the right thing to do, get it fitted out for a bloke who was permanently disabled. I had to persuade them it was a temporary inconvenience. I admit the crutches are hard going, but I'm not giving in. I won't return to the wheelchair if I can help it."

"Have you ever visited Castle Combe, Alex? There's a famous circuit nearby where they run events throughout the year. Race days for cars and motorbikes."

"I can't see me on a bike for ages, guv. So I think I'll stick to four wheels and my two legs in the future."

"With age comes experience. The village in the valley on your left is charming, a typical English village with houses built from that honey-coloured Cotswold stone. So it's no surprise filmmakers have favoured it over the past fifty years. Maggie Monk lives in this part of the village above the valley in a large detached house on a gated estate a mile from the main road on our right."

Twenty-five minutes after leaving the CRT office, they waited for the gates to open. Maggie Monk had replied as soon as Gus hit the buzzer in the panel on the stone pillar.

"Very nice," said Alex, "one of these houses is up for sale. I checked last night. Eight hundred thousand pounds."

"We had better ask Maggie if she's doing a flit. It isn't an estate where they would countenance an estate agency board. Far too vulgar. I wonder if her neighbours know what line of business she's running?"

Gus walked to the front door. Alex collected his crutches and followed him. By the time Alex had reached Gus, the front door had opened.

"You had better come in," said Maggie Monk.

Nothing in the woman's appearance or clothes hinted at how she made her money. Gus reckoned that the massage parlour owner was around fifty years of age. Five-foot-two, eyes of blue. Well, bluey-grey, and although her make-up was a layer more than Tess would have thought necessary, it gave her a chic, sophisticated look. Maggie's bobbed blonde hair suited her, and Gus had to admit she could pass for ten years younger than her birth certificate.

"Thank you for inviting us to your lovely home," said Gus, knowing full well Maggie had no choice. "I'm Gus Freeman, a consultant with Wiltshire Police. My colleague is DS Alex Hardy, a valued member of my team. Our Crime Review Team is taking another look into the murder of Laura Mallinder, an employee in one of your parlours. That occurred in June 2011. I'm sure you remember?"

"I'm not likely to forget," replied Maggie.

"Why don't we sit," said Gus, "I'm guessing this will take a while. My colleague will wear holes in your carpet with his crutches if we have to stand around for long."

Maggie Monk wasn't making things easy. But Gus had ways to deal with her sort.

"May I remind you we're investigating a murder, Mrs Monk? A brutal attack on a young woman left alone in one of your establishments. Alone long enough for someone to walk in unchallenged and stab her in the back eleven times."

"I was there. I saw every bloody mark on her. You don't need to draw a picture."

"I sense a reluctance in cooperating with the police, Mrs Monk. I find that odd. You've prided yourself in running premises that have always maintained certain standards. They've never received a raid, never been the subject of scurrilous rumours of a brothel operating behind those beaded curtains. It would be a shame to see that good work undone. We can carry on this interview at the station if you prefer."

"No, I don't want any trouble. What is it you need to know?"

"Why were you so late that night?"

"I'm always in a rush. My girls will tell you, I haven't got time to breathe some days. I would have been ten minutes late at most if it hadn't been for the phone call. As I was about to leave, I received a message; an update from a courier service. They advised me my delivery would arrive in the next thirty minutes. I didn't have a clue what it was. While I waited for the gate buzzer, I went through my paperwork. I couldn't trace a thing that might have come here. Items for the parlours go direct to whichever premises need them. I waited until the time they said, but nobody showed. So I drove to Broadgreen as fast as I could. Yes, I probably drove over the limit. I got there at twenty to nine. You know what I found inside."

"I'd like you to think back to the phone call before we move on. Was it an automated voice or a human being?" asked Gus.

"Oh, a man's voice, I'm sure of that,"

"Did he have an accent?"

"Local," Maggie Monk replied, "from around here, but not so broad as to pin to a specific area."

"A young voice, or older perhaps?"

"It was so long ago. I didn't pay that much attention. I was rushing to leave the house and racking my brains to work out what delivery they meant. Then, finally, it was just a man telling me it would be with me within the next thirty minutes."

"Did he identify the firm he represented? How did he refer to you? Full name? First name? It would help if you tried to remember. It could be a vital clue to the killer's identity. Any window of opportunity would have closed if you had arrived on time. This fake message confirms the planning that the killer undertook. They deliberately delayed your arrival to increase Laura's time alone."

"You're saying I spoke to the killer?" asked Maggie Monk.

"It's possible, given the information you've told us this morning. Why wasn't this phone call mentioned to the police at the time?"

"I was in shock. You have to understand. I'll never forget what I saw when I opened that door and saw Gem lying there."

"Let's go back a few steps, Mrs Monk," said Gus, "who did he say he worked for?"

"If I'd been on time, I could have been killed. My God."

Gus looked at Alex and nodded towards the kitchen. Alex stood and gathered his crutches from where he'd rested them against the side of his chair.

"Coffee, Mrs Monk?" Alex asked.

"You'll find a cafetière in the kitchen. The cups are in

the cupboard directly above. I'm sure you'll find everything you need."

"Just relax," said Gus, "it's difficult, but we're making progress. Let's take it one step at a time. Did he tell you who he worked for?"

"I'm pretty sure he said: 'Mrs Monk, this is a courtesy call from your courier service. Our delivery driver is on his way with your order. He'll be with you within thirty minutes. Thank you.' That was it. He rang off after that."

"I don't suppose you…."

"Dialled 1471? I hoped it might give me a clue to what was supposed to get delivered, but they withheld the number."

"So, he didn't identify himself or the firm. He knew your name. Is your private number readily available to the public?"

"He knows where I live, doesn't he? I could be in danger. If he finds out, I talked with you."

Alex called from the kitchen.

"Everything's ready, guv. Can someone help carry it through?"

"I'll go," said Maggie, "I never expected this, Mr Freeman. I thought that I'd put this behind me."

She carried the tray from the kitchen. Alex made his way back to his chair.

"Where did I get to?" said Maggie as she retook her seat, "oh yes, my private number. I use my mobile number for everything to do with the business. That's what appears on any adverts I take out in trade magazines and directories. Each parlour is listed in the telephone directories for clients to contact the girls and make appointments. My landline is ex-directory. Living on a gated estate helps restrict the number of people who can turn up unannounced on my doorstep, but you need to avoid being bombarded by cold callers."

"I can understand that," said Gus. "ex-directory will reduce the number of people who had access," said Gus. "Friends and family have it, I suppose? What about tradespeople? Do you get newspapers or milk delivered somewhere outside the main gate? How would you deal with a window cleaner, a plumber, or an electrician if they wanted to know whether you were at home and available for them to visit? Would they have your landline number rather than your mobile? You could be anywhere in three counties if they called that number."

Maggie Monk made her way through the list of things Gus had fired at her.

"I buy my newspapers, magazines, milk and everything else at the supermarket. Nothing is delivered here regularly. I collect my post from the Post Office. If I need something fixed, I sometimes use the landline. I can see how silly that is now with hindsight. When I arrange the annual visit for my boiler to be serviced, I ask the man to call ahead to tell me what time he's arriving. Then I can be sure I'm letting in the right person."

"So, given time, you could compile a list of people who might have your home number or who gleaned it by noting your number after you dialled back?"

"Yes, I would need to think about it for a while, but I could do that. Do you think one of those people will be the killer? Someone I freely let into my home?"

"Again, it's possible. But unless you specifically told people never to pass on your number under any circumstances, a devious person with murder in mind could extract it from them without attracting suspicion."

"Have you had any building work done since you moved here, Mrs Monk?" asked Alex.

"The house was new when I moved here eight years ago," Maggie replied, "there were a few teething problems that the builders returned to rectify. So I've had no work done since."

"Are you happy here?" asked Gus.

"I don't plan to move. The countryside is beautiful, and I'm central to my premises."

"When you compile that list, Mrs Monk, could you also provide us with the details of the staff who worked for you in the months leading up to the murder? Proper names and the names they used in the parlours. Would you include their most recent address if they've moved on from your employment?"

"How soon do you need this information, Mr Freeman? It could take me a while."

"We will call to collect it on Thursday morning at ten o'clock. We can go through other questions with you then."

"What more do you need from me?"

"Details surrounding how the parlours operate. Also, the names of clients in the parlour that evening, plus a list of Miss Mallinder's regulars. We will need to interview every one of them."

"Is that it, then?"

"You were keen to tell us about the room and what you saw, Mrs Monk. Perhaps it would be a good time to hear that now."

"I rushed inside and climbed the stairs two at a time. I knew Gem, or Laura as you knew her, would be mad at me for leaving her alone. I was angry with myself for hanging around for that blessed delivery. It couldn't have been that important.

I should just have let them press the buzzer on the gate. When it didn't arrive, it made me angrier than ever. Then the door to the massage parlour in the alley was unlocked. I've told them to keep it shut so many times. I passed the desk in Reception and paused; I found the first door closed. I thought Gem was with someone. I checked in the drawer to see if the cashbox was still there. Anyone could have run up those stairs and stolen it when nobody was in Reception. Nothing was missing; it was dead quiet. I tapped on the door. It wouldn't be the first time that an elderly client had fallen asleep during his massage. Gem didn't answer, so I eased the door open. I didn't want to disturb whoever was inside. That's when I saw her — sprawled across the carpet, covered in blood — stuff scattered around the room as if there had been a struggle. I wanted to run, but my legs gave way. I crawled back to the Reception desk and phoned the police."

"You saw nobody as you made your way along the alleyway and into the parlour?" asked Gus.

"No, everywhere was dead quiet."

# Chapter Seven

"WHAT DID YOU MAKE OF THAT?" asked Gus as they waited for the main gates to open.

"I found it odd that no one asked why she got delayed in reaching Gentle Touch that night," said Alex. "I would have hoped DI Hickerton didn't merely accept that she was habitually late."

"Anything else?"

"Do we know who built the housing estate? Laura's brothers are in the building trade. One of them could have learned the landline number when they rectified those teething problems Maggie cited. Bristol's only a quick dash up the motorway."

Gus nodded.

"If the delivery subterfuge connected to the murder, then we learned that a man was involved."

"A local man who was working alone or with a partner. A partner who could be female. We can't rule that out yet."

"What did you make of Maggie's response to the request for the client's details?"

"I thought she might plead ignorance or that the information was confidential. But, instead, she didn't bat an eyelid."

"Maggie's last comment was interesting. Before I asked her to describe the murder scene, she asked, is that it? Didn't that strike you as odd?"

"It seemed a natural reaction after the list of things you had asked for."

"Maybe, but I wondered whether she had expected us to ask about something else. I'll have to think about what that might have been."

As they drove back to the Old Police Station, Gus felt they had finally made progress.

"Where to next, guv?" asked Alex.

"I reckon I should visit Bedminster and start digging into the Mallinder family history. You can take it easy, Alex. I'll take Neil with me this afternoon."

"Fair enough, guv," said Alex, "I'm sure Lydia and I will have plenty to keep us occupied."

"Now you raise the subject...."

"Nothing's happened yet, guv. Lydia's keen, but I'm wary. You've already told us the ACC is keeping tabs on her. I'm afraid they'll transfer her miles from here, and it will be a bugger trying to maintain a long-distance romance. It's hard enough for a copper when the girl lives on your doorstep. I've avoided having my heart broken so far. I want to keep it that way. My love of motorcycling came before any of the girlfriends I've had in the past. They were happy to share a week in Majorca or a weekend shopping in the Big Apple, but a bike trip through the Pyrenees, forget it. That life may be behind me now. Time will tell. It was hard to make that first car trip after being laid up for so long. I don't get the shakes these days, but climbing back into the saddle would be a whole new ball game."

"You know we'll support you, Alex," said Gus, "I've mentioned several times to take things steady. I won't labour the point. I want you to remember that although Lydia isn't strictly a serving officer, this CRT role is a stepping-stone, a probationary period if you will. Her academic qualifications may play a large part in her future role within the Wiltshire Police; they may not. There are many routes to the top. Our new Chief Constable studied Film and Media Studies at University. That doesn't appear to have held her back. Our attitude toward relationships between officers working in the same station may seem old-fashioned, but it's for a reason. From a selfish position, I would hate for this team to disband. We're starting to gel. I can't order you to do anything, Alex. I can only advise. If this thing between you and Lydia becomes more serious and the top brass finds out, there's only one outcome. I'm an old romantic at heart. I knew within weeks that Tess was the one for me. If Lydia is your soulmate, then let nothing stand in your way. This is only a job. Life has to be more than that. Finding the right person to share it with is priceless."

"I understand where you're coming from, guv, but I've no idea what Lydia's long-term intentions are. I may be just another notch on the bedpost. She doesn't give much away. Just like my physical recovery, the next few months in our relationship will be small steps, I promise you."

"Right," said Gus, "we'll not mention this again until the situation changes. As for the others, this conversation never happened. I don't want it spread around that I'm an old softie. Got it?"

"Yes, guv. Your secret's safe with me."

Gus opted for a brief stop at the Old Police Station to

swap partners. He wondered how Alex would handle this afternoon alone with Lydia. He'd issued a mild warning, as any superior should do given the circumstances, but as a mere consultant, he'd encouraged Alex to follow his heart.

When did he become an expert in such matters?

"What was Maggie Monk's place like, guv?" asked Neil as they left the first-floor office.

"Sorry, Neil. I was miles away. It was a big detached house with all the bells and whistles you expect when you pay through the nose."

"Why does she need a place that big if she lives alone, guv? The original files said she was a widow."

"Good point, Neil. There were no photographs of children; and no sign of any pets. Maggie told us this morning she's happy. No plans to move. I'll ask when we return on Thursday to collect the information she's compiling. It might explain a lot."

"There has to be a reason for her career choice. Nobody's born a madam, not that Maggie Monk is a brothel owner, but you know what I mean. Women who turn to prostitution or control prostitutes haven't had a happy childhood. Neither have they made successful marriages and surrounded themselves in the warmth of a devoted family."

"You're a cynical sod for one so young, Neil," said Gus.

"I know, the perfect material for a copper. I get it from my father. That was just the comment he'd make."

"Did your Dad ever work in Swindon?" asked Gus.

"Vice was one of my Dad's many areas of expertise, guv. It's no secret he had contacts on the wrong side of the law. If he wanted to get the dirt on a suspect, he learned things in the pubs and clubs across the county. He was in and out of them for a beer, on and off duty, anyway. His best tips often came from strippers and girls who stood on street corners. They've always got their eyes peeled for their safety. They see more than the average person who wanders along staring at their phone or the paving slabs."

Gus filed that away for future reference. It might be worth a phone call to Terry Davis. He might have an insight on this case that no one had tapped into back in 2011.

"Sam Mallinder's our first appointment with Laura's family," said Gus, "that's Church Road, Bedminster. A two-bedroomed terraced house built in the last century's first decade."

Neil noticed the narrow streets and terraced properties were very similar to those surrounding Swindon, where Laura's murder happened. Bedminster and Old Town weren't dissimilar in how they grew after the Industrial Revolution. They had both become tired and care-worn in the century since. Another common trait they shared was it was a bugger to find a parking spot.

"Do you think we'll get a ticket, guv?" asked Neil as they walked a hundred yards towards Sam Mallinder's front door.

"We can only pray the austerity cuts have decimated the traffic wardens and everything else, Neil. I stuck that 'Police-on-call' message on my windscreen. We may be lucky."

"Or the locals will nick the wheels off your Focus, and we'll find it resting on a pile of bricks."

Gus shrugged and rapped the brass knocker on number twenty-seven.

"Are you the police?" asked Sam Mallinder as he opened the door.

"Good afternoon, Mr Mallinder, my name is Freeman, a civilian consultant with Wiltshire Police, and this is my colleague DS Davis. We're here to ask you questions about your daughter, Laura. Our Crime Review Team are taking a fresh look into her murder."

"You had better come in," the old man said and turned and walked away.

Gus and Neil followed him. Neil closed the door behind them. Sam Mallinder had walked to the kitchen at the rear of the house. Gus sensed he spent the afternoons here with the warm sun taking the chill off the place as it moved across the large window.

"This is a nice spot," said Neil, "you've got quite a garden out the back there."

"It gets bloody cold in that front room. I can't afford to keep the heat on all day. My sons help me keep the garden up together. I used to grow more vegetables than grass. Now it's half and half. We don't see as many birds now as we did when they were nippers. Do you want a cuppa?"

"I'll make us one," Neil offered.

Sam sat on one of the four kitchen chairs around the table in the centre of the room. He wore his age well. Gus knew he had retired from an engineering firm last year. That garden would serve him well if he didn't hand the job over to his sons. Sam Mallinder was tall, angular, with thinning hair, but the gloomy character he portrayed this afternoon didn't fool Gus. Sam did what many members of the public did when interviewed by the police. He created a persona that allowed him to assess what they knew or wanted to hear. This conversation could be interesting.

"What do you want to ask me?" he said.

"How was your relationship with Laura?" asked Gus.

"We both loved her. She was our only daughter. So what sort of question is that?"

"When did you learn how she made her living?"

"The day after Laura died. Your lot called on us at eight

in the morning. I was leaving for work. It had taken them a while to identify the body. We knew she lived and worked in Swindon, but Laura rarely came home after she moved away."

"When did she leave home?" asked Neil, bringing three cups to the table. Sam Mallinder added three sugars from a bowl in the centre.

"Not long after she left college. The three of them rented a place."

"Three of them?" asked Gus.

"Laura and two of her school friends. Maureen and Joanne. One of the boys might remember their surnames. Laura came home when we lived in our old house in Bedminster Down. Jean was still alive then. Laura had been working in different offices, and then she suddenly lost her job. There was a falling out with the other girls too. We didn't get involved. Finally, Laura asked if she could come home, and we took her in without a second thought. We were so proud of her when she bought her place in Kingswood. I thought she worked in a solicitor's office. Then she moved to Swindon, into a bigger place. You could have knocked me down with a feather when the detective told us what she'd been doing."

"How did you feel about that?" asked Gus.

"Disgusted. How would you feel if your little girl worked in a massage parlour?"

"Was that why you declined to go to Swindon to identify her body?" asked Gus.

"I didn't want to see her like that. I wanted to remember her as the beautiful young woman we raised."

"When was the last time you spoke with Laura?" asked Neil.

"I don't remember. Laura rang us and talked to Jean,

mostly. Not that often. Every few months. Laura never invited us to her Swindon home. Jean would remind Laura that she knew where we lived. We would always be there if she needed us. Perhaps she was ashamed of what she did. It's not something you can be proud of, you know. The neighbours in our old place never let us forget it after it was in the newspapers. When we moved here, Jean became ill. People either didn't know about Laura or thought we had enough trouble. Cancer took Jean two years ago."

"In a statement that Jean gave at the time," said Gus, "she said Laura was still your daughter no matter what she did. So when did Jean find out she worked in massage parlours? Did Laura tell her in one of those rare phone conversations? Why didn't she tell you?"

"Jean never told me how long she'd known. Why didn't she tell me? Because it would have broken my heart, that's why. But, look, is this going anywhere? All you're doing is raking up bad memories. The Swindon police never found who killed her seven years ago. So what makes you think you can do any better now?"

The real Sam Mallinder was emerging from his alter ego. Feisty. Belligerent. Angry.

"How did you feel when you learned Jean hid the truth from you, Mr Mallinder?" asked Neil.

"All those years we'd known one another. We were only kids when we got married. There was never anyone else for either of us. We argued from time to time, but secrets? There had never been secrets between us. We brought our kids up properly. Laura was bright; she studied harder than Gary and Tyrone. So why would she have to turn to a job like that?"

"You say that you never visited Swindon?" asked Gus.

"Never. Not before, not while Laura lived there, nor

since she got killed. I told your lot that. We went to the Hippodrome for a matinee performance with Tyrone and Emma, his wife. We left at half-past five, returned to Bedminster Down Social Club and stayed there until ten o'clock. Tyrone dropped us at home. I don't know why I'm telling you this. You've heard it before."

"We like to check these things, Mr Mallinder. Where was Gary that night? Do you remember?" asked Neil.

"Ask Gary. While you're at it, ask Tyrone if he remembers what he did the night of his sister's murder. It might have slipped his mind. Bloody daft, this is. Our Gary was where he said he was. We all were. None of us had a reason to kill Laura."

"You admitted you were disgusted at her chosen profession," said Gus, "if you had known about it, that could have led to you confronting her."

"But I didn't know, I swear."

"What happened to Laura's Swindon home?" asked Gus.

"Tyrone and Emma dealt with the solicitors. I couldn't face it. Jean and I were struggling to come to terms with Laura's death. It took forever to get everything resolved. We had planned to move to a smaller place when we both retired. Tyrone found this place. They were renovating a house in the area, and although it needed work, the price was right. So we moved here in 2013. Six weeks of peace we had before Jean got diagnosed. She died in the hospice three years to the day."

"Do Tyrone and Gary work together?" asked Neil.

"Most of the time. The building trade has its ups and downs. When times are tight, they go where the work is."

"I suppose they helped do up this place for you before you moved here?"

"That's right. A new bathroom and kitchen. The rest was cosmetic."

"Do they ever get involved with new builds, housing estates, further afield?"

"Bristol's a big city. There's usually enough work for them to never need to travel. Gary might have had the odd contract out of the city when Tyrone didn't have work for him."

"We'll talk to other family members, Mr Mallinder," said Gus, "to confirm you were where you said you were that evening. However, if someone outside the family killed your daughter, who might that be? Did you ever suspect anyone in her past could have had a motive? A jealous boyfriend, perhaps?"

"I told you she moved in with Maureen and Joanne. They were a bad influence. Tyrone and Gary used to see them in the bars and clubs, drinking themselves silly and getting off with a string of blokes. We didn't raise Laura that way. We wanted to see her find someone and get married, but those friends of hers were happy to play the field. We were glad when that finished, and Laura moved home for a while. She went out with a lad called Ian for a while."

"Ian Hewson, the footballer?" asked Neil.

"Oh, you've got his name on your list, have you? At first, he seemed nice, but Laura said he wanted to stop her from going out unless it was with him. Ian was concentrating on his football, so he wasn't free to meet with her as regularly as a lad with a nine-to-five job. Laura told me she caught him sitting in his car outside her offices. Ian thought she was seeing someone else."

"Hewson stalked her?" asked Gus, "I don't think we heard this before."

"Well, Laura just said he was getting 'clingy', and she didn't want to see him anymore."

"How did he take that?" asked Neil.

"Not well, but Tyrone and Gary had a word with him."

Neil and Gus shared a look.

"What happened after that?" asked Gus.

"The City received an offer for him from a big club in the Midlands. Ian moved away."

"Any idea where he's playing now?" asked Neil.

"Hewson doesn't get his name in the papers much these days. Perhaps he's mellowed. Ian had a quick temper, and if a defender hacked him down, he wouldn't be satisfied with a free kick or a penalty. He got sent off half a dozen times for violent conduct. As a result, he moved clubs regularly."

"Was he ever violent towards Laura?" asked Gus.

"If he had been…."

"Tyrone and Gary would have had more than a word. Have your sons ever been in trouble with the police, Mr Mallinder?"

"Ashton Gate was less than two miles from our door. They had a few scuffles with opposition fans back when they were teenagers. But they stood their ground in the streets around our home. There weren't the gangs and knives there are today; you settled things with your fists. You had to, or people would walk over you."

"I think we'll get the rest of the story from your lads," said Gus, "they'll be working this afternoon. Will Emma be at home?"

"Not until she finishes work. It will be six before anyone's home at Tyrone's. As for Gary, he goes to the pub before going home."

"Is Gary single?" asked Neil.

"He's not bothered either way; he never was. Gary's not gay. He isn't interested in having a woman in his life."

"Thanks for the cup of tea, Mr Mallinder," said Gus. "Sorry you had to go over old ground, but we've got things clearer now. It will help in our search for the murderer. Let's hope we can bring you good news soon."

Sam Mallinder followed Gus and Neil to the front door.

"Tyrone will be your best bet to find out about Ian Hewson," said Sam Mallinder, "he's done work on places up in Bradley Stoke. It's not in the same bracket as the Golden Triangle in Cheshire, where the Premiership footballers live up around Wilmslow and Alderley Edge. Those buggers can be on three hundred grand a week. Scale that down to clubs from the West Country, and they gravitate to the same neck of the woods."

"That could be very useful, Mr Mallinder," said Neil, "many thanks."

The front door had already closed.

"We got more from that than I imagined when we walked in the door," said Neil.

"He's probably cursing himself now for revealing those new snippets of information," said Gus, "do we have a number for Emma Mallinder?"

The Focus was intact when they reached it. No sign of a ticket either. When the pair sat inside, Neil checked his notebook. Gus drove away from Church Road. No point pushing his luck.

"Emma is a primary school teacher, guv. I have a number. If you don't mind sitting on those tiny chairs, we could contact her to arrange a meeting at the end of the school day."

"Do that, Neil. We'll have to walk a distance this time, no doubt. The Mums on the school run will clog up the approach roads way before the final bell. Parking will be a nightmare. Where is this school, anyway?"

"Cheddar Grove is a two-minute drive from where we are, guv. We can park here and walk."

"What you mean is we could have left it parked where it was. So keep your eyes open for a gap."

Emma Mallinder was on duty at the school doors. She ensured the little ones didn't leave the building until the appointed parent or guardian arrived. So as soon as Gus and Neil walked up to the school gates, she knew who they were.

"Only a few latecomers to deal with," she called out, "Please wait by the main door. I'll join you as soon as I can."

The little ones in her charge clearly loved Tyrone Mallinder's wife. She reminded Gus of Tess. Attractive, warm and someone who had found their perfect job.

Ten minutes later, they sat on normal-sized chairs in the staff room. The place was buzzing with activity. Gus couldn't believe teachers made so much noise in their inner sanctum when they yelled at kids to be quiet for most of their careers.

"There aren't many places we can go for a quiet chat," said Emma. "This concerns Laura, doesn't it?"

Neil explained the reason for their visit.

"Where did you go to that Sunday, Mrs Mallinder?" asked Gus.

"The theatre in the afternoon, and then Sam insisted we went to the Social Club."

"You weren't keen?"

"Not my scene, Mr Freeman. Tyrone enjoyed it. Jean and I chatted while the men played darts and pool."

"Were you married at that time?" asked Neil.

"We'd just had our first anniversary."

"Did Laura attend her brother's wedding?" asked Gus.

"We got married on a beach in the Maldives. It was me, Tyrone, Gary, our best man, and my bridesmaid, Amanda."

"Did anything happen between Gary and Amanda?" asked Neil.

Emma laughed out loud. Several of her colleagues stopped talking.

"I don't think he noticed her. The World Cup was starting in South Africa. Gary's happiest in a bar with a pint in his hand, watching a big screen."

"We won't delay you any longer," said Gus, "we'll talk to Tyrone and Gary later. Just one more thing. We know Jean knew what Laura did for a living. Did she hear it direct from her daughter, or did someone else tell her?"

"Laura told her," replied Emma.

"So, you knew too?"

"Only because Jean told Tyrone and Gary. She thought they might hear a rumour. Laura worked in Bristol and Bath before she switched to Swindon. So if they did hear anything, Jean made them swear they wouldn't tell Sam."

"Because he would have been angry enough to do something rash?" asked Neil.

"Not Sam, he would have been mad, but Tyrone and Gary would have been encouraged to sort things out. If you get what I mean."

"The same as they did with Ian Hewson?" asked Neil.

"Was it Sam who told them to have a word with Hewson?" asked Gus.

Emma Mallinder nodded.

"How did you and Laura get on?" asked Neil.

"We only met three times before Tyrone and I got married. Laura was beautiful. She dressed smarter than your average girl that worked in a solicitor's office. Nobody ever picked up on that. Laura didn't talk about work. Her parents didn't push it because, well, she wouldn't gossip about a client's personal affairs. I never saw Laura again after we came back from the honeymoon."

"How did she get on with her brothers?" asked Gus.

"They treated her like most older brothers treat a younger sister. They teased her, and they were very protective. I never heard them argue once."

"That's all, Mrs Mallinder. We'll be on our way," said Gus.

As the staff room door closed behind them, the conversation level rose again.

"It's bedlam in there, guv," said Neil.

"A scene of uproar and confusion? I agree, Neil. The teaching profession sometimes veers towards the same word but with a capital letter, after the Hospital of St Mary of Bethlehem, the most famous mental hospital in history. I spotted the message on Emma Mallinder's mug. It said, 'You don't have to be mad to work here, but it helps.'"

The walk back to the car gave Gus time to reflect on what they had learned today. There was a germ of an idea forming. Too soon to see what shape it would take yet, but what they had heard this morning and this afternoon had helped move things forward.

***Wednesday, 2 May 2018***

"HAVE we got our files updated from yesterday?" asked Gus.

He was feeling chipper this morning. He had thought through yesterday's events as he tended to a few odd jobs on the allotment. Bert Penman had left a list tacked to the door of the shed. The carrots, onions and parsnips he'd sown for Gus needing thinning out while they were still young. Gus had remembered to water along the rows so the disturbed seedlings would settle in again.

Bert had suggested using three poles to construct frames for his runner beans. He'd scribbled a sketch on a scrap of paper that resembled the framework for a teepee. Then, finally, Gus got the idea. He found he had enough five-foot poles to strap together for four frames.

Almost enough for a reservation.

"All present and correct, guv," said Neil.

Alex and Lydia nodded their agreement.

"Who's first on our list today, Alex?" asked Gus.

"Tyrone and Gary Mallinder have agreed to meet us at lunchtime today. They're working in Brislington, adding a conservatory to a detached house on Bath Road. Tyrone said they'd be in the King's Arms, on the corner of Hollywood Road after twelve."

"What do they think this is?" asked Gus, "a quiet chat over a pint? It's an interview."

"Your notes from yesterday suggest Gary will be in a familiar environment, guv," said Lydia, "and Tyrone was in that Social Club on the night of Laura's murder. They will relax in their comfort zone. If you dragged them into an interview room, they'd clam up. The conversation might be hard work. They might be more willing to talk in the pub with a drink inside them."

"I agree, guv," said Neil, "what is it you always tell us? We want witnesses to tell us something they hadn't remembered before or suspects to tell us something they didn't intend us to learn."

"We'll run with it then, Neil. Same team as yesterday.

You and I will stick with the Mallinder clan. Alex will accompany me tomorrow morning when we visit Maggie Monk. Once we've got those details from her, we'll split the list. We need to pick up the pace now."

"Is there something specific Lydia and I can tackle today, guv?" asked Alex.

"Find out where Ian Hewson is," said Gus, "search for him in Bradley Stoke. Then dig into the three Mallinder men's history. Sam Mallinder used an odd phrase yesterday. He said Tyrone and Gary 'stood their ground' in Bedminster as teenagers. Sam looks as if he could handle himself when he was younger. Check social media for the sons. See if you can find links to the football club up the road from where they lived. Football hooligans come in all shapes and sizes, and they don't always grow out of it. If the boys follow in their father's footsteps, they'll be aggressive and argumentative. Sam and Tyrone weren't in Swindon that night, but Tyrone and Gary knew about Laura's job. So we can't discount their involvement."

"I added a comment to my notes, guv," said Neil, "after Sam had confirmed what we knew about their whereabouts on Sunday evening. I asked him where Gary was. He tried to hide something from us, do you agree?"

"Let me read that piece again," said Gus. He checked the Freeman File. "You're suggesting that phrase suggested a strained relationship, is that it?"

"It was the way he hurriedly added we should check with Tyrone. Even though we were only getting him to confirm what he told Theo Hickerton and his team seven years ago. Maybe he wanted to hide the fact that perhaps Gary's alibi wasn't as watertight as theirs."

"It's a worry that the solid alibis this family had, according to Hickerton and Latimer, are falling apart like a house of cards," said Gus. "What else did they skim over in the original investigation? We need to see Tyrone and Gary in separate areas of the bar. Work on the other items I asked for this morning, and then the four of us will head for Brislington. We'll leave at a quarter-past eleven."

"Clever, guv," said Neil, "the brothers will have had time to get the drinks in and order their food. So we won't be upsetting Geoff Mercer with a huge expenses claim."

"I wasn't born yesterday, Neil," grinned Gus, "anyway, we're on soft drinks as we're on duty. I'm sure there will be a wide selection of crisps and nuts."

Gus tried not to smile as he heard a collective groan.

# Chapter Eight

THE DRIVE to Brislington took just under an hour. They took Neil's car because it had more legroom than any of the others. Alex sat in the front with his crutches. Gus and Lydia sat in the back.

"I don't imagine we'll be making a habit of this, will we, guv," asked Neil, "only in six months from now, I'll have a baby seat where you're sitting."

Gus thought back to what the new Chief Constable had told him.

"Six months is a long time, Neil. This team could be history by then."

"I hope not," said Lydia, "you lot are family. I'd miss you."

"That must be their van," said Alex as they drew into the King's Arms car park. A battered white van with ladders on the roof was one row in front. Alex could see Mallinder - General Builders stencilled on the side and rear doors, together with a mobile phone number.

"I can see how you got to make detective, Alex," said Neil as they walked to the main entrance.

Lydia trotted ahead to hold the door open for Alex. Neil followed the couple inside. Gus brought up the rear. The bar area was functional, and there were only a handful of customers. It wasn't difficult to identify the Mallinder brothers. They had the same tall, angular appearance as their father but were twenty-five years younger and more muscular.

Tyrone, the elder brother, was now forty-one, according to the murder file. Gary was two years younger. Gus imagined the gap between Gary and Laura being a significant factor in how the brothers treated her. She would have been their little sister.

There were differences in appearance between the boys and their father. Both had shaved heads and tattoos on their arms and upper bodies. The wife-beater vests they wore reinforced Gus's opinion they were dealing with two hard nuts. There would be no intellectual sparring in any conversation they had with the police. It would be brief and to the point. If matters deteriorated, he and Neil would have their hands full. Alex wasn't fit enough to tackle one of these two yet. If he ever had been. Time to tread softly.

Gary gave his brother the nod that the Crime Review Team was in town.

"Hope this won't take long," said Tyrone, turning towards them.

He had a pint of lager in his hand; with one good swallow, he'd be ready for his second. Gus looked at the bar clock. If Tyrone had a dry neck after grafting on that conservatory, he might already have started on his second pint.

"It will take as long as I say it will," said Gus, forgetting he'd decided to tread softly, "my name is Freeman, and this is my Crime Review Team. DS Hardy and DS Davis will chat with your brother, Gary. It's a sunny morning. I suggest you take your drinks outside to the beer garden. You won't disturb anyone. We'll find a corner for our conversation, Tyrone. My colleague, Ms Logan Barre, will join us once she's bought our drinks."

Gus had asked what everyone wanted to drink as they sped along the Keynsham bypass. Lydia went to the bar with the crumpled twenty-pound note Gus had given her. Alex and Neil steered Gary Mallinder towards the door. Tyrone and Gus were left facing one another by the bar.

"Do you still follow the City," asked Gus.

"I thought you wanted to talk about Laura?" replied Tyrone, strolling over to a comfortable leather-covered bench. Gus sat in a chair facing him; he said nothing.

"We go to every Home game. Can't take time off to travel to Away matches these days."

"What did you make of Ian Hewson?"

"What, the lad our Laura went out with for a while? Ian was quick and skilful, but he had a temper."

"I meant more as a person, not a footballer."

"Ian Hewson wasn't right for Laura. He was too controlling."

"Your Dad proved very helpful yesterday. He confirmed where you were in the afternoon and evening on the day Laura died. He suggested I ask Gary where he was. Sam didn't seem to know. Do you know, Tyrone?"

Tyrone took that last swig of his pint of lager. He was ready for another; Gus didn't move.

"Gary told the police where he was. You'll have that recorded somewhere. Your blokes in the beer garden will ask him that question. Why don't you ask them when they come indoors?"

"I asked you, Tyrone," said Gus. Lydia returned with their soft drinks. Gus pocketed the change.

"Gary was where he always is on a Sunday. Sat in a pub, listening to music, earwigging other people's conversations and getting pissed. It's what he does."

"When did you last see Laura alive?" asked Gus.

"At our old home in Bedminster Down. Emma and I hadn't long got engaged. We dropped in on Mum and Dad. No, I tell a lie. I caught sight of her in Kingswood after that. Laura was getting off the bus from Bath; she lived in a new one-bedroomed flat just up the road. That's where she moved to after she left home the second time."

"You didn't visit her in Swindon?"

"No way. I work sixty hours a week minimum with Gary. Emma and I make the most of our weekends. Laura didn't put herself out to see any of us, so we let her get on with it."

"How did you feel when your Mum told you Laura's occupation?"

"Sick."

"Emma was accommodating yesterday too. She said you and Gary were very protective of your little sister, and you never argued. It seems odd then that you didn't drive the short distance to Swindon. To see if you could help Laura see the error of her ways. You and Gary have done something similar in the past. Sam asked you to have a word with Ian Hewson, didn't he? Why didn't you talk to whoever was employing your sister?"

"You don't understand," sighed Tyrone, "Mum kept pressing Laura for details of where she worked. She couldn't fathom why Laura didn't visit them at weekends.

Laura always maintained she worked in a solicitor's office. Then one day, she snapped at Mum. Alright, she said, I work in a massage parlour. I make twice as much as I would in any old office. Mum was devastated; she thought Laura was selling herself. Her daughter was a whore. Laura explained it wasn't like that. She gave a proper massage but with extras. They never had sex with the clients. That was bad enough for Mum, Gary, and me when she told us."

"Mum told you soon after and persuaded you to keep the matter secret from your father, is that right?"

"Yeah, if Gary and I had gone to Swindon to sort out the owner and bring Laura home, how would we have explained it to Dad? Laura couldn't have carried on living in that house she bought. Once she was back living under their roof, it would have come out. Dad would have lost his rag. You know how he is. You're right; he sent us to thump Hewson. That was for stalking her. Imagine what he would want us to do to whoever persuaded Laura to work in one of those places?"

"Did you ever find out who owned the parlours?" asked Gus.

"The less I knew about what she did, the better," said Tyrone. "I stayed away from Swindon until we had to deal with the solicitor and settled Laura's estate. Emma and I visited the house, but we never went near where she worked. We heard it had closed by then."

Gus was inclined to believe him.

"Emma helped you through that sad time, didn't she?" asked Lydia.

Tyrone nodded.

"She's been a rock. Emma took control. Dad was useless. He couldn't handle knowing what Laura had been doing and how she died. Then, when he was on his knees,

Mum's diagnosis crushed what spirit he had left. Emma cared for her through her final months. It was hard for everyone, but Emma got us through it."

"How did Gary handle things?" asked Gus.

"Gary did what he always did. Never mentioned it, got stuck into his work and drank."

The door to the beer garden opened, and Gary returned to the bar. Alex and Neil followed him in.

"Can we get back to work now?" asked Gary, "have you finished harassing my brother?"

"We've established a better understanding of the case after chatting with Tyrone," said Gus. "It remains to be seen whether you were as forthcoming as the other three members of your family. We welcomed their cooperation. If you wish to get back to work, please do. Just remember that until we close this case, it's always possible we'll return with further questions. Please make yourselves available without us having to chase you when the time comes."

Tyrone and Gary Mallinder didn't hang around. The team heard their van's racket as it left the car park. Another police department could deal with the dodgy exhaust.

"What did you learn?" asked Gus.

"Sam is an overbearing father. Laura was his princess. He had put her on a pedestal and didn't believe she could do any wrong. We asked Gary where he was that day. He told the same story, word for word, as he did to Jake Latimer. A pub in Bedminster for two hours as soon as they opened at noon. He returned home until five o'clock and then visited many pubs, arriving home in the early hours. Latimer visited each one Gary could remember, and someone confirmed they had seen him in there that night."

"Latimer assumed that because there was never a long enough gap between sightings for Gary to drive to Swindon and back, he couldn't have committed the murder," said Gus.

"Tyrone described Gary's typical Sunday routine to us," said Lydia. "What's to say the bar staff Jake Latimer interviewed just assumed he was there as usual that Sunday night?"

"What else did you ask him?" asked Gus.

"The things we agreed, guv," said Neil, "about the City, Ian Hewson, and where Tyrone and his father were that Sunday."

"Anything?"

"He clammed up about the football," said Alex. "I don't believe Gary goes for the match as much he does for the chance of a fight. As for Hewson, those two got on better than we thought. Tyrone carried out the punishment beating. Gary said he disagreed with his father but went along because it was less hassle. His Dad has a temper. Sam expects the boys to do what he tells them.

"Sam and Tyrone were at the theatre in the afternoon and a club at night," added Neil, "Gary never saw them that day."

"When was the last time he saw Laura alive?"

"He couldn't be sure, but at least two years, maybe three," said Alex.

"Did Gary ever visit Swindon?"

"He says not," said Alex. "They've done no building work that far from Bristol. As for socialising, Gary said Swindon was off-limits."

"That will result from the football hooliganism," said Neil. "The derby matches between City and Swindon are mental. They might travel with a gang and look for trouble outside the stadium, but the word would spread if a lone

Mallinder got spotted in Old Town. Gary would be in for a right kicking. Those fans have long memories."

"What was Gary's reaction to Laura's secret?"

"The same as his father. It disgusted him," said Neil.

"Let's head back to the office now," said Gus, "we'll update the Freeman Files and carry on the search for Ian Hewson."

As they travelled through the outskirts of Bath, Gus remembered something.

"Did any of those derby matches occur between the time Laura moved to Swindon and her death?"

"I wish I still had my Rothmans Football Year Books, guv," said Neil. "They're a great reference for trawling through to dredge up memories of long-forgotten matches, players and statistics."

"We'll take your word for it, Neil," said Gus, "just google it."

"I went to school with a football trivia fanatic," said Alex, "he studied those things for hours. You could ask him for team colours, home ground, highest attendance, trophies, and highest transfer. Any detail for either of the ninety-two League clubs. He was rarely wrong."

"How boring," said Lydia.

"You're Scottish," said Neil, "what do you know? You've only got Celtic and Rangers. Everyone else makes up the numbers."

"What did he do when he left school?" asked Lydia.

"Formed his own IT company," said Alex.

"I was right. Your school friend was boring."

"He sold it for seventy million in 2007."

"Now he's just bloody annoying," said Lydia.

"Found it, guv," said Alex, "I did as you suggested and looked it up on my phone. City and Swindon didn't face one another in League or Cup for a few seasons around that time. If Gary travelled with Bristol Rovers to Swindon in March 2010, he might have bumped into his sister."

"It's not usual for fans as committed as the Mallinder family to switch their allegiance," said Neil.

"Perhaps, he drove to Swindon with a mate," said Gus.

That germ of an idea started to grow.

## *Thursday, 3 May 2018*

THE WEEK WAS SLIPPING AWAY from them. It felt like he'd made progress, but it was mighty slow. Gus drove to work with a dark cloud over the Ford Focus. He hadn't heard from London Road for a few days. When would Geoff Mercer call for an update? Would Sandra Plunkett be waiting to pounce the second he reached the first-floor landing?

Neil was in the office when he stepped from the lift.

"This is early, even for you, Neil. Everything okay?"

"Melody was restless last night. Then she was up early with the sickness, you know."

"No, I don't. Tess and I never wanted kids. She had thousands pass through her life at school or college. I had children to handle in the office every day. I reported to several of them."

Neil laughed out loud. Some of last night's tension was released. The lift doors opened; Alex and Lydia had arrived. They wondered what they had missed.

"Before Alex and I head back to Castle Combe, is there anything you thought of last night to add to what we learned yesterday?" asked Gus.

Lydia thought it typical that Gus believed they thought of nothing other than the case in their leisure time. The case became all-consuming. She realised that something *had* been niggling her as she drove in this morning.

"Our meetings with the four members of the Mallinder family gave us more negatives than positives, didn't they, guv?" she asked.

"Explain," said Gus.

"Well, three alibis haven't been weakened one bit. Sam, Tyrone and Emma could not have been in Swindon. Therefore, they weren't involved in Laura's death. Gary's alibi isn't watertight. He may not have visited every bar DS Latimer checked. Gary went there so often the staff may have got the day wrong. There might have been time to allow him to drive to Swindon."

"How did he know where to go?" said Gus. "Tyrone was adamant they had been nowhere in Swindon, let alone near the massage parlour. He wasn't even aware Maggie Monk was the owner. He told us Sam would have ordered him and Gary to sort the owner out if Laura's secret had come out. Tyrone naturally assumed it was a man. I'm not sure Gary's our killer. One or two of the bar staff could have suffered brain fade when DS Latimer talked to them. They couldn't all make a mistake on the timing. The gap between the murder and the verification of the witness statements was a matter of days, not months."

"The timeline is very tight, guv," added Neil. "Gary reckoned he left home at five in the afternoon and was out on the lash for around eight hours. Laura got attacked at around a quarter to nine. Bristol to Swindon on a Sunday night? Forty-five minutes on the M4. Thirty-five minutes if he pushed it. Let's assume he lied, stayed off the drink, and had a meal before leaving Bristol at eight o'clock to murder his sister. The attack lasted no more than fifteen minutes. If he drove back straightaway, he could have been in one of his regular haunts before a quarter to ten. For at least one hundred minutes, Gary had to be missing, and nobody noticed. It's tight, but just possible he made that trip. I don't think we can rule him out yet."

Gus stood and walked to one of the wallboards and began to list the main events as he saw them.

"Laura left school in 2000. Two years at college, and then she began work in a solicitor's office. Laura left home to share a place with this Maureen and Joanne, whom Sam Mallinder mentioned. According to Sam, they had boring jobs and partied hard at weekends. In 2006, Laura learned that the agency work paid peanuts compared to what she could earn as a masseuse. Who told her that, another girl-friend? Was she ever identified? That needs chasing. Laura had moved back in with her parents because she'd lost her job. The massage parlour work started at that point. She worked in parlours in Bristol and Bath. Laura moved into a new one-bedroomed flat in Kingswood in 2007. That suggests she earned good money over a reasonably long period. Tyrone said a chance sighting as she got off the Bath bus was the last time he saw Laura alive. The brothers work together. We can assume Gary was in the van with him that day. He told you yesterday it was two years, maybe three, before she died that he last saw his sister. Kingswood was four years earlier; that's interesting. Emma and Tyrone were newly engaged. Tyrone corrected himself when I asked the last time he'd seen Laura. At first, it was when he and Emma visited Sam and Jean one weekend. Laura lived with her parents for ten months. We should confirm that. We know that Laura moved to Swindon in Spring 2008 to run the new parlour. Tyrone and Emma got married in 2009. There's one other date that's missing."

"When did Laura tell her mother how she earned a living," said Alex.

"Exactly," said Gus, "how long did Tyrone and Gary keep a lid on that secret?"

"Who will you ask, guv?" asked Lydia.

"All three of them," said Neil, "to check we get the same answer."

"Oh, I would only ask Emma to begin with," said Lydia, "if Gary's not in the clear, it wouldn't be wise to alert him to the fact, surely? Or am I being naïve?"

"Neil's right," said Gus, "we always try to substantiate what a witness says. The more confirmations, the merrier. Tyrone and Gary are close. We can't discount them lying to provide one another with an alibi, no matter how they reacted to the questions we posed yesterday. Lydia could be on to something. Give Emma a ring at Cheddar Grove, Neil. Try her around break time. She should be in the staff room. Keep it casual. You may need to shout. With luck, she won't tell Tyrone you called the minute she gets home from school. Right, Alex, we'll get moving now, shall we?"

Maggie Monk had anticipated their arrival. As Gus approached the estate entrance, the gates opened at dead on ten o'clock.

"Still no signs of which of these neighbouring properties are for sale, guv," said Alex looking around him.

"No building work is being done at present either. Well, would you look at that? Mrs Monk already has the front door open. She's eager to get us indoors before anyone puts two and two together."

"Don't worry, guv. You might look like a copper, but my crutches will confuse them."

"Good morning," said Gus, "a lovely day for it."

"Come on in," said Maggie Monk, "I think I've got everything."

Gus noted the various sheets of paper on the hall table. Maggie was keen to get rid of her visitors as soon as possible. He had other thoughts on that subject.

"We have further questions, Mrs Monk," he said, "perhaps we could take a seat and run through them first?"

"If we must."

They walked through to the same spot as on their previous visit.

"You're a widow, Mrs Monk, am I correct?" asked Gus.

"Charles, my husband died some years ago."

"How did you meet?"

"Is this relevant?"

"I believe so," said Gus.

"I was his secretary. Charles owned a successful precision tools engineering firm. I was in my early twenties. He was married and in his mid-forties. One morning five years after I'd started working there, he called me into his office and asked me to close the door. I thought he was a good boss, and we got on very well. I asked him what was wrong. Charles told me he'd been in love with me from the first day I'd started working for him. He couldn't imagine life without me. He said he had left his wife, and he wanted us to marry after his divorce. I had no idea. We had grown close, I suppose, as one does when one sees one another every day."

"Did you love him?" asked Gus.

"I liked and respected him. Charles offered me the chance of expensive holidays, and good clothes. A life I could never expect to match with someone my age. Expediency coloured my choice. It wasn't romantic love, if that even exists. We had a good marriage. Charles was seventy when he died. The company was still thriving, so I sold up and began to build my investment portfolio. I enjoyed what I could do with the money. I could afford to buy this place outright. Even if it's far too big for one person, it reminds me just how far I've come. I enjoy seeing the envy on people's faces. The income from the properties is more than enough for me to continue to take those exotic holidays and buy whatever clothes I fancy. My decision to marry Charles might seem mercenary to you, Mr Freeman, but a girl has to live."

"Is that what influenced the business model you installed in the properties you purchased?" asked Gus.

Maggie Monk looked at Alex and back to Gus.

"Charles had needs. I'm sure you sympathise, even if you wouldn't admit it. He wanted to be with a younger woman and sacrificed everything to be with me. That showed me the power I had as a woman. I kept him happy in the bedroom; he lavished money on me. He left me everything in his will. His first wife never saw a penny. So after I'd bought a few properties and leased ground floor units to hairdressers, DIY shops and cafes, I thought, why don't I help more women with my windfall? I started with Cleopatra's in Knowle. I employed several girls who did as I asked or were out on their ear — no funny stuff. I took a basic massage fee from them per customer. They charged the men various options for a happy ending. Everyone went home happy."

"How did you meet Gem or Laura Mallinder?" asked Gus.

"Gem was recommended to us by one of my girls, Amber. Her real name is somewhere on the list I've prepared for you. I believe they met at school."

"You told us you received a call regarding a courier delivery just before you left home that night. Can you be more specific about the time you received that call?"

"No later than twenty-five past seven. The man told me the parcel would arrive in the next thirty minutes. I waited the whole time, then gave it up as a bad job. Finally, at around eight o'clock, I raced over to the parlour. I got there at twenty to nine."

"Excellent," said Gus, "that makes sense now. Can we go through the items you've gathered for us now?"

Maggie Monk picked up the sheets of paper in the hall and brought them through to where Gus sat.

"As you can see, the list of people who had direct access to my landline was short. I don't have many friends. The list of people who might have had indirect access is longer, but I can't see why anyone would note a number they had no reason to call. If I need a tradesperson, I call them. They don't call on the off-chance you need a painter and decorator, do they?"

"We'll call them and ask them, Mrs Monk," said Alex.

"The additional sheets contain the staff at the parlours I owned at the time. Look at this one: Bristol, Knowle, Cleopatra's, Amber. That's the girl I told you about, Carol Gullis. She's been with me since the beginning. As for where Laura worked, Swindon, Broadgreen, Gentle Touch and the girls there were Gem, Janina, Ebony, Kathy and Camille. All the details I have for them appear beside each name."

"This is comprehensive enough, I think," said Gus, "I assume you've included the other sites because after the Broadgreen parlour closed, you gave the girls jobs elsewhere?"

"The girls needed a job, Mr Freeman, and as we were still successful, I opened new premises in other towns."

"This last sheet includes the clients Camille and Laura saw that evening, yes?"

"These were Laura's regulars that booked her on a Sunday. Camille had clients of her own. I've listed the four men: Walter Shadwell, Don Green, Ryan Black and Jeff Naylor. They were the only men Gem had booked. Jeff Naylor would have left her at about eight forty-five. But, perhaps, a little earlier."

"Why don't we have the names of the men who visited Camille?" asked Gus.

"They never came into contact with Gem that night," said Maggie Monk.

"Maybe not, but they may have returned to the parlour. What if someone left something in the room where Camille entertained them? Something which had the potential to damage their marriage or their business reputation? Your girls held information about clients that could get used to blackmail them."

"I hope you're not suggesting I was ever involved in anything illegal. I've run a clean business from the outset and did my utmost to protect the girls from exploitation. Apart from this awful exception, I've kept them safe from harm. Trust works both ways, Mr Freeman; I trust my girls will obey my rules. Our clients trust the girls will keep their liaisons secret. If this rumour got out, my business would collapse overnight."

"I still wish to interview the men who visited Camille. I want to discount the possibility that the person allowed into the parlour after Jeff Naylor left wasn't one of those men. Why that man then killed Laura Mallinder, I don't know, but I can't ignore the possibility he was here earlier. You said they wouldn't contact Gem, but the parlour had a Reception area, stairs, and passageways. Camille could escort a client from the front door to a room while Gem got herself a coffee. Or they could cross paths as she took a customer downstairs to see him off the premises."

"I suppose so," sighed Maggie Monk. "During the week with five rooms in action, the footfall can be significant. It's like Piccadilly Circus. It's plausible that Gem recognised another girl's client. If he returned for some reason, she might let him in."

"We'll wait while you look for those names, Mrs Monk," said Gus.

Fifteen minutes later, Alex and Gus wished Maggie Monk a good morning and returned to the warmth of the car. Unfortunately, the mood had turned decidedly chilly in the Monk household.

"Do you reckon she was deliberately hiding something, guv?" asked Alex.

"No, but I wanted to let her know who was in charge. Witnesses don't get to decide which information they disclose. We decide. These names may be vital, or they may be a complete waste of time. Without them, I would always wonder whether there was someone we hadn't checked out. I want to nail the killer. The more names I can confirm were close to Laura Mallinder on the evening of her death, the better."

"Well, we've got the parlour's visitors now. If none of them was the killer, we're still hunting for the caller's identity that delayed Maggie Monk. As she said the other day, she may have spoken with the killer."

"We'll get a clearer picture soon, Alex. We can start

interviews now we have these lists. Who is most likely to know which of these clients might be capable of murder? The girls who worked alongside Laura will hold the answers."

# Chapter Nine

ONCE THEY RETURNED to the office, Alex and Gus made themselves a coffee.

"The hospitality wasn't great today at Castle Combe then, guv?" asked Neil.

"I won't be losing sleep over it, Neil," said Gus.

Lucky you, thought Neil. Melody's interrupted sleep patterns were taking their toll on him.

It was turning into a long day.

"Have you heard from your Dad, Neil?"

"Not for ages, guv. We ought to let him know about the baby. It will be his first grandchild."

"I plan to call him this evening to get Terry's inside knowledge on our case. I won't put my foot in it by congratulating him on the happy event. Thanks for the warning."

"Tell the old bugger you heard a whisper that I'll be ringing him at the weekend. We might as well get it out of the way. I doubt it will persuade him to fly home, though."

Terry Davis had several reasons for staying in Marbella. Some related to his enjoyment of the Spanish weather after a lifetime in the police force. Others were related to cases involving certain criminals where he had been negligent. Whether that less diligent approach was due to payments received is still debatable.

"Alex and I will update the Freeman Files while the interview with Maggie Monk is fresh in our minds. You two can read through what we learned later. Alex will compile a list of interviews we'll share between us. Lydia, you will sit in with me on the ones involving the clients. The boys will interview the girls."

Lydia raised an eyebrow. Her reaction prompted Gus to explain his reasoning.

"Alex and Neil will need to travel to various properties across Wiltshire, Somerset and Gloucestershire. As far as possible, we'll talk to the girls in their working environment. A thirty-minute session should be enough to learn what we want. We'll invite the male interviewees here to this office. I don't want them to feel too uncomfortable. If we go stomping into their homes asking what they did with their spare time, it could cause ructions. I don't know how many are married. Or whether any of them is in the public eye. This case review isn't about ruining marriages or reputations. We're seeking a single truth. Who killed Laura Mallinder?"

"I hope none of them will expect a happy ending to their interview, guv," said Lydia.

After lunch, Alex gave Neil and Lydia a list of names and contact numbers.

"I've split our interviewees between the three of us. Maggie Monk had a mobile number for each of the girls we were interested in, so you'll be speaking to them directly. These aren't the parlour numbers. If they don't reply, remind them in your message that we know their real names and where they work and live. We will collect them from home and take them to a custody suite for an interview under caution, if necessary. This interview is not optional."

Gus looked up. Alex was on the money. The signs of strain he'd displayed when he emerged from the lift that first morning was disappearing. He'd been correct in his assessment of the man — a solid partner to have alongside a Detective Inspector. Fingers crossed, his health didn't impede his progress. Everything crossed that Geoff Mercer didn't realise he was a great asset and transferred him.

"I'm calling the male customers," Gus said, for Neil and Lydia's benefit. "I'll be telling them the same thing. They can choose a discreet chat in the comfort of a well-appointed office or be dragged out of their armchair and taken to a police car. When most of their neighbours will be at home."

"If the girls try to avoid us, will you send uniformed officers to remove them from the parlours, guv?" asked Lydia. "If not, doesn't that look like we're approving what goes on in these places?"

"Maggie Monk's girls aren't breaking the law, Lydia. She's not running a brothel. When I referred to our approach with the customers just now, I said we didn't wish to ruin reputations. In Maggie's case, we're not looking to ruin her business. It's not for us to judge the rights and wrongs of the services she offers. We merely enforce the laws this country has in place."

The team spent the rest of the afternoon chasing dates and times when the various people were available. The schedule in the Freeman File was soon filled with appointments. When the team left the office at five o'clock, they were waiting for only three callbacks.

"None of Laura's four regulars had any objection to

travelling across the county, guv," said Neil as they descended in the lift to the car park. "Did you consider using interview rooms at Gablecross?"

"Because it's on their doorstep, did you mean, Neil? No, I want to avoid Hickerton and Latimer learning we are digging deeper into a mismanaged case. Try to get to sleep tonight, Neil. Your head was dropping this afternoon."

"Sorry, guv. It was warm in the office. You're off tomorrow, aren't you?"

"I won't be in first thing. The security camera firm will be at the bungalow at nine o'clock. After that, I'll get into the office for the afternoon interviews. Never fear."

As he drove home, Gus remembered that he hadn't asked whether Neil and Lydia had uncovered Ian Hewson's whereabouts in Bradley Stoke. It shouldn't be too hard to find him despite the size of the place. The first houses in Bradley Stoke, six miles northeast of Bristol, were built in 1987. The area now had thirty thousand residents.

The town council had worked hard to establish a community spirit. It was still a young town with many people and families. It takes time to develop a community spirit - it doesn't happen overnight. Gus knew that first-hand from the village a few miles ahead of him. The spirit there had developed over the centuries.

Gus hoped they could lift Ian Hewson out of the rabbit warren of houses and sit him in a quiet room for a face-to-face chat very soon.

Once inside the bungalow, Gus prepared his evening meal. He looked at the scene from his kitchen window. How long had it been since he tidied the garden? He had spent most of his spare time on his allotment. The lawns and borders that Tess had been so proud of looked uncared for and drab. He couldn't transform it overnight, but two hours of remedial action could prevent its terminal decline.

At nine o'clock, he sat in the lounge with a well-earned cold beer. Even the climbing roses Tess had cherished looked happier with life. Gus was more content too. The physical benefits of manual labour were secondary to the freedom it provided for clear thinking. There was no background noise of chatter, phones ringing or office equipment humming away to disturb his thoughts.

There was one more thing to do tonight. Gus called Terry Davis.

"Good evening, Terry," he said, "Gus Freeman here. Are you free to chat?"

"I'm not working tonight, Freeman, so you're in luck. Although. I told you I wasn't keen on these chats becoming regular. So who have you upset this time?"

"Nobody that I can recall. We're taking a closer look into the murder of Laura Mallinder in 2011. She worked as a masseuse in a Swindon parlour. Someone stabbed her to death. Does it ring any bells?"

Terry Davis retired to Marbella in 2013. Gus knew from the murder file he wasn't on the team that carried out the initial investigation.

"I heard a few rumours,"

"That's what I hoped, Terry. That network of informants and colleagues you established over the years gave you a comprehensive appreciation of what was happening around you."

"You have a way with words, Freeman. I was looking after Number One."

"If you hadn't kept your ear to the ground, you may not have made it to Marbella before Internal Affairs paid you a visit."

"I think you'll find they're called the Independent Office for Police Conduct, Freeman. They never had enough to make a case because I did nothing wrong. That's my story, and I'm sticking to it."

"What rumours did you hear?" asked Gus.

"It pleased Hickerton to be dragged away from that case to concentrate on the knife crimes business. Jake Latimer is a good copper. Maybe he takes after me too much for his superior's liking. Jake's fond of a shortcut. He will do it if he can solve a case by taking the odd risk. If they'd left him to get on with this murder you're on about, Jake would have found the killer. Hickerton is a plodder who didn't want to investigate crimes involving the sex trade. He considered Laura's death as a self-inflicted wound. Theo's no different from most of the county force's top brass. They sweep the trade under the carpet. Pretend it isn't there. They'll dash out for a blitz on kerb-crawlers or streetwalkers to appease the locals, but anything more than that isn't part of the overall plan."

"We've identified glaring omissions from that initial investigation," said Gus. "Hickerton's covered his backside by running an annual token check on the fingerprints collected from the murder scene. But, other than that, this is one of the coldest cold cases I've ever encountered."

"Where did this girl work?" asked Terry.

"Gentle Touch, in Broadgreen," said Gus, "opened in early 2008."

"If you can use the term to describe places such as that, then Gentle Touch was one of the clean ones," said Terry. "I never heard a whisper of anything illegal occurring there."

"Maggie Monk, the owner, prides herself on providing a service that means they never risk a raid. She would be horrified if her premises got thrown into the same basket as those catering for the grubbier end of the sex trade."

"The public might take a different view. Many want every parlour closed for good. The force's policy can be ambivalent. They allow brothels to operate, providing they create a safe environment for the women. I could show you a dozen properties in towns surrounding Devizes that couldn't be further from what you might expect of a brothel. It's just as likely to operate in a smart, two-bedroomed flat or a semi-detached three-bedroomed townhouse. They will be modern, pleasant and warm places, not the dirty hovels you associate with the sex trade."

"That's all very well," said Gus, "but many girls trafficked across the UK are drug-addicted and controlled by vicious pimps. For example, look at the Albanian gangs, such as the Rexha brothers. The brothers were in that line of business before they moved into marijuana."

"Look," Terry said, "say nothing to Neil, but call around to chat with a friend of mine, Donna. I'll text you her address later after I've warned her you're coming. She won't charge you full whack for her time. She knows I can make things difficult for her. You'll see the bigger picture. Who knows, she may have crossed paths with this girl, Laura?"

"Donna, you say?" said Gus, "I suppose she's the ubiquitous tart with a heart?"

"We bumped into one another in bars several times over the decade," said Terry. "Donna's getting too old for the game now, but she won't retire while a few of her elderly gentlemen are still breathing."

"There was nothing else relating to the murder?" asked Gus.

"Nothing specific. I needn't tell you, Freeman. It's nearly always personal."

"We've found a discrepancy in one of the brother's statement. The other family members are out of the frame. We have yet to interview Laura's regulars."

"I'd give you long odds against it being one of them, Freeman. They don't go to Gentle Touch looking for love. How old was she?"

"Twenty-seven," said Gus.

"There you go. That girl's regulars will be my age or five years on either side. Am I right?"

"We've only got names and phone numbers so far. Walter Shadwell doesn't sound a youngster."

"Walter? Bloody hell, he's pushing eighty. He was the landlord of an Arkell's pub in Old Town that I frequented. It was the end of civilisation as he knew it when he had to let women into his public bar. Walter was the last person I dreamt would visit a massage parlour. He reckoned a woman couldn't pull a good pint. Now he's trusting them with something else entirely. The world has gone mad, Freeman."

"One thing we've already learned since we began reviewing this case, Terry," said Gus, "it takes all sorts. Do you recognise any other names on the list? Don Green, Ryan Black, Jeff Naylor."

"None of them ring any bells, Freeman, sorry."

"If you think of anything else, give me a ring. Oh, or you could pass a message through Neil. He said to say he might call at the weekend."

"I wondered how long it would be before I heard from him. I suppose Melody's expecting, is that it? Her family are prolific. There's hardly one of them that hasn't got five kids. I don't suppose any little Davis's will fly over to see their Grampy in the future. Money will be tighter than ever."

"You could always pop back to Devizes to see your grandchild," Gus suggested.

"Not a chance," said Terry, "my friends will keep me informed of what's happening. I can catch baby pictures on Facebook. Melody hasn't blocked me yet, and no doubt she'll plaster them everywhere. I'll be able to see more of the little beggar's progress day by day than I did of Neil's. Being a copper, I missed all his 'firsts' because I was never home."

"I can well understand, even if I never had that problem. Kids weren't on our wish list."

"Are you still seeing Monty's missus?" asked Terry.

"We've been out together twice," said Gus. "Hardly news for your eyes and ears to think was worth calling you for."

"I was only pulling your leg, Freeman. Good luck to you. Vera was always too good for Bernard Jennings, anyway. What did you make of your new Chief Constable?"

"Sandra Plunkett seems to have the right credentials,"

It was no surprise to Gus to learn that Terry Davis knew about Sandra Plunkett.

"You really should listen to me when I give you a word to the wise, Freeman. You almost got yourself killed by those Albanians when you ignored my advice. In case you hadn't realised yet, that Plunkett woman is gunning for you."

"I met her for the first time earlier this week. Frosty summed up how I thought she felt about my coming back into the fold. So why would she be targeting me in particular?"

"Sandra Plunkett and Dominic Culverhouse worked together in the past. I'm not doing the donkey work for you, Freeman. You'll have to discover where and what they did. Culverhouse knows about your first two successes. He doesn't enjoy looking foolish. Any chance he has of taking the next step up the chain of command will get scuppered if you solve another case from his back catalogue. So, you have to stop. Plunkett is looking for the slightest excuse to close you down. She has to be clever with it. Don't step out of line this time, Freeman. Keep your wits about you."

"Thanks for the heads up, Terry. I remember you saying that I was a mug to come out of retirement the first time we spoke. What's done is done. I'm enjoying it far too much to walk away now. In my innocence, I hoped that if we kept solving cold cases, there was no way any Chief Constable could object to my continued presence. It's clear now that it's the Culverhouse threat we have to handle ahead of anything else."

"I sense you and Geoff Mercer have thought of something along those lines. Am I right?"

"What, your informer hadn't given you a ring?"

Terry Davis gave a dry laugh.

"Nice try," he said. "Even if I do have people at London Road who keep tabs on things for me, they don't overhear every conversation. Especially if those conversations should be top secret, Culverhouse has friends in that building, so tread carefully."

Gus wondered who that might be. Was it someone he and Geoff trusted? He wasn't ready to entrust Terry Davis with the knowledge that they were looking for evidence to bring down Culverhouse. There was too much at stake.

"I can see I'll need to start digging this weekend, Terry," said Gus.

"None of it should involve that allotment of yours, Freeman,"

Gus was thinking of a witty response, but Terry Davis had ended the call.

***Friday, 4 May 2018***

BIRDSONG AWAKENED GUS. It was a little after seven. He made his way to the en suite bathroom and started his shower. The gardening he'd done last night had offered two benefits. He had no niggles in his shoulders that needed a massage. The local birds had returned to feast on what goodies his freshly dug soil and mowed lawns had yielded.

As the hot water cascaded over his head, he thought he should ask Bert Penman a question. Do birds only sing in a well-kept garden? There were always plenty of visitors to the allotment.

Once dressed, Gus ate a light breakfast. One poached egg on toast washed down by a cup of coffee, black, no sugar. Then, finally, he was ready for the security camera installers. A black van with garish advertisements for famous products edged through the gateway a few minutes after nine. Two men in their early thirties sat inside the cab staring at the front of the bungalow. Gus watched their antics from the lounge window.

Once you've seen one bungalow. Clearly, these British workmen expected him to believe this building would take a lot of effort to find four positions to fix his cameras.

Odd, considering the sales representative had assured him it would be a doddle. Gus waited for the fitters to risk stepping from the safety of their black chariot. What dangers did they see lurking behind his red bricks? Had they forgotten to bring a ladder to enable them to reach what he could manage standing on a kitchen chair? Then, at last, there was movement. The front doorbell gave a reluctant ring.

"Good morning," said Gus, trying to sound cheerful and confident.

"We're here to fit your security cameras," said the driver. His mate was removing items from the back of the van.

"What a relief," said Gus, "where do you want to start, front or back? Your rep assured me my kitchen was the best place for the receiver."

"We'll need to check. I'm Adam, and that's Daryl. Will you be here all day?"

"I hope not. I'm working on a murder case and have places to go, people to see,"

Adam looked at his watch. He pursed his lips. Gus waited for the bad news.

"I can't promise anything. But, if we don't hit any snags, we should be out of your hair by three o'clock."

Typical, thought Gus. A leisurely trip back to the Bristol depot, unload the van and clock off by four-thirty. Another gruelling week was completed. He would have to drive through heavy traffic to the office to get those interviews sorted and his schedule organised for next week.

He hoped Alex had remembered it was a Bank Holiday on Monday. The parlours would be busy. Maggie's girls might not want to give up thirty minutes without financial compensation. It was one problem after another.

Daryl appeared beside Adam. He held a schematic diagram of the bungalow.

"Are you sure you want your cameras there, Sir?" he asked.

"That's where your sales rep told me they gave the optimum coverage," replied Gus. He realised as soon as he spoke that he was a little brusque.

Adam and Daryl shared a glance. Adam smiled.

"We'll do our best," he said.

Gus decided it was time to withdraw. If he made it to the lounge without tripping over one of those snags, perhaps Adam and Daryl would realise he wasn't falling for their tactics and get on with it. There was no point antagonising them.

He tried to read for a while, but Daryl had found a radio in the van tuned to a station Gus would pay good money to have banned. Despite the loud music that spewed forth, Adam and Daryl tried to carry on a conversation. That involved shouting to one another at the top of their voices, no matter where they were working around the bungalow.

Enough was enough. Gus changed into his gardening clothes and went outside.

"I've got an allotment next to the cemetery in the village," he shouted to Adam as he passed his ladder. "If you hit a snag, pop along, and I'll return to help sort it."

"OK," said Adam. "we're taking a tea break soon. Can we use your toilet if the need arises?"

"Of course," said Gus, "I'll be back for lunch at around one o'clock. If I don't hear from you."

Adam gave him the thumbs up, which probably meant he hadn't heard him over the noise. Gus walked smartly up the lane.

Bert Penman saw Gus arrive, stopped working and leaned on his fork.

"Are you having work done, Mr Freeman? I saw a van in your driveway earlier."

"Security cameras, Bert. I believed that I needed them after that break-in last month. But, the fuss those two fitters are making, I'm wondering whether I've overreacted."

Bert shook his head.

"We can't afford to lose you, Mr Freeman. Better safe than sorry."

"You're right, Bert, but it seems like too much hard work for the fitters they've sent,"

"They can't get the wood, can they, Mr Freeman?"

"Where did that saying come from, Bert? Do you remember?"

"I reckon it was the Goon Show on the radio when the wife and I were just married. Everything was simpler in those days, somehow. Perhaps, it was because it was in black and white."

Gus couldn't imagine the changes Bert had seen in his lifetime. Yet, the pace of change is rapid, and technology was out of date before it got fitted. He groaned. Why had he thought that? Would his cameras be superseded by a newer model before Adam and Daryl connected everything? At least the snags hadn't materialised yet.

Bert Penman had resumed his gardening. Gus worked alongside the older man until the church clock struck noon; Bert started to pack up his tools.

"Off for lunch, Bert?" asked Gus.

"A liquid one today," said Bert, "I've got a doctor's appointment this afternoon."

"Nothing serious, I hope," said Gus.

"Just the annual service," said Bert, "he'll tell me to drink less and eat healthier. Then I'll drop a few spring vegetables and early potatoes to his house later. That's usually enough to convince him to leave me alone until next year."

Gus watched his old friend wander up the road towards the Lamb. Then, he returned to his digging and forking. He was listening for the church clock's chime to send him on his way home when he spotted Daryl ambling through the gateway. They must have hit a snag.

"Problem?" asked Gus, not wanting to know the answer.

"Adam wants to run through the system with you. First, to make sure you have what you need on your phone. You do have a smartphone, don't you?"

"Of course, Daryl. What do you take me for, a dinosaur?" said Gus. "You made better progress than you thought, then?"

"The music helps keep our spirits up," said Daryl.

Daryl watched as Gus cleaned his tools and stored them in the shed.

"Do you save much money by growing your own vegetables?" he asked.

"Not much," said Gus, "but the exercise is useful, and it's a place where I can hear myself think."

Daryl didn't look that impressed. They walked up the lane side by side in silence. Adam was in the kitchen, testing the wireless receiver when they walked indoors.

Thirty minutes later, the two fitters were ready to leave. Everything was in its optimum position. Gus could access the view from the four cameras on his phone. If he spotted someone loitering in the garden, he could ask them what they thought they were doing. Or words to that effect.

"We thought we'd stop at the Lamb up the road," said Adam, "do they do a decent pub lunch?"

"They do," said Gus, "if you sit and let your meal go down, you'll reach the depot just on finishing time."

Adam and Daryl loaded the van and disappeared through the gateway with a beep of their horn. Gus inspected their handiwork. You could see the two cameras at the front of the bungalow from the lane if you were looking for them. He was pleased.

He prayed they would never be more than an expensive deterrent.

The drive through Devizes and the CRT office didn't vary much, no matter what time Gus attempted it. The traffic was always manic. Thank goodness those fitters had finished two hours earlier than their initial estimate. He could conduct the interviews they had arranged.

Gus parked his car and entered the Old Police Station lift. Their first interview in the afternoon was due at two o'clock. So he had a few minutes to spare.

"Is everything ready for our guests?" he asked as he exited the lift.

"Lydia popped out to get a tin of biscuits," said Alex.

"I told her boxes of tissues might make them more at home, guv," said Neil.

"Ignore him, guv. We've found an address for Ian Hewson," said Lydia.

"Happy days," said Gus.

"He doesn't live there now, though," she added, "Hewson appears to drift from house to house. Neil's chasing his registration as a player. When we know who he plays for, it will be simple to pick him up on a Saturday afternoon."

"The season's almost over," Neil warned, "with the World Cup starting soon. So we'll need to move fast, or he'll be off to one of the hotspots the football crowd favour."

"Concentrate on finding Hewson," said Gus, "and bugger the biscuits."

"How did the security camera installation go, guv?" asked Neil.

"It went, Neil. My cameras are now in full working order. Why it cost so much escapes me. Please ring your Dad this weekend. Alex, have you made allowances for Monday being a Bank Holiday?"

"It wasn't necessary, guv. Laura and Camille's regulars are here for interviews this afternoon or Tuesday morning. All the girls we confirmed times with were working on Sunday or Monday, whether it was a Bank Holiday or not. We haven't had a call back from those outstanding from yesterday. So I'll chase those this afternoon."

"Keep on top of it, Alex," said Gus, "Neil, can you see if our first guest is outside?"

"No sign of him on the CCTV, guv. He might find it difficult to park. It can be busy at this time of day."

"Get it sorted, Neil. We need to make headway in this case," said Gus.

Neil returned a few minutes later with a swarthy-looking individual who looked to have just finished a shift on a building site.

So, this was Ryan Black.

# Chapter Ten

NEIL LED their first guest to a chair in front of Gus's desk.

"Come on in, Mr Black," said Gus, "take a seat. You know why I asked you to come here this afternoon. You were the first customer to be seen by Gem at Gentle Touch on the night she was murdered."

Ryan Black was nervous. He knew three people sat behind him, listening to every word he said. Lydia thought if this were an example of Gus not making the men too uncomfortable, she would hate to be in his bad books.

"Yeah, I visited Gem twice a week, sometimes three; my back plays me up something chronic in cold weather. I'm a bricklayer by trade; Gem kept me in work, earning money. I got there just after six and left after thirty minutes."

"Did the police ask you about the parlour after the murder?" asked Gus.

Ryan Black shook his head.

"I didn't kill her," he said, "Gem was okay. I would never have harmed her."

"Did you see anyone else inside the parlour or as you left?"

"No, Gem walked to the door with me and said she'd see me in the week. That was the last time I saw her. It was a terrible shock when I heard what had happened."

"You didn't hear any rumours of a client getting too attached to her or someone she had argued with in the past?"

"Nothing like that. I didn't go there to socialise. I haven't spoken more than a dozen words to another customer in the last ten years."

"How's your back?"

"I still get days when I can hardly get out of bed. So I use Cleopatra's now, over by the Designer Outlet site. A girl called Ebony fixes my problems."

"You're single?" asked Gus.

"No, married with two kids. A boy and a girl. Why?"

"Do you ever mention where you're going to your wife?"

"Are you serious? My wife thinks I visit a chiropractor. She won't need to hear about this, will she? We weren't married seven years ago, anyway."

Gus shook his head.

"Can I get back to work?" asked Ryan Black.

"Yes," said Gus.

The bricklayer eased himself up from the chair and walked towards the lift.

Ryan turned as he reached the door.

"Is that it then?" he asked.

"Yes," said Gus, "we won't need to speak to you again."

A relieved Ryan Black took the lift to the car park.

"Are we sure about him, guv?" asked Alex.

"Check whether his firm ever worked on Maggie

Monk's place. Either the original build or the running repairs. If not, we can discard him."

"Someone is coming up in the lift, guv," said Lydia, "he must have arrived just as Black was leaving."

"Remind me. Who do we have on the list now?" asked Gus.

"Derek Gosling. Fifty-five-year-old lawyer. Divorced. The last client to visit Camille," said Alex.

Gus met the lawyer at the lift door and invited him to sit. Derek Gosling looked petrified. Gus went through the same rigmarole as Ryan Black and tried to get their visitor to relax.

This is painful to watch, thought Neil. This bloke was a wet lettuce, not someone who could carry out a vicious stabbing. The only thing he might have that could help their investigation was sighting a person they hadn't yet identified. He had left the parlour at around eight o'clock.

"Do you live alone, Mr Gosling?" asked Gus.

"Since Mother died, yes, I've been on my own."

"How long had you been visiting Gentle Touch?"

"I first went there not long after it opened. It was convenient, only two streets across from my office. Camille was the first girl I saw, and I decided not to book anyone else."

"Were you aware that wasn't her real name?"

"She didn't tell me what it was, but it wouldn't be high on the list for Thai families."

"Take me through that Sunday evening. What time did you arrive?"

"My appointment was for half-past seven. I arrived five minutes late. Camille let me in. I paid her the basic fee in Reception, and we went to our room."

"You're very nervous, Mr Gosling? Is there something you're not telling us?"

"No, not at all. It is very embarrassing. After the massage, Camille asked if I wanted the usual. I paid her, and I got dressed and prepared to leave when it was over."

"Did Camille escort you downstairs to let you out?"

"Yes, but for the first time, she asked me to wait while she got her things. She was rushing home to her husband. He was ill. I felt awful that I had kept her from her family. We walked downstairs and left via the alleyway together. I worried in case someone had spotted us. Camille even crossed the road with me. We were heading in the same direction. It appeared she lived within five minutes of my home. When we went our separate ways, she said she hoped to see me next week. I said I hoped her husband was better soon. It was a most unusual evening."

"Was that the last time you visited Camille?" asked Gus.

Derek Gosling smiled.

"Can you imagine my reaction the next day when the news broke of the murder? I didn't leave the house for days. Work was the last thing on my mind. I waited and waited for a knock on the door."

"You expected the police to learn that you were there maybe an hour before the killer struck?"

"I couldn't rule out that the parlour would release the names of customers who booked sessions that evening. If my name got linked with that business, my career would have been in ruins. I'm a lonely man, Mr Freeman. A sad, lonely man who craves company. I risked everything for a few minutes of excitement with someone little more than a stranger. Except for that night when I glimpsed the real person behind the made-up name."

"In the event, the police didn't contact you, did they?"

"They did not. As the days and weeks passed, I realised they weren't after the customers. The police must have believed the killer was someone much closer to the poor woman who died."

"You allowed yourself a brief smile when I asked if that was the last occasion you saw Camille. Why was that?" asked Gus.

"Gentle Touch never re-opened, as you are no doubt aware. I was reticent about looking for somewhere new. Several months passed. In late November, I walked near my home and bumped into Camille. We discussed the murder of her colleague. I asked Camille what she did now. She said some of the girls had moved to the parlour on Cricklade Road. She hadn't returned to work yet as her husband had died in August. I don't think she had many people to confide in; their children lived with their grandparents in Thailand. I told her I was a lawyer and offered to help in any way I could. At Christmas, she dropped by my office with a card. Not a Christmas card, but a business card. She started working again in the New Year. I visit her every Sunday at Cleopatra's. She works under the name Therese now."

"Do you meet her at any other time, outside the parlour?" asked Gus.

"Never, but it's the closest I've ever been to a real relationship. I hope you won't tell Therese how you learned of her change of name. I would hate for her to stop letting me visit her."

"We have no intention of damaging anyone's reputation or relationships, Mr Gosling. We're seeking a vicious killer. Nothing more. When you left the alleyway that evening, you were keen that nobody saw you. I imagine your senses were on high alert. Did you see or hear anyone in the vicinity of the parlour?"

"The street was empty. I could hear someone singing

nearby. They were singing and whistling; they must have been happy in their work. I saw no one, however."

"We needn't detain you further, Mr Gosling. Thank you for attending this afternoon. Please inform us if you remember where those sounds might have come from. DS Davis will see you out."

"Another relieved customer," said Lydia when Derek Gosling had left the office, "I wonder how often they've gone over their part in that night's events? For seven years, they've held onto snippets of information, waiting for someone to ask what they saw and heard. Gablecross screwed up the investigation the first time, didn't they?"

"Remember what I told you not long after you walked through that door for the first time, Lydia? DI Hickerton would have been under pressure. New crimes hit his desk every day. If they didn't make immediate inroads, the detective team would move on to another case which offered a better chance of success. They decided early on it was a family member and focused on that. I need to have a word with Maggie Monk about one thing. She told Hickerton she believed Camille returned home with her husband. That was a lie. Maggie hid that she moved on to another parlour after her husband's death."

"We didn't make much progress other than learning Maggie lied, did we guv?"

"We've learned something new this afternoon which could prove worthwhile. Someone was working on Sunday evening at around eight o'clock, close enough to the alleyway for Derek Gosling to hear. Who was that? Where were they? What did they see?"

"Jeff Naylor, the last client, may have heard something, guv," said Alex.

"Naylor's not due here until Tuesday," said Neil.

"Only two left to interview this afternoon," said Gus, "first up is Cyril Harrison, a banker, forty-five years old. Then we have Babar Ahmed, a retired dentist who lives in Wroughton. He's seventy-two now. Both clients of Camille. Harrison was her six o'clock appointment, and Ahmed her seven o'clock."

"Why the full hour for Harrison and not the usual thirty minutes?" asked Neil.

"Camille may not have had as many regulars as Gem. Although, we won't have a long wait to discover the reason for the gap," said Gus, "in the meantime, why don't we have a coffee?"

"I'll go," said Lydia.

Gus was ready to offer to help when his phone rang. It was an unfamiliar ringtone. What was that? Heck, someone had triggered his security system. Who was snooping around his bungalow? He checked the app.

An off-duty Suzie Ferris stood near his front door. She was studying his camera. When she disappeared, he soon caught sight of her in the back garden. The camera covering the kitchen door now held her in its gaze. Gus knew Suzie was intelligent enough to realise he could see her. What was she doing? Adam had shown him how to contact intruders via his phone, so he tried it.

"What do you think you're doing? You're on private property. Please leave before I call the police."

Suzie did something unexpected.

She lifted her t-shirt and bra in a single motion exposing her breasts. Then she beckoned for Gus to get home. Suzie looked on the verge of tears.

She must be drunk, thought Gus; some bugger has upset her. I can't leave her like that. The neighbours will have a field day.

Lydia had returned with the coffees. Neil was collecting Cyril Harrison from downstairs.

"Alex, do me a favour," asked Gus, "something's cropped up. You've heard the pattern of these interviews. Follow my lead and then get them to tell you what they saw and heard when entering and leaving the premises. Next, ask about this one-hour session Harrison had. It might be the first chink in Maggie Moon's armour relating to what was actually on the menu. I'll be back in the office first thing on Tuesday morning. Have a good weekend, everyone."

Gus passed Neil and Cyril Harrison at the lift door.

"Neil, while Alex is chatting with Mr Harrison here, can you and Lydia redouble your efforts to trace this footballer? He's a person of interest. I want him found before Tuesday."

Neil nodded.

Gus left the banker in capable hands. Alex swung across to Gus's chair on his crutches. Neil made sure Cyril Harrison sat in the chair opposite.

Gus kept just under the limit as he drove home. He tried to work out what had upset Suzie so much. The Detective Inspector was usually unflappable, relaxed and calm in a crisis. He found her sitting on the step outside his kitchen door. She was now correctly dressed.

"Come inside, Suzie," said Gus, "I'll put the coffee on. Where's your car, by the way?"

"In the car park behind the Lamb. I went there for lunch. Things went pear-shaped."

"I assume you didn't drink alone. I spotted you in Devizes the other evening as I left the supermarket. You were with someone. Was he your lunch date?"

"Tim Yarwood. We went out together when we were younger. He played rugby for a Championship side. You wouldn't know him. Tim's a player-coach now for one of the local clubs. We met up by chance again a few weeks ago. We both thought there was something worth pursuing. Last week we spent time together; it felt right. Last night we spent at my place. I'd chosen the red wine we shared the night I came here and slept in your spare room. I cooked us a meal, plied Tim with red wine, and convinced him he couldn't drive home.

Lucky bloke thought Gus. Why tell me, though? Suzie knew the situation between him and Vera. But, of course, it would be a big surprise if the events of last weekend didn't reach her ears.

"Everything was going fine," said Suzie.

Gus wondered if he needed to hear this.

"You know what it's like when the passion of the moment grabs you, and you lose control?"

Funny you should mention it. Something similar happened to me recently, Gus thought.

"It's your fault," said Suzie.

"Sorry? How can it be my fault?" he said.

Suzie carried on unloading her problems as if Gus hadn't spoken.

"Suddenly, Tim jumped out of my bed, got dressed and dashed out to his car. I scrabbled around, searching for my underwear. Then, when I was decent, I shouted at him from the bedroom window to come back. I knew he shouldn't be driving, but he was long gone."

This conversation might make sense in a moment, Gus thought.

"Did he get stopped on his way home and get done for driving under the influence?"

"No," sobbed Suzie, "I kept ringing him this morning, asking him to meet me today in the Lamb. We needed to talk. Tim turned up. I wanted to understand why what should have been a lovely moment suddenly turned to crap."

"These things happen," said Gus, "what did he say?"

"I've told you. It's your fault. It was your name, I cried out, not Tim's."

There wasn't much chance of the poor bloke making a mistake. Tim. Timmy. Timbo. Gus.

He knew what he said next was crucial.

If only he knew what to say.

Gus bought himself a few seconds of thinking time by wrapping his arms around Suzie and allowing her to soak the front of his blue work shirt with her tears; it seemed to help. The tears subsided. Suzie lifted her head; her mouth was less than an inch away. Suzie wasn't making any attempt to move.

"So, Tim buggered off and left you in the pub," said Gus, trying to keep things light. "You had a few drinks and staggered up the lane to find out if I was home."

"I didn't know whether you would have gone to work this afternoon. But, then, I spotted the camera firm's van in the car park, so I realised they'd installed your cameras."

"They work very well, based on the trial run you gave the system."

"It was the only way I could think of getting you to return home."

"I'm sorry about you and Tim."

"Don't be. I appreciate my timing is terrible, but there's only one way to solve this problem."

Suzie closed the gap between them.

***Saturday, 5 May 2018***

THIS IS BECOMING A HABIT, thought Gus as he awoke to find a naked woman beside him for the second Saturday running. He told himself he was a fool. Last night had been a mistake.

Suzie had been on the rebound from this Tim Yarwood character. As much as Gus had loathed the bloke from the second he had laid eyes on him in the supermarket car park; it wasn't right. He and Vera may have agreed they would take things slowly, but last weekend was a commitment.

Gus couldn't avoid that fact. There was never any mention of either of them seeing other people. He was old enough to be Suzie's father. He should have let her down gently, continued the black coffee treatment to sober her up and then driven her home.

"I know what you're thinking,"

A tousle-haired Suzie stretched and yawned as she threw back the sheet that covered them. The camera hadn't done her justice yesterday. She looked stunning.

"Do you now?" said Gus, lifting his underwear from the floor.

He needed to move out of the danger zone. But, unfortunately, his body hadn't listened to the arguments in his head.

"I am a detective," said Suzie, grabbing his arm, "don't run away. You think it was a mistake; it wasn't. It was wonderful. I believed I could turn back the clock with Tim. Rekindle a romance that died over ten years ago. I should have remembered that it died for a good reason. We weren't right together. So why did I do it? I tried to stand by while you and Vera grew closer. It's been agony. Since we met,

I've wanted to be with you. I said the timing was terrible, but last night was perfect."

Nobody used a name out of place; Gus had to give her that.

"I'm old enough to be your father," said Gus.

"Bugger the difference in our ages," said Suzie. "Can you tell me, honestly, that you don't feel the same way as I do?"

"I feel a heel for letting it happen when I slept with someone else this time last week. I can't deny I was jealous when I saw you and Tim together, but that's no excuse. You're right. I wanted last night just as much as you. What's done is done. What do we do now?"

"We have a shower, and then you cook us breakfast. I'm starving."

"If only it could be that simple."

"It can be. I'm going riding this morning. I don't know what your plans are."

Suzie dragged Gus towards the bathroom. Showering together would be cosy. He didn't rate his chances of making it to the kitchen to start that breakfast for a while.

Suzie left the bungalow a few minutes after eleven. Gus offered to drive her to the Lamb car park.

"Sorry if I've made you late for your horse ride," said Gus.

"I'm as much to blame. I can ride out this afternoon. But, every step of the way, I'll think of you. What did you plan to do today?"

"I'm ringing Vera later to check if we're going out for a meal. If not tonight, then tomorrow at lunchtime. At some point today, I expect to be visiting a prostitute."

That stopped Suzie in her tracks. She turned in the driveway and walked towards Gus.

"Excuse me?"

"Terry Davis agreed to put me in touch with one of his old drinking pals. A lady called Donna. Terry thought she was my best chance of getting the lowdown on Laura and Gentle Touch."

"Good hunting," said Suzie. With that, she left.

Gus closed the door; the bungalow felt empty. He had no excuse this time; he initiated their love-making in the shower. So, far from finding a way out of the mess he had gotten himself into, he realised he was more attracted to Suzie than ever.

Gus waited until after lunch before plucking up the courage to call Vera. When his phone rang, he thought his time had come. Vera had found out already.

"Hello," he answered.

"Is that Gus?"

"It is. Who am I speaking to?" said Gus. It didn't sound like his old sparring partner, Dorothy.

"Terry Davis said you wanted to talk. I'm Donna,"

"Donna, great to hear from you. Where are you? Can I visit you later? For a chat."

"I'm free at four o'clock," said Donna, "Terry said you would see me right. Is sixty okay?"

Gus thought that was rather steep, but he wasn't familiar with the going rate. Terry had said Donna would give him mate's rates. Sixty would be a small price if he picked up a lead that led to Laura's killer.

Donna must have thought the silence ominous.

"I couldn't go any lower than forty," she said.

"No need. Fifty, and it's a deal, Donna. Just tell me where you live. I'll be there at four."

A relieved Donna gave Gus an address in Devizes and rang off.

Gus waited for an hour. Still no news from Vera. He called her.

"Hi there. Are you free tonight? Or do you prefer a Sunday lunch somewhere?"

"Let's make it tomorrow," said Vera, "and so we don't get the premium service you're so jealous of, I'll leave you to book a table. Surprise me."

"I'll look for somewhere we can park in a municipal car park and walk to," said Gus, "that will fool the management. It will only be the second we walk through the door they realise Royalty is dining there."

"You're incorrigible," said Vera.

Gus thought Vera didn't know the half of it.

"I'll text you the details later," he said, "I'm working on the case later this afternoon."

"No rest for the wicked," said Vera.

Gus closed his eyes. Could life get any more complicated?

Donna's house was a twenty-minute drive from the bungalow. He felt self-conscious, strolling up the path to the front door even though the street was quiet. Perhaps Terry had been right. The neighbours wouldn't know Donna's profession from the outside appearance of this townhouse. It looked very stylish. He rang the bell. The tune that announced his arrival was Tina Turner's 'Simply The Best.'

Donna opened the door, and Gus stepped inside. Donna closed the door behind him.

"If anyone remembers you from your time as a copper, it will damage trade for my girls," said Donna.

Gus studied the woman in front of him. Her next big birthday would start with a sixty. When she was in her twenties and thirties, Donna would have been a beauty. The extra weight she had put on since then was evenly spread.

She reminded him of Diana Dors, the Swindon-born film star. With more make-up. Gus realised Donna was holding her chubby hand out for the money. He handed over his fifty pounds.

"Come through to my lounge," she said, "we can get more comfortable."

The room was another surprise. It was like stepping into an eighteenth-century drawing room.

"This is elegant, Donna. You've got a good eye for décor," said Gus, and he meant it.

"I know what you thought, Mr Freeman. Nobody believes women like me can have a bit of class. You reckon the men who visit my girls and me exploit us. No way we are exploited. It's our choice. We have the right to do any job without people making a moral judgement. But, because I choose to work four days a week and earn a thousand pounds selling sex, they get antsy. What do they want me to do, work a twelve-hour shift in a supermarket on minimum wage? No thanks. I'm not on drugs. Nobody coerced me. All I want is to be allowed to secure a future for myself."

"What sort of clients do you entertain?"

"The other girls get more young blokes than old these days. It's easier than dating, and they're sure to score. I have a few old friends who drop by. I'm winding down now, almost ready for retirement. Do you want to do the tour?"

"We're not disturbing anyone?" asked Gus.

"We don't need to work all day, every day. I've got girls working tonight. Saturdays can be busy."

Double doors off the lounge led to a small hall which gave access to two en-suite bedrooms on the ground floor. Cream walls, a double bed with maroon bedding and gold silk cushions.

"What do you do between clients?"

"We sit around, drinking tea, checking our phones and laughing about the kinky stuff clients ask for."

"How many rooms are there upstairs?"

"Three decent-sized en-suite bedrooms on the first and second floor. Eight rooms. Up to sixteen girls use this place. They work different shifts to fit in with their kid's schooling and babysitting duties if they're mothers or grandmothers."

"It takes all sorts, doesn't it?" said Gus, "you must run a terrible risk of being raided by the police?"

"Why would the police raid us? I would go to prison, and fifteen girls would be on the streets looking for work. I run a good house. We offer customer satisfaction. You're right, of course; it takes all sorts. Different strokes for different folks."

Gus thought it was time to change the subject.

"Terry wondered if you had heard of Laura Mallinder, or Gem as she called herself. She worked in massage parlours in various local towns and cities. Unfortunately, Laura got stabbed to death in June 2011."

"I remember reading about it in the papers. As for the girl, I never met her. I haven't worked in one of those parlours. They're not my expertise. A few of my girls have worked in them at various times. You know they offer different things in different places, don't you?"

"We do, Donna. Laura never had sex with any of her clients. It was a house rule. The owner believed it helped to keep the riff-raff out."

"We had the same problem, Mr Freeman. Especially the younger blokes, when they get out on the lash at the week-ends, they think what a lark it would be to visit a brothel. We used to get plagued with stag weekends and sports club tours. The worst offenders are professional footballers;

they've got stacks of money. Most spend it on gambling; others spend it on flashy cars. Quite a few spend it on women. More often than not, they want to stick together in a group. God knows why. Six blokes with two or three girls for the whole night. Money, no object."

"You don't allow that here?" asked Gus.

"Not on your life. The parlours are their preferred target these days."

"Where do these footballers come from?"

"Plenty of clubs around here pay their youngsters a damn sight more than the money I could earn after I left school. I don't know much about football, but there are many young lads with money to throw around living on the big estates around Bristol and Swindon."

"Places such as Hayden Wick, Blunsdon or Bradley Stoke, is that where you mean?"

"Those are the places where people with money live and congregate. They tend to socialise together."

"Interesting, Donna, that could be useful. Thanks for your time."

Donna came closer to him.

"While you're here, Mr Freeman is there…."

"Now, now, Donna. Information was what I paid for."

"A pity, you're a fine-looking gentleman. Not like Terry Davis. Is he still in Marbella?"

"He's out there alone, Donna. Perhaps you've earned enough for a holiday?"

"I might do that, Mr Freeman. That would surprise the old bugger, wouldn't it? Terry wouldn't get it for free, mind."

Donna led Gus to the door. He looked around him as he made his way to the car. Not one curtain twitched.

Terry was right. The neighbours didn't have a clue.

# Chapter Eleven

***Sunday, 6 May 2018***

NEIL HAD PHONED Jake Latimer late on Friday evening. The detective had offered to ride shotgun if Neil needed to visit any premises where the parlour girls now worked. Their first port of call was to Cleopatra's in Swindon. They were visiting the girl who called herself Ebony.

She told them how she met Gem in Knowle and why she had moved to Swindon.

"I was one of her trainers," she said, "when she moved here, I missed her company. So I asked Maggie if I could split my shifts between Bristol and Swindon. It meant I could watch more sports that way."

Ebony gave Neil a brief tour of the recently refurbished facilities. It was a rabbit warren; Neil saw a corridor to his left. A large mirror and twinkling lights invited him forward. To his right was a table waiting for a prospective massage customer to arrive. A warm reddish-orange glow from behind a beaded curtain illuminated a Jacuzzi.

"Here, you can have a relaxing bath and invigorating massage," Ebony told him, "it improves circulation and restores your energy levels; all your stress soothed away."

Neil walked further along the corridor. The décor was more opulent here. It must be the premium area of the parlour. He peered through the half-open door. A large double bed dominated the room. Neil gave a quizzical look to his guide.

"Our elderly gentlemen struggle to climb onto our tables," said Ebony, "they're too narrow."

Neil didn't detect a hint of a smile. Did Ebony think he swallowed that?

"Do customers ask for sex?" he said.

"Every day. Some ask many times. We run a massage parlour, not a brothel. The police would never allow us to stay open if they suspected we were not above board."

Ebony had last seen her friend Gem on the Thursday before the murder. They were due to work together again on Monday. Ebony had never heard rumours that Gem ever argued with her family. None of the customers caused them sleepless nights.

"Did you know Ian Hewson?" asked Neil.

"I watched him play when we were younger. I haven't heard of him lately. We saw players in the Bristol parlours, especially out of season, or if they were in town celebrating a win. They're like you. Coppers stick together, don't they? Nobody else will drink with you in case they say a word out of place. Athletes can be like that in my experience; they can't talk about their sport to someone who hasn't played at that level. They think they wouldn't understand."

Neil and Ebony had returned to Reception to find Jake chatting with the girl behind the counter.

"Sorry to break it up," said Neil, "but we must get to our next appointment in Marlborough."

"She was tasty," said Jake when they returned to the car, "I was thinking of giving her a call."

Neil shook his head. He was glad to be happily married, despite the broken sleep.

"Who are we visiting now?" asked Jake.

"She called herself Janina. I wondered if she might be Polish, but I'll reserve judgement."

When they met Janina, she turned out to be a Lithuanian girl in her early thirties. Naturally, Jake was keen to ask the questions.

"What's a typical day? Me at present, I work an eight-hour shift from two o'clock. That means I can lie in, go shopping, read, and relax in the morning. Whatever I choose to do. When I start work, the lunchtime rush is at an end. I can spend more time on social media, from two to five, than in a room. We get a mixture of regulars who pre-book and those who are in Marlborough for the day. They search through location-based apps for afternoon delight. The pace picks up as office workers finish for the day. Our parlour closes before the pubs shut, preventing the drunks from deciding they need something other than a kebab to complete their night. I can be home before eleven when I'm on this shift. My earnings are still high, and you wouldn't get me to swap for a nine-to-five job."

Janina was another girl who followed Gem to Swindon from Bath and Bristol. Gem was a good friend to all the girls and a pleasure to work alongside. Gem was only three years older than her, so Janina thought of her as a sister.

Neil thought Jake was more interested in Janina than finding out something that could identify the killer.

"Were you and Gem ever more than good friends?"

"Gem was not like that."

"There were no men in her life other than her clients. That seems odd for an attractive young woman. What about you? Do you meet men outside of the parlours?"

"I don't have a boyfriend at the minute. I was married when I came to this country. He hit me, so I left him. This work was all I was qualified to do. Since then, I have seen men who come here that I like. Off the books, nothing to do with the parlour. They don't pay me. A night out for a meal and a few drinks is enough."

"Gem didn't do the same as you, though, did she?"

"There was never anyone she liked enough to meet away from work. Several asked her for sex in the parlour. She always said no. The Turkish man asked her on a date. She wasn't interested."

"The Turkish barber? Was he a customer?" asked Neil.

Janina laughed.

"Not him. That guy was old-fashioned. He bought her flowers and talked to her when she arrived at work one day. Gem thought it sweet, but she wanted to keep herself to herself."

"Did he continue to pester her?" asked Neil.

"I don't think so. Gem still waved to him as she passed the shop window. She never wanted to fall out with anybody. That's why we loved her."

Neil and Jake drove across to Cirencester in the afternoon. There were two girls at Gentle Touch they wanted to interview. One was Carol Gullis, who introduced Laura Mallinder to Maggie Monk initially.

"Do you still work as Amber?" asked Neil.

"Why change?" she replied, "I blamed myself for Laura's death. If I hadn't bumped into her in a bar one night all those years ago, she would still be alive. So I convinced her this life was better for her than slogging away in a dead-end job. So here I am, seven years later, and although the money is still great, it's no different to swiping goods through the scanner at checkout. Same thing, every day."

Neil glanced at Jake. He shook his head. Amber could supply little more than background to how Laura got into the business.

"When was the last time you saw her?"

"We worked in Bath at the end of 2007. She called me now and then after she bought her own house in Swindon. We talked about taking a holiday together, but nothing came of it. Six months before she died was the last time. She called to wish me a Happy New Year."

They left Carol Gullis and sought their second interviewee.

"Kathy, what can you tell us about Gem?"

"We met in the parlour in Knowle. I hadn't been there long. I'd been unemployed for three months. It stings a bit when you can't even get a job at a call centre. My roommate wondered whether I'd ever move from the sofa again. She spotted an advert for a receptionist in a massage parlour. I was desperate. The owner told me it would be the easiest job I'd ever had. Could I start straight away? That's where I met Amber. She knew Gem and had encouraged her to join. We worked together in Bristol and Bath. Then Maggie asked Gem to run the Swindon parlour. After a few months, the place became busy. Gem asked Maggie for extra girls. I offered to go because Gem was such a good friend."

"When was the last shift you worked together?" asked Jake.

"I can't remember. I did Monday, Wednesday and Thursday in Swindon. She may have worked Thursday."

"Were there any troublesome clients? Any arguments you recall?" asked Neil.

"Not with Gem in charge. She didn't stand any nonsense from the customers or the girls. Gem made it a pleasure to go to work. That's why it seemed so wrong that someone wanted to kill her."

"If there's anything else you remember that might help us, give us a call," said Jake handing Kathy a card.

"You haven't found yourself a girlfriend yet, Jake," said Neil as they drove towards Swindon.

"We're rushed off our feet at work, as you can imagine. I can't be bothered with going on half a dozen dates before sealing the deal. I reckon I'll call one of the girls we met today. It might be expensive, but you save on having to remember birthdays and anniversaries."

"Who said romance was dead," laughed Neil,

MEANWHILE, on the other side of the county, Alex Hardy and Lydia Logan Barre moved their relationship forward inch by inch towards the precipice.

That's how Alex viewed it. It was tearing him apart. His heart wanted to jump into bed with Lydia, but his head knew that the odds against her leaving him would shorten if he did.

Today, Lydia had cooked a meal for them at her place. They watched a football match in the afternoon and then lounged around chatting. Finally, after another large glass of wine, they sat together on a leather sofa.

"What influenced the career change you made," asked Alex, "you need a flair for acting, and it's quite a switch to forensics. That's a part of your life that you've not mentioned."

"Growing up in Dundee, my childhood was a happy one," said Lydia, "I always knew I was adopted but didn't give it much thought. Then, on my twelfth birthday, I received a file with information on my birth parents. There were only a few details: My birth mother was eighteen when she had me. She worked in a gift shop on George Street, Edinburgh. My birth father was a Nigerian sailor who had arrived in the port of Leith two days before they met for the first time. He was on shore leave for five days. My parents had agreed to a closed adoption, which meant that the basic information I received was all the specifics anyone gets. My parents didn't even know my birth mother's name. I've been badgering the adoption agency and adoption support groups for the last eight years. While studying, I spent countless hours in libraries and trying internet searches."

"It must have been a difficult time for you and your parents," said Alex, "but I can appreciate the desire to find the woman who brought you into the world."

"The adoption agency wrote to say I was now entitled to learn my first name given at birth. My birth mother, Eleanor, named me Lisa Marie. It was the only thing she could do after giving birth before the baby got whisked away. Eleanor didn't have any family support during her pregnancy. I kept questioning what I was doing. What if I found her and she didn't want that? When I plucked up the courage to contact Eleanor, it was through a mediator. I said I wasn't asking Eleanor for anything but was curious to learn more about her. Communication began between us. Months passed before either of us was ready to meet in person. I had often tried to imagine my birth mother. When we finally met face-to-face, Mum turned out to be so completely normal it threw me. Instead of trying to force an instant bond as mother-daughter, we decided to be friends. We get in touch now and then. There's no pressure."

"That's great, Lydia," said Alex, "but it doesn't answer my original question."

"The next step is to find my father. That won't be so easy. I need to find the ship he arrived on; where it went when it left the Port of Leith five days after they met, it's something I *have* to do. I won't rest until I find out who he is and what part of him has made me who I am today. While I sat in the library searching for a way to find my mother, I wondered which occupation might offer the most access to information impossible to unlock online. I started reading books on forensic psychology to fill in the time between the results of internet searches. I viewed the police as a career that allowed me to search for him without raising red flags, so I switched courses. Am I an idiot?"

"Of course not," said Alex, "we would never have met for a start. You'll not find it easy to trace your father unless he's in the UK and has committed an offence. You would still need a valid reason for accessing information. We can't just log on and root around without alerting someone."

"Are you saying you would help me?"

"I'll do what I can, Lydia, I promise, but we must tread carefully."

"You're my hero," she said, punching his arm. Then, she lifted her head and kissed him.

"Were you going home?" Lydia whispered.

Alex looked into those big brown eyes and knew it was a lost cause.

IN URCHFONT, Gus had spent a leisurely Saturday evening at home. The batteries needed re-charging. He had booked a table for one o'clock on Sunday.

When he and Vera arrived, they found another country pub with a roaring trade. Gus wondered how many people ever bothered to learn to cook for themselves. He'd seen the evidence with his own eyes in Salisbury that the fast-food outlets catered for the younger set.

Here in the heart of Wiltshire, families and senior citizens queued to get seated for a meal. Why did they show so many food programmes on TV? They gave the impression everyone was at it. He gazed around the bar restaurant and decided he could solve the obesity crisis crippling the nation. People needed to be taught to either cook at home or eat out, not both.

"What did you get up to yesterday?" asked Vera.

"I visited a lady in Devizes who gave me useful information. I was sure that a young footballer we were keen to talk to could assist us in our enquiries. Now, I believe he's the key to solving the case."

"It would be good if you found something to take the wind out of the Chief Constable's sails. She's a force to be reckoned with; several senior officers are fretting over their futures. There's bound to be a knock-on effect on those lower down the ladder. The ACC doesn't seem too worried, though."

"Kenneth Truelove will be happy if he doesn't survive the cull she's threatened. He can't wait for retirement. A new broom always has to be seen to do something meaningful. We can only do one thing at a time with the CRT. This case is moving forward at last after a very sluggish start. Whether it will be solved before the axe falls or not, who knows? Do you know anything about Sandra Plunkett? Had you heard she and Dominic Culverhouse worked together?"

"That must have been before my time," said Vera.

"You knew him, didn't you?" asked Gus.

"I knew of him, and I didn't like him much. I can't think where those two worked together. You should ask Geoff Mercer."

Lunch had been excellent. He and Vera strolled in the local park for an hour before returning to her rented house. Gus had driven back to the bungalow the next morning.

***Monday, 7 May 2018***

AS THE SUN rose higher in the sky, the temperature climbed too. Gus couldn't remember a Bank Holiday with such glorious weather. He pottered around indoors, waiting for a phone call. Suzie hadn't been in touch since she left on Saturday morning. Vera had been asleep when he awoke; he had let her stay there.

"Time to visit the allotment," he said to himself.

If anyone wanted to speak to him, they knew where he'd be.

Bert Penman was busy on the adjoining patch when he reached his shed.

"You're gaining a new neighbour, Mr Freeman," said Bert.

"They've got someone to take on Frank North's patch already, have they?"

"A newcomer to the village, I expect," said Bert, "the waiting list must be shorter than I thought."

They must play their cards close to their chest if Bert

doesn't have chapter and verse on who they were and where they originated.

"You won't need to worry over the weeds running riot now, Bert,"

"No, but I'll miss the extra vegetables Frank provided."

The church clock struck four before Gus made his way back up the lane. He decided to drop into the Lamb for a cold one. It was thirsty work in the heat.

Bert perched on a stool by the bar. His pint of cider looked almost empty.

"Can I buy you another, Bert?" asked Gus.

"Only a toothful left in this glass, Mr Freeman. That's very generous."

As they sat beside one another enjoying a quiet drink, the bar door opened and in walked an unfamiliar face.

"That could be your man, Mr Freeman," whispered Bert, nudging Gus's arm.

The stranger ordered a gin and tonic. Then, he went to sit at the other end of the bar to read the newspaper.

"Not very sociable, is he?" said Gus, "and he's not got the look of a gardener."

"I'll keep an eye on him," said Bert, "next time we meet. Then, I'll be able to tell you more."

Gus thought he'd better get home. Another cider and he wouldn't be able to drive anywhere this evening. But, of course, he may not get an invitation.

"I need to get myself a meal, Bert. I'll catch you one evening in the week."

"OK, Mr Freeman. I'll be making my way home soon. The doctor drops in here on a Monday evening. No point pushing my luck."

As Gus left the Lamb, the stranger glanced up from his newspaper.

***Tuesday, 8 May 2018***

"DID YOU HAVE A GOOD WEEKEND, GUV?" asked Neil as Gus walked into the CRT office.

"It had its moments, Neil," Gus replied.

Not last night. He had returned to the bungalow, cooked his meal and sat with a glass of single malt, listening to music alone until he had gone to bed at eleven.

"Did you solve your emergency?" asked Lydia.

"What emergency? Oh, that was just a fox or something that tripped the motion sensor on my cameras. Nothing suspicious."

"Do you want to read through the reports in the Freeman Files from Friday afternoon's interviews, guv?" asked Alex.

"I'm updating our files with my interview from Saturday afternoon," said Gus, "I talked to a friend of your Dad's, Neil. They gave me useful information about footballers spending time and money in regional parlours. Did you find Ian Hewson?"

"Yes, guv. Hewson's registered for a team playing in the National League South. He's thirty-four now. His playing career is coming to a close. He might have a couple more seasons left."

"What time will he be here?" asked Gus.

"Two o'clock this afternoon, guv," said Neil.

"I'll read those Friday reports later, Alex. Give me the headlines?"

"Harrison had booked a bath, guv. Do you need to learn what that entails?"

"Too much detail, Alex. So, that meant the session overran the thirty minutes?"

"He reckoned Camille saw him off the premises at ten to seven. He didn't hear any whistling or singing. Nobody was working nearby then."

"And Babar Ahmed, the elderly dentist?"

"A taciturn man, guv. Gentle as a lamb. Anxious that his wife never found out. Ahmed heard nothing and saw nothing. He hasn't visited a parlour since the murder."

"Anything sound off with his answers?"

"No, guv. No way could he be our man,"

"The reports from my visits to the parlours will be updated in the next hour, guv. Jake Latimer came along for the ride. We got a similar story to the one you picked up on Saturday afternoon. Several of the parlours had footballers among their clientele.

"Thanks, Neil. I look forward to hearing what the girls could add. We still have girls to catch. Keep hunting for them."

"I'll get on it, guv," said Alex.

"Jeff Naylor is in this morning, I believe?"

"He's your noon appointment,"

Gus nodded. A quiet morning in prospect. Jeff Naylor and Ian Hewson should bring them closer to the truth. Still, they had to go through the process with the others, just in case.

Don Green was in his early sixties. He was a greengrocer and married three times. A somewhat overweight man whose nose suggested his five-a-day included something closely related to a Pinot Noir. Whether the other four items were vegetables or another grape variety was difficult to tell.

Lydia wondered how the parlour girls could stand being in the same room. Somehow, Laura had agreed to Don Green becoming a regular. Gus followed the same line of questioning as the other men. The greengrocer may have looked like an old soak, but his replies were brief and never wavered. He arrived on time. Gem took him to the room, conducted their business, and left. Gem walked downstairs with him and closed the door behind him.

Walter Shadwell was as Terry Davis had described him. In his eighties, short, bald-headed and with rounded shoulders. He was shrinking with age. Gus could imagine him standing straight and proud behind the bar as mine host in the Swindon pub Terry described. Now he was collapsing in on himself. He looked in a sorry state.

Gus cut to the chase.

"We don't want to keep you here any longer than necessary, Walter," said Gus.

Lydia wondered if Gus feared the older man might keel over and draw his last breath on the carpet in front of his desk.

"I should hope so," replied Walter.

"What time did you arrive at Gentle Touch?"

"Seven o'clock on the dot,"

"Did you see anybody outside the parlour; or hear anyone in the vicinity? Inside one of the nearby buildings, for instance?"

Walter thought for a while.

"I don't remember anything like that. I saw nobody. My hearing isn't what it was; someone could have been talking. I'm afraid I wouldn't have heard a conversation on the other side of the street."

"We understand that you visited Gem often,"

"Not for what you think," said Walter, "my wife died when she was forty-seven. So I've been on my own for nigh on thirty years now. But Gem, let me talk to her. I didn't go for anything other than the female company."

Gus helped Walter Shadwell from his chair and escorted him to the car park.

"An expensive way to get someone to chat with you," said Neil.

"What, you think he should have signed up for something similar to Tinder?" asked Lydia.

"We're no closer to our killer," said Alex, "but Laura wasn't just a masseuse, was she? The more we learn, the more caring she appears to have been."

"Which makes it vital to understand why someone stabbed her repeatedly," said Lydia. "Who could she have hurt or upset that much?"

Gus returned to the office.

"We don't need to bother Walter again, guv," said Neil.

"I asked him in the lift what he did for company after Gentle Touch closed," said Gus, "he told me he joined a dating agency for Over Sixties. I asked how that had gone for him. He said he received hundreds of emails from young Russian women. They were all beautiful. Every one of them was desperate to come to the UK to meet him. Sadly, they couldn't afford the airfare. I told him it was a scam. He said he was aware of that, but he had an extensive library of candid photographs they attached to their emails designed to convince him to part with his money. The girls got nothing from him, but Walter had enjoyed writing backwards and forwards to them. It was a company of sorts, and it hadn't cost him a penny."

"Crafty devil," said Lydia.

"Did you get the name of the site he used, guv?" asked Neil.

"You shouldn't be messing around with things like that with your wife in the family way, Neil," said Gus.

"I wasn't thinking of myself, guv. You're over sixty and thought you might need the company."

I've got more than I can handle, Neil. Thank you very much, Gus thought.

"I don't speak Russian, Neil," he replied.

The less they knew, the better.

Jeff Naylor found parking spaces at a premium when he arrived at noon. As a result, he looked hot under the collar when he arrived at the CRT office.

Some of that was due to the warm weather. An altercation with a bollard had caused damage to Naylor's brand-new Audi, which irked him.

"What a shambles," he moaned, "these council-run car parks are useless. The lines they paint on the ground take no account of the room required for the wide variety of models on the market. They seem to imagine everybody drives a Mini or a Smart car."

"When you're ready, Mr Naylor," said Gus, "perhaps, you could sit here and answer a few questions?"

"Right. Sorry. A bad start to proceedings. The phone call I received indicated this meeting concerned the murder of the Swindon girl in 2011. Is that correct?"

"Laura Mallinder was the young lady's name. You knew her as Gem. You were a regular customer of hers at Gentle Touch in Broadgreen."

"I hadn't realised she used a different name until I read it in the newspapers."

"You were her last client," said Gus.

"I had booked for eight in the evening, as I had every week since the place opened. Gem was very proficient. Without a doubt, she gave the best massage I have ever experienced. I'm on my feet all day in my job. There's a lot of lifting and carrying. I don't think I could keep up with the others where I work if I didn't have the kinks worked out of my muscles every weekend."

"Did you find somewhere else to get this weekly treatment once you realised Gentle Touch wasn't re-opening?"

"Not immediately. I was shocked to hear that Gem, well Laura, had been murdered. The police contacted me and asked about my session. They wanted to know if we had argued. Whether anyone else entered the building to wait in Reception until one of the girls was free. I don't think there was anyone else there on that occasion. When Gem walked me downstairs, all the doors to the rooms were open. There was nobody in Reception either. That was strange, but I didn't comment on it to Gem. I wished I had."

"What do you mean?"

"Well, I suppose it would have been awkward for her, given the circumstances. But she could have made me a coffee, and I would have stayed until she was ready to close."

"Why would she be closing the parlour?"

"The opening times on Sundays were displayed on a board in Reception. Six pm to nine pm."

"Where did you move to when you realised the parlour had closed for good?"

"The new parlour on Cricklade Road. Heaven knows what her real name is, but a girl called Janina sees to me now. She's not a patch on Gem, but I can't afford to retire yet."

"What work do you do, Mr Naylor?" asked Gus.

"I work for a firm of funeral directors," replied Jeff Naylor.

Gus heard a cough from the back of the office as Neil tried to stifle a laugh.

"I want you to think carefully now, Mr Naylor. You

arrived at eight. Did you see or hear anything as you approached the parlour? What about when you left, thirty minutes later? Did you notice anyone singing or whistling?"

"I heard a mechanical sound. Wait. That would have been upstairs. There was a utility room. They always kept the door closed. It was further along the corridor. Next to the small room where the girls had their lockers and made themselves drinks. There was a constant need for fresh towels. One of the girls must have started a washing machine."

"Nothing more you could hear?"

"When I came out of the alleyway, I turned left to walk home. As I passed the shop window, I realised someone was inside."

"In the barber's shop?" asked Gus. This was new.

This revelation alerted Alex Hardy. He checked the murder file they had inherited from Gablecross. There was no mention of Ahmet Tekin, the Turkish barber who leased the ground floor unit.

According to the statement he had given to DS Latimer, he had closed at half-past five on Saturday afternoon. The shop opened at nine on Monday mornings, but the police wouldn't allow him inside until they had completed their investigations. Alex noticed Jake Latimer had added that Tekin was annoyed at having to turn customers away.

When Alex looked up, Gus had finished his questioning of Jeff Naylor. Neil was taking him downstairs to the car park. Gus had asked Neil to photograph the damage to Naylor's new car. It was the least they could do. Knowing Gus, he would pass it on to the correct department and then forget it. It wasn't their problem.

"Did you hear that, Alex?" asked Gus.

"Yes, guv. The owner Ahmet Tekin is a Muslim, as are

most Turks. He attends the mosque on Manchester Road. Tekin may have needed to attend to something on his way home. However, he didn't tell Latimer when interviewed."

"What time would he have been at the mosque for prayers?"

"Isha is the last prayer of the day, guv, between sunset at around a quarter past nine that day and midnight. Which suggests he worked at something before he visited the mosque. We need to speak to him."

"I agree. Get in touch with Tekin. We can interview him on his premises. I stopped across the road with Theo Hickerton the other day, but I haven't stepped inside to check the layout of the building. We need to rectify that."

Gus checked his watch. They had over an hour to wait before Ian Hewson arrived. After that, he had time to dig into the Culverhouse and Plunkett link. What should the others be doing?

Neil was still outside in the car park. Alex was phoning the Turkish barber.

"Lydia, can you do something for me?"

"If I can, guv. What do you need?"

"Laura Mallinder was an attractive girl. In her teens and early twenties, she had a series of boyfriends. Then, for at least six years, she worked in massage parlours. When we spoke to her family, there was no mention of a relationship after she split up with Ian Hewson. Maggie Monk didn't allow sex on her premises…."

"You want to know why a sexually active teenager suddenly becomes celibate?"

"Laura must have had urges, surely?"

"We can't profile the poor girl based on the details we've learned since her death. From a distance, it seems strange she helped hundreds of men gain sexual release and yet apparently denied herself the pleasure. We don't know Laura's mental state during that period. Nor did her family, by the sound of it. The interviews with the girls she worked alongside tomorrow might offer better insight. We must seek emotional causes, such as stress, relationship problems, depression or anxiety. There could have been a memory of sexual abuse or rape, unhappiness with her body. We can't rule out physical causes, such as hormone problems or pain from an injury either."

"Everything we've learned of Laura so far suggests she was caring, compassionate and not a nervous, troubled individual. So what are we missing?"

"Perhaps, we'll soon find out," said Lydia, "Ian Hewson has a wild streak, according to his football persona. It would be unusual for that to stay within the confines of the pitch. It's bound to spill over into his relationships."

Gus agreed. He was keen to question Hewson over his relationship with Laura. Donna had given him an idea that Hewson may have been among the crowd that visited parlours splashing the cash.

Neil had returned to the office.

"Did Mr Naylor leave us in a happier frame of mind, Neil?" asked Gus.

"He'd done a grand's worth of damage, guv. I saw him out of his parking space, so he didn't make matters worse. He had a point. When they made room for our vehicles, the remaining spaces must have got squeezed to ensure they didn't lose revenue."

"He might win a claim against the Council. Then, pigs might fly," said Gus.

"That comment about the barber being in the shop, guv," said Neil, "one girl told me he fancied Laura

Mallinder, but she knocked him back. He didn't bug her, according to her."

"We're following up on that, Neil," said Gus, "it might be something."

Gus tried to recall what had struck him about the barber's shop when he'd sat across the road from it with Theo Hickerton. Then, finally, it would come to him.

## Chapter Twelve

IAN HEWSON ARRIVED at two o'clock. He was a fit-looking thirty-four-year-old who looked after his body. His hair was cut short, and his face, arms, and legs were tanned. Lydia thought he was a poser, wearing a club t-shirt and shorts to a police interview, but typical of the sporting jocks she had known at university.

Hewson's trainers were top-of-the-range. The designer sunglasses tucked into his shorts would have set him back several hundred pounds. The Ferrari keyring he twirled on his forefinger wasn't a nervous tic. It was to let them know what car he drove. Lydia revised her opinion. Not a poser. A dickhead.

"Good afternoon, Mr Hewson," said Gus, "you're a difficult man to find. Please sit."

Hewson looked around, then realised the only unoccupied seat meant he had the three younger people behind him. So he sat and inspected the old face opposite him.

"My name is Freeman," said Gus, "a consultant with Wiltshire Police. My Crime Review Team and I are eager to solve the brutal murder of Laura Mallinder seven years ago."

"Why do you think I could help?" asked Hewson. He had relaxed in the chair and spread his legs. He looked bored.

"You were in a relationship with Laura, were you not?"

"We met at a nightclub and saw one another for a few months. So what? That ended years before she died."

"Who ended the relationship?"

"Laura. She messed me around."

"In what way?"

"Laura knew I was serious. I wanted to get engaged. I hoped she would settle down. But, unfortunately, her mates, Mo and JoJo, messed with her head. They turned her against me. I thought she was seeing someone behind my back."

"You followed Laura and waited outside the place where she worked. We have laws against that these days. Mr Hewson. You stalked her, didn't you?"

"Laura wouldn't see sense. She thought me too intense. We parted company. I tried to get back with her, but I got a big break. I moved away."

"You transferred to a bigger club and secured a well-paid contract?"

Hewson sat up in his chair. Gus had mentioned something that allowed him to brag.

"I got paid way more than I earned at the City. I could take home sixty, even seventy grand a week with winning bonuses."

"You are keen to display the trappings we associate with the wealthy young footballers of today," said Gus, "yet we struggled to find a permanent address. You moved from house to house, and that made finding you difficult. But,

Ferrari or no Ferrari, your high-earning years are behind you. The National League South is one step from whatever life you have planned after you retire."

Hewson's right leg began to bounce. Gus knew he was getting under his skin. Just a few more barbed comments and he would be a prime candidate for a red card.

"When did you last see Laura?" asked Gus.

"Before I left for West Bromwich."

"You never had cause to return here, to visit family or friends, perhaps? Or to try your luck with Laura again? After all, you were earning big money."

"I came back to visit my mother, but I never went near the Mallinder family. I didn't want any more trouble."

"Ah yes, they had a word with you, didn't they? Sam and Tyrone told us about that. Gary was your friend, though, wouldn't you say?"

"We met up from time to time in the old days when I played with the Academy."

"Did Gary tell you what his sister did for a living?"

"Who says I knew until it appeared in the papers? Whoever it was, they're a liar."

"You seem agitated, Mr Hewson. You have a temper. There's plenty of evidence in televised games where you made brief appearances. You got sent off on various occasions. Your disciplinary record contributed to the decline in your fortunes. The bigger clubs off-loaded you because they prefer players who can be relied upon to stay in control of their emotions for ninety minutes."

Hewson's leg bounce became even more rapid.

"I was quick and skilful. I scored eleven goals in my first season. Defenders targeted me. They were jealous."

"It's only a game. Mr Hewson. You lash out with your fists if you don't get your way. Is that what happened with

Laura? Did you attack her when she refused to have anything more to do with you?"

"I never hit her. Laura wouldn't see sense."

"I'll ask you again. When was the last time you saw Laura?"

"In 2004, I took her a bunch of roses on October the twenty-third. She never even came to the door."

"Do you spend much time in Swindon?" asked Gus.

"I've played there. I've been to watch the team once or twice when I was injured. If you're not playing, it helps to travel to the local clubs to feel the buzz. I've watched City and Rovers more often."

"Well, that would only be natural since you came from the city and now live in Bradley Stoke. When did you move there?"

"I moved back five years ago. It's where I lived as a boy. My mother still lives there."

"Ah, you visited her while Laura worked in the massage parlours. You only moved back after her death."

Hewson did not comment.

"Did you ever spend an evening in Swindon with your teammates between 2006 and 2011?"

"Never,"

"What about in Bristol in the eighteen months before that?"

"I would have been on the town in Birmingham, Manchester or London,"

"Was that where your money went, Mr Hewson? You have told me you earned obscene amounts every week. Surely you spent it on items other than clothing, sunglasses and sports cars?"

"I got cheated," said Hewson, "I made poor investments. My mother promised to help, but that never happened. So I couldn't move in with her. I'm still earning good money and getting back on my feet, but I can't afford to buy a place yet."

"Are many of your old colleagues from the Bristol Academy still living in Bradley Stoke?"

"Only three or four. Lads who still play for local teams but never made the grade. Not to the level I did."

"Is that where you heard about Laura and the men she entertained in the massage parlours?"

"You keep asking me whether I knew. I told you. I didn't know."

"We find it hard to believe, Mr Hewson. Footballers mix in the same circles; you play one another with different clubs; there are rivalries. You have a temper, and the opposition knows how to push the right buttons. Hey, Hewson, your bird has a gentle touch, hasn't she? I bet you miss that?"

Hewson flipped. He sprang from his chair and slammed the palms of his hands on Gus's desk. Neil moved forward to intervene. Gus raised a hand to tell him to wait.

"Time to tell us the truth, Ian,"

"I was there, okay. I was there that night, but I didn't kill her."

"Sit down, Mr Hewson. Start from the beginning. When did you find out what Laura did for a living?"

"March 2010 - I was injured. I wanted to watch a fellow ex-trainee playing for Rovers, and we drove to Swindon. After the game, we spotted Laura in Broadgreen enter the alley."

"By we, you mean you and Gary Mallinder?"

"Yes,"

"What did you do?"

"Nothing much; Gary was upset; I was mad as hell. We

had a haircut and then we went for a meal. We found a club, got drunk and spent the night in my car."

"So, you both knew for over a year. Are you saying you never visited Gentle Touch to try to talk to her?"

"You were right. Several West Country teams play in the National League South. Laura must have seen players in Bristol or Bath before she moved to Swindon. Then, they started taunting me, making snide comments. I didn't believe them. Gary didn't know; he thought they had mistaken her for someone else."

"What caused you to visit the parlour that night?"

"I'd had enough. I'd been transferred yet again in the summer. The injury I had picked up that put me on the sidelines in 2010 left the club wondering whether I was worth the risk. The only way from there is down into the lower leagues. My money dropped, and the side I joined wasn't successful, so the bonuses disappeared. In the spring of 2011, I made one last attempt to get the money. When that failed, I was angry at the world. I wouldn't have been on the verge of bankruptcy if we'd married. Gary wanted his sister to stop what she was doing before Sam found out. The knowledge was already killing his mother."

"Who came up with the idea of the phone call?"

"How do you find out about that?"

"He's a detective," said Neil, placing two cups of coffee between Hewson and Gus on the desk.

"I did. I met Gary in our usual pub. Gary phoned the owner as he walked from pub to pub. I drove to Swindon to confront Laura. He rang to confirm I had thirty minutes before anyone would be there,"

"How did you know Laura would be alone?"

"Ryan told us,"

"Ryan Black?"

"He went in there often, so he overheard things — especially on weekdays when five girls are available. In a slack period, the girls gather in the locker room and drink coffee and chat. Ryan overheard the Thai girl saying she had asked the owner to cover for her when she left early on Sunday."

"So, you created a window where you could talk to Laura to persuade her to give up the work she did. How did you know Ryan Black?"

"I didn't. Gary did. They worked together from time to time."

"Did Gary tell Ryan why he needed to see her alone?"

"Gary told him it was a surprise. They hadn't seen one another for ages. He didn't tell Ryan I was going instead of Gary."

It dawned on Gus why Ryan Black had been the second person to ask if that was it when they interviewed them.

"Laura wasn't concerned when you rang the bell?"

"Laura opened the door and asked what I was doing there. I followed her upstairs. OK, I dragged her upstairs. We argued for five, maybe ten minutes. She was screaming and shouting. Finally, I lost my temper and picked up the nearest thing to me and threw it at her."

"You missed and smashed the mirror?"

"Yes, that was me. I realised I was wasting my time. Laura was happy with the way her life had turned out. I couldn't believe what I had heard. She kept shouting at me to get the hell out. Finally, I ran downstairs, slammed the door behind me and drove back to Bristol. She was alive when I left her. You've got to believe me."

Gus sat back and thought for a while.

"Did you see anyone outside when you left? Did you hear voices?" asked Gus.

"Not that I remember. I was angry and upset. It was probably just as well I didn't run into anyone."

"Stay close to Bradley Stoke. Don't leave the country, Ian. We need to check your story. I'm sure we'll be in touch with further questions. DS Davis will escort you."

Ian Hewson left the office with Neil. His coffee cup sat half-empty on the desk.

"We can't use it, can we, guv?" asked Lydia.

"We didn't even caution him," said Alex.

"It doesn't prevent us from checking whether he lied about being in the parlour," said Gus. "get his prints tested against the ones found at the scene."

"Who's next, guv? We can visit Ahmet Tekin's shop this afternoon."

"If you feel up to it, Alex, we'll take a spin out to Castle Combe first."

"I THOUGHT WE FINISHED THIS," said Maggie Monk as she opened the door.

There it was again, thought Gus. What had he missed?

"Why? Was there something we forgot?" asked Gus.

"You didn't ask me about Charles the other times you came here."

"We knew you were a widow and that you moved here in 2010. Difficult to see how your late husband could have been relevant to the case. You had already been running the massage parlour business for four years. You told us last time that selling your husband's business provided the capital. We wondered where the money came from, but it was logical that you inherited enough money to launch your enterprise. We never suspected you came by it illegally."

"Charles died in 2004," said Maggie.

"I suspect there's more," said Gus.

"When he divorced his wife, she married again almost at once. Elizabeth was forty. She and Charles had never had children. Within months she gave birth to a son. Charles was never sure whether he was the father or Elizabeth had been having an affair. We didn't sleep together until after his divorce. Charles thought it rich for Elizabeth to be committing adultery throughout while he had only been guilty of loving his secretary for five years and not acting on it."

"I'm sure we'll get to the relevant part soon," said Gus.

"Elizabeth's second husband's name was…."

"Hewson," said Gus.

"Oh, I thought that would come as a surprise. How did you know?"

"Ian Hewson was Laura's boyfriend. He played football with the Bristol City Academy Under-23. After he and Laura split, he transferred to a Midlands club. We have been trying to locate him for ages until today."

"Ian came here," said Maggie, "he was angry. He had proof Charles was his father. He blamed me for the divorce. I robbed him of the inheritance that should have passed to his mother."

"When did this happen?"

"Early in 2011,"

"How did he gain access to the estate?"

"The builders were here, seeing to the last of the teething problems."

"If I showed you a photograph, would you be able to say whether it was one of those builders?"

"Perhaps, they were only here for three days."

Gus searched for the image caught by their CCTV of Ryan Black.

"Do you remember this man?"

"No, he wasn't here then. He worked for the firm that built the estate."

"A different firm did the repairs, then?"

"No, the same firm, but most of their workers were on another site. So the foreman phoned for someone to drive up from Bristol for three days of work."

Gus described Gary Mallinder to her.

"That's him, lots of muscles and tattoos. Didn't like the look of him one bit."

"I reckon we've got everything we need from you, Mrs Monk."

"I hope so. My neighbour came around yesterday. She's got her place up for sale. She was worried that seeing the police here so often deterred people."

"You weren't shocked to learn about Hewson, guv," said Alex when they returned to the car.

"I hadn't got a clue, Alex. I kept wondering why people thought we hadn't asked something they expected. Ryan Black believed Gary only wanted to surprise his sister. He didn't think he meant her any harm. When the police discounted her close family from being involved in her murder, that reinforced Black's belief that it was someone else. So, he didn't come forward."

"When Maggie Monk seemed to have something to add and revealed the details of her late husband's extended family, it fell into place."

"Something like that. Let me ask you this. Is Hewson our killer?"

"Hewson denied knowing what Laura did for a living. At first, he denied visiting Swindon for a night out, but he caved in after you kept the pressure on him. Finally, he admitted to being in town with Gary in 2010 and was in the room with Laura minutes before she died. Do we have enough for a search warrant?"

"What could we hope to find," asked Gus. "A murder weapon after seven years? I don't think so."

"So, we must add Maggie Monk's information to what we have and tackle Hewson again? It has to be him."

Once they reached the CRT office, Gus trawled through the Freeman Files. He was searching for that impression he had formed of the building in Broadgreen. There it was. The nail bar and barber's shop looked bright and shiny, but the building was crumbling. Gus read Neil's latest updates; he was almost there.

"I want to apply pressure on this Ahmet Tekin. He must have withheld information. Tekin was on the premises that evening. Gosling heard him singing and whistling at eight o'clock. Maggie Monk said everywhere was dead quiet when she arrived and walked indoors at twenty to ten. When did he start his work? When did he leave?"

"Shall we drive to Swindon to talk to him this afternoon, guv?" asked Alex.

"He'll be upstairs in his refurbished shop for a few hours. Tell you what. Call Theo Hickerton. Find out if he and Jake Latimer are available. I want to see their faces when we expose such a blatant error. How could they not even ask him if he visited the premises between closing time on Saturday and Monday morning? They must have had people working at the parlour when Tekin arrived to open his shop. He was annoyed at being unable to serve his customers. Did he show any signs of being upset to learn of the death of a young woman who worked on his doorstep? A woman he had asked out."

"They didn't know Tekin fancied Laura and asked her to go out with him, guv," said Alex.

"Tekin bought her flowers after she'd rejected him. However, Laura continued to be friendly towards him. She wasn't angry with him," said Neil.

"Tell DI Hickerton to meet us in Broadgreen," said Gus, "if they don't know which questions to ask, we'll give them a list."

"Who do you want with you this afternoon, guv?" asked Neil.

"You get on well with Latimer. Perhaps it would be better if you came. No offence, Alex."

"That's okay, guv. The stairs would be an issue."

Neil drove to Swindon. As they approached the street where Laura's murder had occurred seven years ago, Neil remembered his red-light tour with Jake.

"Jake told me the history surrounding the red-light district when we did the tour, guv. Manchester Road, where we are now, was the centre for years. For a while, the street girls had disappeared. Jake said it was on the increase again. There are at least two mosques in the area. Add in the massage parlours, and Tekin had plenty to complain about if he was a devout Muslim."

Hickerton and Latimer sat in his Kuga on the opposite side of the road from Tekin's business. Neil parked behind them.

"Nothing like being discreet, is there?" said Gus, "I wonder how long they've been here?"

Gus and Neil walked forward. Gus tapped on the passenger window.

"Everybody ready?" he asked.

"Hop in the back for a minute," said Theo. "Explain to me again why you've dragged us out here."

Gus made Neil walk around to the driver's side door.

Gus clambered into the back seat; the lack of legroom annoyed him.

"It's quite straightforward," he said, "seven years ago, you two screwed up. Nobody asked Ahmet Tekin what he was doing on the night of Laura Mallinder's murder."

"Who?" asked Theo.

"The Turkish barber, guv," said Jake.

"Well, he closes at half-past five on a Saturday. He never came back until Monday morning to open at nine."

"Tekin was in the shop, working. A regular customer heard him singing and whistling when they left at eight. It might help our enquiries if you ask him why he was there. When did he arrive? When did he leave? Did he overhear the argument between Laura and her former boyfriend?"

"Anything else? Do you want to know if he can fit you in for a trim before he shuts?"

"No, but you could ask him if he had a key for the massage parlour."

Neil glanced at his boss. What was he driving at this time?

"Where will you be while we're interviewing this guy?" asked Jake.

"We'll let you two get things started. You understand algorithms, don't you? So if you get answers that allow us to continue interrogating Ian Hewson until he admits he killed Laura, we can do that."

"What if we don't get the right answers?" asked Theo.

"We'll ask him different questions. Then, Neil and I will wait at the bottom of the stairs to keep the nail technicians occupied."

The four men crossed the street. DI Hickerton and DS Latimer announced their arrival, waving warrant cards and asking for the owner. There were four young female technicians, three of whom dealt with customers. An older lady, clad in a lilac blouse and a black pencil skirt, the same uniform as her assistants, checked their ID and pointed upstairs.

Gus and Neil stayed in the nail bar.

"Please," said the manageress, "we don't want any trouble."

"The detectives are here to speak with Mr Tekin. It won't take long. Are you related to Mr Tekin?"

The lady shook her head.

"He's not married, I take it?" asked Gus.

Another shake of the head.

Neil heard raised voices.

Three men came downstairs; they weren't happy. Hickerton must have told them to leave.

The first two had been waiting their turn. A sign on the door said appointments weren't always necessary. The third man's hair looked lop-sided. He must have been in the chair.

"We apologise for the inconvenience," said Gus, "but this is part of a murder enquiry."

Neil expected them to hang around, waiting for Tekin to become available, but they shot through the door and walked away.

Theo Hickerton had started to question Ahmet Tekin.

"What time did you arrive here the evening Laura Mallinder died?"

"A quarter to eight."

"Why did you need to come?"

"There was such a mess. I couldn't start on Monday morning if I didn't get it clean."

"What time did you leave?"

"I was here for forty-five minutes."

"Hang on," said Jake Latimer, "the Thai girl, Camille, left then. Did you see her?"

Tekin shook his head.

"Did you see anyone else arriving as you left?"

"I saw nothing. I heard nothing."

"Did you have a key for the massage parlour?"

"Why ask that?"

"It's something we need to know," said Hickerton, not knowing why it mattered. He was bored; this was a waste of time.

"Come on," he said, raising his voice, "did you have a key for the massage parlour?"

"Watch it, guv," yelled Jake, "he's got a knife."

Neil sprang up the stairs two at a time.

Jake Latimer had rugby-tackled Tekin to the floor. Theo Hickerton sat on the floor, leaning against a barber's chair. A metal object was sticking out of his chest.

"Guv, call for an ambulance," Neil shouted, "the DI's been stabbed."

Gus pulled his phone from his trouser pocket and made the call.

His instinct had proved right yet again. Tekin wasn't happy being asked about the key.

Gus walked up the stairs to join Neil.

"Have you cautioned him, Jake?" he asked. The DS nodded.

"Record this conversation on your phone. As my old teacher used to say. Read, mark and inwardly digest,"

"Why did you have a key, Mr Tekin?" he asked.

"The building is old; it has many faults. They were always using the washing machine, day after day. It was old. It leaked. The water gathered in the ceiling space, and the tiles gave way; my shop flooded. Mrs Monk came to see me;

she inspected the damage. When her back turned, I used a soap bar to take an impression of the Yale key. I had a copy made. She didn't do a thing to stop it from happening again."

"When did this take place?"

"A year before my Gem died. I wanted to check the pipework was secure. So I went in when there was nobody there."

"So, let's recap," said Gus, "Gem came to work here in 2006. You took over from a record shop owner around eighteen months later. Gem passed your shop several times a week for over three years. She was beautiful, a pleasant girl; you were attracted to her. You asked her out more than once, but she declined your offer. Does that sound right?"

"Gem was beautiful. She was too good to be working there,"

"When did you meet her brother?"

Tekin strained against his handcuffs. He was becoming agitated.

"Gary came here a year before her death, didn't he? Gary saw his sister arrive to start work. He was with a mate, Ian Hewson; they had been to a football match. The stadium is a ten-minute walk away. Although your signs say you close at five-thirty, you don't turn trade away. Instead, you switch the sign in the window to 'closed' and lock the door. Those men waiting take their turn, and you finish at six o'clock, even later. Am I right?"

"Yes. So, what?"

"You had ample time to listen to their conversation. Gary had just learned where his sister worked. Hewson watched a girl enter a massage parlour without a care in the world. A girl he wanted to marry. How did the things they said make you feel?"

Neil heard a siren in the distance. Just as well, that wound was high on Hickerton's chest. Anywhere vital, and he could have bled out before help arrived. The DI was ashen-faced, and it was safest not to move him. Jake knelt beside him, keeping him as comfortable as possible.

Neil dashed downstairs to show in the paramedics. But, instead, he found the nail bar empty. Both the staff and the customers had fled.

Upstairs, Gus had asked Tekin again about the conversation between Hewson and Mallinder.

"The one with tattoos was angry, but he kept it hidden. The other one wanted to do something to stop Laura from working there."

"A year later, that man returned, didn't he? You saw him arrive in his flash car and go inside."

"I heard them arguing. There was so much noise. The washing machine was spinning like crazy. The ceiling tiles were loose. Water seeped through again. My Gem yelled at him. She enjoyed giving pleasure to the men she saw. She never wanted to settle down and raise a family. I was angry. I heard the door slam. The man left."

"You left your shop and let yourself into the parlour. What did Gem say when she realised it was you?"

"She was crying. Her ex-boyfriend had trashed the room. There was glass everywhere. I put my arms around her and told her I loved her. I would look after her. Nobody would ever abuse her again."

The ambulance crew helped Theo Hickerton downstairs to the waiting ambulance.

Jake stayed behind. Neil sat on the barber's chair.

"How did she respond?" asked Gus.

"She laughed at me," said Tekin.

"Where did you get the knife? Did you take it with you?

Tekin indicated with his head towards the staircase.

"Are you saying that was the knife you used? The one in DI Hickerton's chest?"

Tekin nodded.

"It's not a knife. It's half of a pair of scissors. I carry it with me always."

"Would you do the honours, Jake?" asked Gus, "in the absence of your boss?"

Gus walked away as DS Latimer charged Ahmet Tekin with the murder of Laura Mallinder.

"BLOODY HELL," said Neil, "I was convinced Hewson did it."

"So was I for a while, Neil. I just had an inkling. Why was Ahmet in the shop out of hours? I remembered the poor state of the building, and then Hewson told us they had a haircut and went for a meal. They stood across the road from Tekin's place. It made sense they came here. Both men were angry and upset; they talked. Barbers are famed for listening. Tekin stored away what he heard. The flooding that occurred last year was on the verge of being repeated. It just needed one more thing to produce the final straw. Then he saw Hewson go upstairs. Tekin thought he was the white knight riding to the fair damsel's rescue. She laughed at him. Everything we know of Laura suggests that laugh held no malice. Yet Tekin lashed out with that makeshift weapon. The red mist descended. He struck her time and time again."

"What do we do now, guv?" asked Neil.

"Get back to the office. Tidy up the Freeman Files for this case and wait for what the future brings."

# Epilogue

***Wednesday, 9 May 2018***

GUS HAD SPENT the day at London Road HQ. His meetings with Geoff Mercer and the ACC were more convivial than in the past. Geoff was over the moon. Kenneth Truelove had a new folder relating to the 2004 murder of a scientist. He had been shot at close range with a sawn-off shotgun. The ACC told Gus to put his feet up for the rest of the week. Monday morning would be soon enough to get their new investigation started.

Sandra Plunkett didn't show her face. Vera Jennings and Kassie Trotter supplied tea and cakes as usual.

Everything was fine for now.

GUS DROVE HOME to an empty bungalow. Time to catch up with those vegetables of his. He visited the allotment. He noticed someone working on Frank North's old patch.

"Good evening," he said. The woman straightened up and faced him.

"Hello, I've seen you somewhere before, haven't I?" said Clemency Bentham.

"Yes, you were the celebrant at Frank's funeral,"

"I made a mess of that, didn't I?" laughed Ms Bentham.

"They'll get over it. Bert Penman not around this evening?"

"He was here earlier, but I don't think he wants to get too familiar. Bert said he'd see me when the time comes."

"He takes the same approach with the local doctor."

AS GUS and his new neighbour passed the time of day, Ricky Gardiner sat in the Lamb. He placed his gin and tonic on a table near the bar and made a phone call.

"Dominic? Ricky here; the bugger has done it again. Another case is solved. Well, decide what you want to do next and give me a call."

## Next in the The Freeman Files series

vinci-books.com/deadlyformula

**One bullet, countless secrets and a past that must be unlocked.**

Detective Gus Freeman probes the unsolved murder of scientist Dr. Ian McGuire, unveiling corruption, a sinister formula and perilous truths from past and present.

Turn the page for a free preview…

## Deadly Formula: Chapter One

"Is the coast clear, Mr Freeman?"

Gus hardly had time to unlock his shed door before the disembodied voice broke into his thoughts on how to spend his unexpected free time.

"What's the matter, Bert?" he asked, realising it was his friend from the neighbouring allotment.

"I can't come here without being pestered by the Reverend," said Bert, emerging from the dark recesses of his six-foot by four-foot hut.

Gus smiled.

Clemency Bentham, the celebrant from Frank North's funeral, had taken over the plot next to Gus. She was young and very keen to learn. Bert was the fount of knowledge in the village for everything related to gardening.

"You can't blame her for tapping into your wealth of experience, Bert," said Gus, "isn't that what I've been doing ever since I came to live here?"

"You keep to yourself, Mr Freeman. I never expect you

to discuss one of your cases with me while digging, hoeing or planting."

"Ah, she's trying to save your soul. Is that it?" laughed Gus.

"The Reverend keeps dropping hints. Why do I only see you here on the allotment, Mr Penman? Why don't you pop next door to the church on Sunday? Have you ever given produce for the Harvest Festival?"

"Were you ever a regular churchgoer, Bert?"

"Many years ago. Anyway, I don't see you going there, Mr Freeman."

"Not my thing, Bert. Tess and I got married in a registry office. We had no children to get christened. So I opted to go straight to the crematorium when she died, as we did with Frank North the other day."

"Cora and I got married in Devizes, at St Mary's; in 1955, I'd come home from Kowloon a month earlier. After my National Service stint ended."

"That tour of duty lasted eighteen months, didn't it?" asked Gus.

"Yes, I went to Oswestry for basic training, then travelled to Woolwich Barracks. That place had been home to the Royal Artillery since the latter part of the eighteenth century. We travelled to Southampton and then sailed out to Kowloon. It took us over four weeks. It was a different world, I can tell you. I missed the Wiltshire countryside, and I could have done without the sights I saw and the things I had to do."

Tonight was the first time Bert had ever mentioned his early life. Gus hadn't realised that he had ever travelled abroad. Let alone see action on the other side of the world. Gus had only just started school in Salisbury when National Service ended.

"Did you go straight into the butcher's shop after they demobbed you?" Gus asked.

"Cora and I spent the weekend in Sidmouth," said Bert, "no exotic honeymoons in those days. Then on Tuesday morning, I started back to work with my father. I'd been learning the butchery trade ever since I left school at fifteen. I took over the shop when he retired."

"Did you and Cora have children?" asked Gus, realising how little he knew, even after three years of seeing Bert several times a week.

"A boy and a girl," said Bert, "David and Margaret. They're both married with children. David lives in Canada. Margaret and her family are in New Zealand."

Bert had a faraway look in his eye.

"Are they able to visit you, Bert?" asked Gus.

"They're too busy. We talk on the phone from time to time. I couldn't travel that far, not with my aches and pains. It is what it is. We were never close after their mother died."

"When did you lose Cora?"

"My wife died in 2005. I lost her to dementia ten years before that. The children had already moved abroad. Neither wanted to return to England to help, so I battled on alone. It was a blessing when her pain ended.

"Had you both gone to church before Cora's illness?" asked Gus.

Bert nodded.

"I've not been through the door since her funeral."

"David and Margaret came home for that, I imagine?"

"They managed to get over for a few days. We have to count our blessings, Mr Freeman. They're fit and well, have excellent jobs, and the grandchildren get a good education. I'll be out of their hair soon enough. There won't be much to share between them when I'm gone. They aren't relying on it; that's a blessing. My little windfall might pay for a holiday or help with the kids' higher education. It won't change their lives."

"When I came here this evening, I wondered what to do with myself for the rest of the week. We cleared another case yesterday, and my bosses told me to take a break. All we've done so far is have a morbid conversation about death. Can we change the subject, Bert?"

"It's that Clemency woman's fault," replied Bert. "She keeps asking me how I'm feeling; and telling me to take it easy, not to overdo it at my age. Working this soil keeps me as fit as I've any right to be at eighty-five. I was here for two hours yesterday, and I distinctly heard her tutting when I passed the church gate and headed toward the pub. I earned a pint as a reward for my labour."

Bert fetched a seed tray from the shed and placed it on its side on the ground. He lowered himself to sit for a while.

"It catches up with you, doesn't it, Bert?" said Gus. "Are you sure you haven't been working too hard?"

"Don't start, Mr Freeman," said Bert, "it's a busy time of the year."

"I'll be helping you for the next few days, Bert. What do we need to do?"

"The sowing and planting are up together. See those rows of vegetable seedlings over yonder. You had better thin those out while they're still small. I put in the beetroots, carrots, onions, parsnips and turnips you love. Water along the rows to settle the disturbed seedlings back in after you've completed the hoeing. That teepee gadget of yours is ready for the runner beans. We'll hoe between the other crops to control the weeds if this weather stays fine. I always try to hold off watering until the evening if we haven't had a shower. It's cooler then, and I can make sure the root areas get a good soaking."

"It's a pity Clemency isn't around this evening. She would have learned so much."

Gus wasn't sure if Bert's noise qualified as a 'harumph', but it was close enough. Bert eased himself up from the wooden seed tray using his trusty walking stick and headed for the Lamb.

"See you in the morning then, Mr Freeman. Don't be late. There's plenty to do."

Gus watched Bert until he reached the entrance to the main bar. The older man was struggling with that arthritic hip. Gus revised his opinion on whether the stick was just for show. Then, with a sigh, he rooted in his shed for a book to read. There was plenty of time to work under supervision tomorrow.

***Thursday, 10 May 2018***

The bin men awakened Gus as they clattered along the lane. Good to know people still started work early in the morning to provide services for those who lived in rural England. He wondered how long it would last.

No doubt he would soon have to take his rubbish to a recycling centre unless he paid an exorbitant annual fee on top of the already eye-watering Council Tax for the pleasure.

Gus listened to the familiar sounds of the vehicle and the workers trotting in front to collect the villagers' bins. They seemed perfectly happy. One was whistling a popular tune; another lad called a cheery greeting to one of Gus's neighbours.

Gus knew where they were. The steady high-pitched

beep told him the driver was reversing his lorry into the small cul-de-sac of council bungalows thirty yards up the lane.

Gus imagined that none of the workers woke this morning with a guilty conscience.

Last Friday afternoon, he had rushed home from work to attend to what he described to his team as a minor issue with a new security system. His cameras had been in place since that morning. Adam and Daryl, the fitters, had lunched in The Lamb pub.

DI Suzie Ferris was in the bar area, too, drowning her sorrows after a brief fling with an old flame ended in a midnight misunderstanding. Gus had arrived home, hoping he could sober her up and say something sensible. Something appropriate that helped her. That was before she told him what caused the misunderstanding and then stopped crying on his shoulder to kiss him.

No wonder he had a guilty conscience.

Saturday didn't bring any relief after Suzie stayed throughout the morning. Gus succumbed to her charms yet again.

Gus lay in bed and tried to hear the binmen. They had moved further along the lane, close to the pub. It was no good. He may as well get up and shower alone. The colder, the better, if he wished to erase the memory of Saturday morning.

He thought that no matter how terrible things got, he always had positives to remember from last weekend. The visit to Donna's house of ill-repute in the afternoon had yielded a new line of enquiry.

On Sunday, Neil Davis and Jake Latimer had trawled around massage parlours across two counties interviewing girls who worked with Laura Mallinder. Every scrap of information helped in a murder investigation. You never knew when a casual remark linked to an event you struggled to explain.

While Neil and Jake sought that elusive casual remark, Gus had fretted over Sunday lunch with Vera Jennings. Nobody could be lucky enough to keep their dark secrets hidden forever. He wouldn't mention what had happened, and safe topics of conversation were always plentiful with Vera.

Somehow, he'd cleared that hurdle and returned home the following morning unscathed. Suzie Ferris had maintained a discreet distance throughout the Bank Holiday. But, unfortunately, Gus knew it was only postponing the inevitable, which didn't help him sleep well at night.

When he had returned to work in the Old Police Station office on Tuesday, Gus found that the odd scraps he'd collected combined well with snippets Neil had gathered. As one after the other Gentle Touch clients told their stories, a viable solution emerged. Laura's ex-boyfriend, Ian Hewson, was firmly in the frame for her brutal murder.

It was typical of Gus that he retained a niggling doubt.

He'd seen it while sitting across the road from Maggie Monk's building, where a Turkish barber and a massage parlour carried on their very different trades.

Gus decided he needed a trip to Swindon to put his concerns to rest. He arranged to meet the two officers from Gablecross involved in the initial investigation into Laura's murder.

Gus didn't have time to pursue the niggle over whether the barber had access to the parlour. While he stood downstairs keeping watch on staff and customers in the nail bar, Theo Hickerton and Jake Latimer interviewed Ahmet Tekin.

Neil raced upstairs as soon as Jake shouted that Tekin had stabbed Theo Hickerton.

Jake and Neil had grappled with the assailant, and he was now facing a murder charge.

It didn't take Gus long to work out the sequence of events that fateful evening.

Hewson had burst into the parlour, and there was an almighty row between the former lovers. Tekin had waited until Hewson left and then gone upstairs to comfort the woman he loved. Laura had already rebuffed him on several occasions. This time, her reaction proved too much for Tekin to take. She laughed at him. He stabbed her to death.

It might have been a double murder if his make-shift weapon had struck Theo Hickerton's chest a few inches lower. Laura Mallinder's murder was solved. It was another cold case closed by Gus and his Crime Review Team.

Yesterday morning he'd driven straight to London Road and the Wiltshire Police HQ. Some meetings were more pleasant than others. Gus knew a warm welcome awaited him. ACC Kenneth Truelove stood by the window as he entered the room with Geoff Mercer. Geoff had been waiting at the top of the stairs when Gus signed in at Reception five minutes before ten.

"Excellent work, Gus," Geoff had enthused.

"We got there in the end," said Gus, "even if we arrived in Swindon thinking the lad Hewson was the guilty party. I imagined Tekin would give us information that confirmed Hewson was the only person upstairs with Laura Mallinder that evening."

"Ah, but you must have imagined another likely scenario?"

"All I had to go on was the distressed look of the fabric of the front of the building when Theo Hickerton took me to the murder site. You know, those old Victorian buildings. Hundreds of shops and offices are housed in similar premises across any sizeable town or city. They have had several guises over the years. The shop fitters come in, rip out the old fittings, slap on a fresh coat of paint and tart the place up to reflect what a modern shop or office should resemble. Another firm repeats the process eighteen months, ten years or several decades later, depending on the enterprise's success."

"What doesn't alter much is the original bricks and mortar," said Geoff, nodding his understanding.

"Exactly, until the building's fabric crumbles," said Gus, "and that got me thinking whether Tekin might have had access to the parlour upstairs. It was a record shop for years before Tekin opened his barbershop. Did the owner live over the shop? Was it a storage space for his business? Maggie Monk wanted two businesses in operation, providing her with a regular income. When Tekin took over, did he hold on to a key for that side door without her knowledge? Tekin got a key made, and as soon as Hickerton asked about access, he realised the game was up and lashed out."

"We'd better get in to see the ACC," said Geoff, "he was checking on Theo's progress. I want to hear how he is."

"I heard that," said the ACC as he took his seat at his desk, "if I might add my hearty congratulations on another successful case, Freeman. The Chief Constable will echo those sentiments when she has time. She's otherwise engaged today."

"I'll miss her smiling face, Sir," said Gus.

"Yes, well, moving on. You'll be happy to hear that DI Hickerton will leave the hospital early next week. When he returns to duty at Gablecross is undetermined."

"The good news is he didn't die," said Geoff Mercer, "the bad news is his handling of the original case wasn't textbook."

"It was a shambles; let's not dress it up any other way," said the ACC.

"What do you think will happen?" asked Geoff Mercer.

"When these things come to light, it's vital that the public keep their complete trust in the service. DI Hickerton's next appointment need not be well-publicised, for instance."

"That would only happen if he were moving further up the ladder," said Gus.

The ACC nodded.

"I imagine Theo will learn that he has reached as high as he will ever go. To demote him seven years after the event only attracts unwanted attention. Far simpler to shunt the officer sideways."

"Nothing to see here," said Gus, "move along, please."

"Exactly," said the ACC.

"Theo's got a way to go before retirement," said Geoff, "he might jump ship and move into private security. If he feels he needs a greater challenge; or a larger salary."

"You're not tempted, Sir?" Gus asked the ACC.

"Never in a million years, Freeman. The wife would kill me if I didn't end my time here and leave at the earliest opportunity. Money isn't a motivator for me."

"There are those keen to scale the greasy pole, despite the associated problems," said Geoff.

"Forget it," laughed Gus, "you've already blagged your way to dizzy heights."

"I wasn't thinking of myself," said Geoff, "I'm happy enough with my lot. Suzie Ferris is ambitious, and our new Chief Constable is keen on advancing the careers of young females. Ms Plunkett encouraged Suzie to attend a training course this week. That's why you haven't seen her here this morning. I know you two are as thick as thieves."

"Suzie's a sociable person," Gus agreed, trying to keep things as brief as possible in that regard, "we always find something to discuss."

"I can't think what's holding up our morning coffee," said the ACC, "I'm parched. I hope Mrs Jennings is fit and well."

Gus could confirm she was fit but declined to mention it.

Geoff Mercer went to find Vera and Kassie Trotter. As soon as he opened the door, Kassie wheeled in her trolley.

"Thanks, Mr Mercer. Sorry for the wait," she chirped, full of the joys of Spring as usual.

Vera followed her in, carrying a tray covered with a cloth.

"We waited until Her Ladyship left the building," said Vera as Kassie poured three cups of tea. "We couldn't risk her catching sight of Kassie's fancies."

"No, that would never do," smiled Kenneth Truelove.

"Kassie has excelled this weekend," Vera said, removing the cloth with a flourish worthy of a magician's assistant.

"Ooh," said Geoff Mercer, "I can't remember the last time I had a cream horn."

"Those are for a special occasion," said Kassie, "they're to celebrate the official end of Vera's marriage."

Vera and Gus exchanged a glance. The ACC didn't spot it.

He was deciding which cake on the tray was the least damaging to his waistline.

On the other hand, Geoff Mercer chose the largest on offer, grinning from ear to ear.

"We are here to celebrate the decree absolute of the marriage of Vera and Monty Jennings," he began and winked at Gus.

Kenneth Truelove tutted.

"Monty and I had several wonderful years," said Vera, "but it was over ages ago. The children will continue to see both of us whenever the opportunity allows. Divorce doesn't bother the younger generation too much. They've carried on as if nothing has happened ever since the initial split. My first task is finding somewhere closer to work to set up my new home."

There was an awkward silence.

"Well, if everyone's happy with their mid-morning refreshments, we'd better get on," said Kassie, "I'll pop back in fifteen minutes for the empties. I'll leave the tray, Mr Mercer, just in case."

With that, Vera and Kassie left the room.

Gus battled with his cream horn, praying he could avoid getting its contents on his clean shirt. He hoped the ACC didn't continue discussing Vera's altered circumstances.

"Young Kassie is one of your success stories, Sir," he said, hoping to steer him away from the topic. "She's a ray of sunshine, and we'll miss her baking skills if she were to get married or move on to new pastures."

"Marriage and Kassie Trotter's life have something in common," said the ACC, shifting his cup of tea around the saucer with the tips of his fingers.

Geoff Mercer thought there was a joke on its way, but he realised his boss was serious.

"In what way, Sir?" he asked.

"They both have occasions when everything balances on a knife-edge, and one false move can lead to disaster. Kassie was experiencing a life-changing moment when I spotted her. Without the right help, she might have fallen into a life of drugs and prostitution. I'm sure we know colleagues who have been happily married, and an extended undercover operation or a social occasion offers the opportunity to stray. It's tough to resist in such circumstances."

Geoff looked at Gus. Was the ACC admitting to an indiscretion from his past? If he was, it had been a well-kept secret.

"I can't speak for Gus," said Geoff, "but a colleague of either sex has never propositioned me during my time in the police."

"What about members of the public?" asked Gus.

The ACC sat up in his chair; he ignored his cup and saucer. He was all ears.

"Don't panic, boss. I wasn't accusing DS Mercer of any impropriety. It happened to me last Saturday afternoon, and not for the first time. Donna, the madam that Terry Davis put me onto, suggested I stay longer than our interview session concerning potential suspects in our case. So I made my excuses and left in a time-honoured fashion. Several girls in Salisbury asked if I was interested while working as a beat constable or a young Detective Sergeant. I always declined, whether single, engaged, or married at the time."

"Glad to hear it, Freeman," said the ACC, "I was talking in general, you understand, not implying there had been any wrongdoing on anyone's behalf. Especially my own. However, our old friend Culverhouse has skeletons in his closet, as we know. Do we have any more information to aid our cause of getting our retaliation in first?"

"I appreciate the turn of phrase, Sir," said Gus, "but no, we've not found any further indiscretions to add to the ones we identified earlier. There was just one thing, though."

Gus had remembered something.

"There's an unfamiliar face in the village. A man in his fifties who drinks gin and tonic and reads one of the broadsheets. He's been in the pub frequently when I've been there. Nobody knows who he is. I might be barking up the wrong tree, but he could be in league with our new Chief Constable. Terry Davis told me his informant reckons she's actively seeking an excuse to close the CRT."

"How many more times will Davis do that?" said the ACC, exasperated. "His intelligence-gathering is superior to that of GCHQ. If I ever discover who he's receiving these tip-offs from, they'll be for the high jump."

"We need to discover who Culverhouse and Plunkett have in common," said Geoff.

"Exactly," said Gus, "somewhere in their past, these three have worked together."

"I'll let you two dig deeper into those matters," said the ACC, "I'll try to keep Ms Plunkett out of your hair. So that brings me to your next assignment."

"Ah, you have another cold case for us to tackle," said Gus, rubbing his hands.

"I do, and I'll give you the details in a moment. However, you and your team need to take the time to recharge your batteries. I suggest you start work on this case on Monday; I insist on it. Once we've finished here, I want you to get off home. The weather forecast is fine. It would be best if you spent time on your allotment and caught up with your reading by that Kierkegaard fellow you enjoy. I don't know your team's leisure interests, but I encourage them to pursue them for the next few days. They may not get a break for ages. This next case will be a challenge."

Gus imagined Neil would hate being home with Melody while she fretted over the early months of her pregnancy. As for Alex Hardy and Lydia, well, that might be a problem. Despite his warning, if Lydia wanted to move their relationship along, Gus imagined Alex couldn't stop her, even if he tried.

"I can always catch up with the tasks on my allotment in the evenings and at weekends, Sir," said Gus, "I need to keep busy."

"Never ignore your social life, Freeman," said the ACC.

Geoff Mercer almost choked on his second cream horn. Gus gave him the stare.

"What is it you have for us to look into, Sir?" he asked as Geoff Mercer brushed tears from his eyes.

The ACC handed both officers a copy of the murder file.

Late on a quiet afternoon on Saturday, 10th January 2004, Dr Ian McGuire, a Southampton football fanatic, was working at his home in Amesbury. He had one eye on the kitchen door he was repainting and the other on the TV screen for the football scores.

McGuire had just boiled the kettle for a well-earned cup of tea. He paused his painting, laid the brush on the open can, and picked up his red-and-white mug.

Outside in the darkness, a killer crept silently through the small back garden.

McGuire blew on the hot tea and offered a prayer as the newsreader gave the Premiership results for the afternoon's matches.

'Birmingham City 2, Southampton 1.'

He gave a deep sigh. Both teams expected to finish mid-table, but he had high hopes for a draw today. Prutton getting sent off just after the hour mark was a disaster. One advantage of the fixture list was that the Saints were home to Leeds on Monday night. That was a chance for three points.

Fingers crossed; work wouldn't prevent him from travelling to St Mary's stadium to watch the game. McGuire took several sips of his tea and placed the mug on the worktop beside him.

As he picked up his brush to resume painting, he caught another result. Bristol City had won away at Notts County. Typical. The Robins were having a successful season in the Second Division. His colleagues wouldn't miss the opportunity to rib him over the Saint's reversal of fortunes at St Andrew's.

Those colleagues never had that opportunity.

The person outside in the back garden fired two shots through the kitchen window from a pump-action shotgun.

The first shot whistled past Ian's ear and crashed into the door jamb. He turned as he heard the spent cartridge hit the concrete patio. The second shot hit him square in the chest. He fell to the floor, mortally wounded.

His attacker collected the spent cartridges and scaled the wooden fence at the bottom of the garden. He soon disappeared into the maze of properties on the estate.

Ian McGuire struggled to the doorway into the lounge. His mobile phone was on the couch. If he could reach it, there might be time. The Scottish League results faded into the background as he dialled 999. When the call connected, Ian McGuire found it impossible to speak. He was too weak.

The emergency operator heard groans and shallow breathing and traced the call. An ambulance raced to the scene, but by the time they arrived, Dr Ian McGuire was dead.

"How on earth did this Dr McGuire deserve to get murdered?" asked Geoff Mercer, "did he upset one of his patients?"

"He wasn't a GP," said the ACC. "When you read further than the first page, you'll learn he was a research scientist with a stellar list of awards and accomplishments. He was a highly regarded man in his field, as they say. That's what made this case so baffling. The detectives investigated several motives. None of them emerged as the definitive reason for the attack. One idea proposed was that it was a case of mistaken identity. As far-fetched as that may seem, the investigating team clutched at straws after several fruitless weeks."

"No wonder you want us to take a few days off," said Gus, flicking through the weighty murder file.

# Deadly Formula: Chapter Two

Gus found it hard to relax. It was all very well for the ACC to send him home on Wednesday lunchtime and insist he didn't think about work until Monday. Ever since he'd handed him a copy of the Dr Ian McGuire murder file, he'd been itching to get stuck into the detail.

His first job when he reached the bungalow in Urchfont had been to phone his team members. They were in the office clearing the decks of paperwork from the Laura Mallinder case and refreshing the digital version in the Freeman Files. He'd spoken to each of them. Gus passed on the ACC's congratulations on a well-done job and instructed them to follow his wishes.

Neil, Alex, and Lydia weren't aware of the contents of the murder file, so they wouldn't get burdened with thoughts of the case until Monday morning when they started the week at the Old Police Station office. Nevertheless, certain aspects were already scratching away at the dark corners of his brain. For Gus Freeman, it was ever thus.

Neil Davis hadn't been as glum as Gus expected to learn he had a free weekend ahead. Neil had news of his own. His father, Terry, was flying in from Marbella. It was his first trip home since he retired to the Costa del Crime in 2013.

Neil told Gus that Terry thought they needed to wet the baby's head, even though it was seven months before the new Davis family member was due.

Terry Davis hadn't struck Gus as a full-on family man based on the few conversations they'd had over the telephone. Perhaps he was mellowing.

Gus wondered if he could tear Terry away from the bosom of his family for an hour to question him further on his local contacts. He could threaten him with Donna's idea of flying out to catch up with him again after she retired from the game for good.

It might be a way to get something useful out of the enforced layoff, and it could help reduce the ACC's blood pressure.

Alex Hardy was planning to spend his free time in the gym. His leg muscles were recovering from the extended period he'd spent in his wheelchair, but work was still needed now that he was more mobile on his crutches. In addition, his upper body strength required attention.

Gus wished Alex well. He hoped his gardening kept him as fit as a sixty-one-year-old had any right to expect. Unfortunately, there was no way anyone could persuade him to invest in a gym membership.

Lydia Logan Barre sounded less engaged than usual when he spoke with her. The prospect of time off didn't receive the enthusiasm Gus thought it warranted. When Tess was Lydia's age, she would have squealed with delight. Instead, Tess always had a lengthy list of things to do and places to go and greeted every hour of unexpected leisure time with unbounded enthusiasm.

Gus reckoned Lydia had other things on her mind. He wondered as Alex was seeing his physio later and planning frequent visits to the gym. It signalled he was aware things were getting too serious between them. Perhaps Alex was erecting a few barriers; that chat they'd had last week might have hit home.

"What are your plans?" Gus had asked Lydia. "Anything in particular in mind?"

"I might travel home to visit my mother," she'd replied. That was the end of the conversation.

Gus helped Bert Penman on the allotment throughout the daylight hours on Thursday and Friday. The older man was in his element. Bert manoeuvred Gus around the plot on a succession of tasks. Gus knew that he would benefit when the vegetables they worked on were ready to eat. The prospect of an infinite supply of fresh produce made the back-breaking effort worthwhile.

Bert disappeared to the pub on Thursday evening. Gus checked his watch. Ten minutes after six o'clock. The list of items Bert had suggested Gus could complete before finishing for the day would keep him here until eight o'clock. The weather was perfect. It was no hardship to potter around on such an evening.

"Good evening,"

The Reverend Clemency Bentham had arrived. Bert must have an early warning system, thought Gus.

"Mr Penman not around today?" she asked.

"We've toiled away together since half-past nine this morning. Bert's taking refreshment after his labours," said Gus.

"You mean he's in the Lamb drinking cider and avoiding me," said Clemency.

"Don't take it personally," said Gus, "he avoids the local GP too. Bert knows the Doctor drops into the Lamb two evenings a week. Thursday isn't one of them. He fears he will scold him for having the occasional drink."

"Thank you," said Clemency, "I can see I need to do my homework. But, once I learn which nights the Doctor is in the pub, I can guarantee Bert will be here or at home."

"If you're that desperate to save his soul, you could always visit the Lamb yourself," suggested Gus.

Clemency giggled.

"The Church doesn't concentrate on that stuff these days," said Clemency, "I want to learn what I can from him. Mr Penman's a proper countryman. So much knowledge could disappear if we don't talk with our old folk before they're gone. He's bristly toward me, but I know that Irene North thinks the world of him. Those gifts of vegetables he leaves on her doorstep when she's out are very much appreciated. He never gives her a chance to thank him."

That's a guilty conscience, thought Gus. Frank North's hapless gardening skills had allowed Bert to pinch fruit and vegetables from his allotment for years.

"What about you, Mr Freeman?" asked Clemency, "should I be concerned for your soul?"

"What have you heard?" asked Gus.

"Irene North tells me you're a widower. As I am, you're a newcomer to the village and destined to be an outsider for at least twenty years. However, you've returned to work as a consultant attached to Wiltshire Police and enjoy female company."

"Ah, the curtain twitchers have been busy," laughed Gus.

"Very little escapes villagers in any corner of the country, Mr Freeman. It's the nature of the beast."

"If the parties involved are unattached, I hardly think it's anyone's business," said Gus.

"Oh, you'll get no argument from me. I thought you should be aware, that's all."

"Duly noted," said Gus.

"Irene North also told me you have someone monitoring your bungalow,"

"A tall, angular-looking gentleman, aged around fifty-five, who carries The Times under his arm as he strolls along the lane. Is that who you mean?"

"Oh, you knew already. Do you have an undercover policeman keeping you safe? I didn't realise you needed protecting."

He's undercover, okay, thought Gus, and not doing a good enough job of it here in the countryside.

"Had you moved into the village when the police raided the outbuildings behind Cambrai Terrace?" Gus asked.

"I read about it. I was still buying my place here, but Irene told me the men involved in that nasty business were responsible for Frank's death."

"That gang broke into my bungalow and tried to scare me. So, I had a protection officer on duty in the lane for several days. That protection has now ended. The gentleman you mentioned has been in the Lamb when I've had a drink with Bert Penman. Nobody knows who he is or what he's doing in the village. He's not attempted to speak with me. As a consultant, restrictions are placed on me, so I'd need to report any potential crime through the right channels. I can't act on the information myself. On the other hand, walking along the lane and admiring the view isn't a criminal act."

"I moved here looking for a quiet life," said Clemency, "as each day passes, it gets more like Midsomer Murders. I've taken up enough of your time, Mr Freeman. It's time to get my digging done and let you continue your work."

Gus relayed everything Clemency said on Friday morning to Bert; and persuaded Bert to meet Irene North face-to-face to thank him for the produce. He was less successful in getting Bert to accept that the Reverend only wanted advice on her brassicas. Gus decided to bide his time. He could try to mend those fences another day,

"Our mutual friend was in the Lamb last night, nursing a gin and tonic," said Bert.

"Irene North and others from the village have spotted him," said Gus, "Clemency tells me he's keeping an eye on my place."

"What will you do about him, Mr Freeman?" asked Bert.

"I've asked my colleagues at London Road to do a little digging. They'll find out who he is and what game he's playing. Remember my warning to Frank North. Keep well away from him, Bert. He could be dangerous. I can't afford to lose you, and nor can the Reverend. She needs to learn from you yet."

Bert didn't pass comment. He had several more chores to complete before the evening. The two friends passed the time, steadily working their way through the list. Gus decided against a drink in the Lamb as they left the allotment just after eight o'clock.

Gus said goodnight to Bert at the pub door and walked home. The lane was empty.

As he put his key in the door, he heard the phone ringing. He was too tired to rush.

The answerphone had clicked in, and Gus played the message once he got indoors.

"Are you free tomorrow? I'm looking at houses. I'd appreciate the company."

It was Vera Jennings. He called back and arranged for her to collect him at ten o'clock in the morning. Gus stood in the darkened room and watched for movement.

Gus saw nothing untoward, so he drew the curtains, switched on the lights and poured himself a cold beer. He realised how hungry he was and wished he didn't have to cook for himself. With a sigh, he placed the half-empty glass on a side table and headed for the kitchen.

"You picked a pleasant day for it," said Gus as he slipped into the passenger seat of Vera's Alfa Romeo the following morning. Passing clouds now masked the sun that had been so prevalent in the preceding days. The forecast was for showery rain by noon, which threatened to last until nightfall.

"We'll be indoors most of the time," said Vera, "quit moaning."

"Ouch," said Gus, "did someone get out of bed on the wrong side?"

"Only Monty," she replied, "my solicitor says he's arguing over trivial items we thought we settled weeks ago."

"I thought the divorce was amicable. You've been apart for so long; surely Monty didn't still harbour hopes of a reconciliation?"

"No, it's nothing like that. Monty's strapped for cash, as usual. He's looking for any angle he can exploit to screw me for a few thousand pounds to keep him afloat until his next get-rich scheme arrives."

"What does your father think?" asked Gus.

"You've not met him," Vera replied, "if you had, you wouldn't ask. My father would have him horse-whipped and thrown into the arms of his creditors. This rigmarole our solicitors are going through is why he placed financial restraints on our marriage in the first place."

"As long as those restraints hold firm, Monty will have to accept that there's no big payday in the offing. I'm not qualified to give legal advice, but if it were me, I might cut short the process by offering a one-time payment to settle all outstanding and further queries. Monty can take it or leave it. For your sanity, you need to draw a line under the matter and know that he's not knocking on your door every few months with another issue to resolve."

"I'll discuss it with my parents tomorrow at lunch. I don't want to commit too much to pay him off; it will leave me with a tighter budget for my next home. Talking of which, this place on the right is a two-bedroomed townhouse on my list."

As they made a tour of the property with a bright young thing from the estate agency, Gus made two mental notes from his conversation with Vera. She had referred to her father and the fact that he hadn't met him. There was no 'yet' in the comment. Their relationship had a way to run then before she needed to introduce him to her parents. Gus wondered if Vera had even mentioned she was seeing someone. It also appeared he wasn't in her plans for Sunday lunch.

"What do you think, Gus?"

"Very nice," he replied, unsure which aspect of the property was under scrutiny.

"Really? The galley kitchen's far too small, and I'm not too fond of the layout of the second bedroom. Time to drive to my next option."

Gus and Vera spent the rest of the morning and early afternoon moving from two townhouses to a bungalow and from the bungalow to a cottage. The showers had arrived with a vengeance.

"Well, that's five places visited," said Vera as they returned to her rented cottage for a well-earned cup of coffee. "Three are a total write-off, and two are still in the frame. I could be happy in the cottage; that's only a ten-minute walk from work."

"The fuel savings will be significant," said Gus, "and the Green people will applaud your contribution to the cause. It benefits me too because that's one more space in the car park at London Road for my old banger."

"I'll weigh up the pros and cons over the rest of the weekend and make my decision. Are you hungry?"

"I've been in five kitchens and not had a nibble," said Gus, "that's a first. So where do you want to eat? I'm free for the rest of the day if you're going home tomorrow."

"The night too, I hope?" said Vera, "actually, we're not lunching at home. My father has booked a table somewhere."

"I imagine the red carpet is getting an airing as we speak," said Gus, "let's find somewhere to eat before the next shower. We can be back before dark and spend a quiet night indoors."

"Sounds good to me," said Vera.

Gus studied the dark clouds overhead as he drove home on Sunday morning. His Friday fling with Suzie hadn't reached Vera's ears yet. Nevertheless, everything that happened between driving into Devizes for an Indian meal, the quiet evening at the cottage, and overnight cemented his opinion he and Vera were compatible. It was as if they'd known one another for years, not months.

Why was there still a persistent black cloud looming over his Ford Focus this morning? It appeared to be tracking him mile by mile as he headed towards Urchfont. With Vera leaving in an hour to spend the day with her family, Gus was alone.

Gus found that his gardening activities were on hold due to the inclement weather. Maybe he could get a head start on the new case by digging further into the murder file.

As he passed the Lamb and the Community Shop, he remembered his unwanted stalker. There was no sign of strangers in the lane today. He pulled into the driveway of his bungalow and parked the car.

Gus checked his phone. He'd received no alarm from his camera security system to warn him of uninvited guests. All this technology was still new to him. He scolded himself for not realising he could check every few hours to see what his cameras captured. Old habits die hard. He didn't want to get anal about referring to his phone screen every five minutes like the youngsters did these days.

Once inside, he visited the kitchen to see what the system had to tell him. Very little, it transpired. He walked into the lounge and found the last message on his landline was Vera's call from Friday evening. Billy No Mates. Whatever happened to Dorothy? No bugger wanted to talk to him, it appeared.

The next place Gus checked was his fridge-freezer. There were dozens of meals in there that he'd stocked up, thinking they'd be backwards and forwards to Swindon on the Laura Mallinder case for weeks. He closed his eyes and picked one. That was lunch sorted.

As he sat at his kitchen table enjoying a glass of red

wine after his beef bourguignon, he wondered what Terry Davis was up to later. Gus dialled Neil's number. Melody replied.

"Melody, it's Gus Freeman here. How are you keeping?"

"I'm better at this time of the day than I am first thing, thanks for asking. Neil wouldn't bother. You-know-who is here this weekend. He's just as objectionable in the flesh as he is on the end of a telephone line."

"I was hoping to have a word," said Gus, "can Terry tear himself away?"

"Terry's not here. He took Neil out for a lunchtime drink. Neil won't get home until after the football's finished."

"Is Terry staying with you?" asked Gus.

"What do you think? I put my foot down. We had to stay in a hotel when we visited him. He'll get no favours from me. Terry's in a B&B in town."

"Where will they go to watch football? I'll take a spin into Devizes and see if I can catch them. Terry might put a name to a face for me."

"Neil likes the Cavalier out on Eastleigh Road," said Melody, "if you see him, tell him his dinner will be on the table at six."

"In the bin by five past six. OK, Melody, I'll pass on the message. You take care of yourself."

Gus rang off before she could sling more barbed comments Terry's way. He studied what remained in his glass and poured it back into the bottle. Waste not, want not; the ACC would blow a fuse if one of his consultants got nicked for drink-driving.

It was no hardship finding the pub. The Cavalier was one he passed as he drove into Devizes, depending on which route he took. The car park was busy, and empty spaces were relatively small.

Still, another dent in the Ford Focus wouldn't notice. Gus didn't bother looking for Neil's car. He would take a taxi home. Melody may have wanted him to cut out the drinking while she was pregnant, but Terry's visit warranted a free pass.

Gus pushed his way past a noisy crowd in the bar. Nobody faced the barman as every head turned towards the giant screen.

There were twenty minutes left in the televised game. Gus couldn't stand around waiting without a drink. So he ordered a slimline tonic with ice.

"Do you want a straw with that?" sneered the barman.

"A smile's out of the question, I see?" Gus replied.

Neil must have spotted him. He tapped his boss on the shoulder.

"I'll get that, guv," he shouted above the roar. Someone had scored. Gus didn't know who and didn't care either way. "Two more of the same for me and my Dad, Skip."

The barman replenished the empty pint glasses that Neil plonked on the bar. Gus's soft drink arrived without a straw. Neil nodded towards the far corner of the crowded room.

"We're over there, guv. What brings you here?"

"Melody said to be home by six," said Gus, "I wanted a chat with Terry. I need to tap into his vast knowledge of creeps that knew Dominic Culverhouse."

"Melody won't leave it alone, guv. Sit with us and enjoy your drink. The game's nearly over, and this place will be empty within five minutes. You can talk without shouting, and there won't be anyone earwigging at the next table."

Neil was right. The final whistle was equivalent to the

barman calling time. Only a handful of die-hard drinkers remained. They weren't close enough to hear any conversation between the three men seated in the far corner of the bar. Even the barman ignored them as he collected glasses from abandoned tables.

"Afternoon, Freeman. You're roughing it today, then?" said Terry Davis.

"I wanted a word. You remember what happens when a copper needs to rub shoulders with the great unwashed to get information."

"I remember, but you're not a copper any longer. You're a consultant who keeps sticking his nose where it's not wanted. I've warned you about that. Why don't you listen?"

"I listen, Terry, but sometimes you can't turn a blind eye."

"They never charged me with any wrongdoing, Freeman. I travelled here without incident. Nobody was waiting for me at Bristol International on Friday afternoon. Come on, spit it out. You wouldn't have come here unless you wanted something."

"Ten days to a fortnight ago, a guy in his mid-fifties, smart dresser, cultured accent, turned up in the village. I've seen him in the Lamb. Other villagers tell me he's watching my bungalow. I wondered if he might have links to Culverhouse or our new Chief Constable."

Terry Davis shook his head from side to side.

"I told you to stop this consulting lark and stick to growing vegetables. This guy stands six-foot-one or two, yeah? He reminds you of a grey-haired Christopher Lee. You've stirred up a hornet's nest this time, Freeman. That has to be Ricky Gardiner. He's an enforcer."

"I thought he was an ex-copper," said Gus.

"Gardiner's worked both sides for so long I don't expect even he knows which way is up," snorted Terry.

"How does he link to Culverhouse, and why is he called Ricky? It makes him sound like a teenager."

"That rich voice is part of his persona. He's from a council estate in South London. He switches accents as often as Mike Yarwood used to when he was on the telly. Ricky started as a beat copper in the Metropolitan Police in the mid-Eighties. They had a succession of corruption problems and rumours of dirty cops wherever you looked. Gardiner went undercover inside a drug syndicate. He gathered evidence on the corrupt officers every bit as much as he helped to bring down the gang. His back story got tested more than once. I heard they took him to a deserted warehouse, and one of the gang members stuck the barrel of his gun into Gardiner's mouth. He swore blind Gardiner was a copper. Your man laughed in his face. Whoever trained him did their job well. Ricky blagged his way out of that tight corner, and an hour later, he was buying a pint for the gunman in a pub in the East End."

"Did they get enough evidence to arrest the gang?" asked Neil. "What about the officers mixed up in the business?"

"Check it out, son," said Terry, "it went the same way as every other operation with a code name ascribed to it. You win some; you lose some. Gang members at the bottom of the tree got sacrificed. Two or three low-ranking detectives got charged. The ladder got pulled up on both sides of the law, so those at the top escaped punishment."

"You haven't explained the Culverhouse connection," said Gus.

"To get chapter and verse on that, you must dig into the time my ex-guvnor and Sandra Plunkett spent together."

"That's not a likely scenario," said Gus.

"I don't mean he was giving her one," said Terry, "your new Chief Constable bats for the other team. I know that. They were at Bramshill together. The staff college in Hampshire. Neither of us received invitations to attend that place during our careers. You might be lucky to go somewhere like that, Neil. If you keep your nose clean."

"OK," said Gus, "they were on the same senior management training course. When was that exactly? Did something happen during that course that led them to become allies? Why should Gardiner target me on their behalf? What on earth is it they're so desperate to hide?"

"Culverhouse was at Bramshill between 2001 and 2002. I can't be sure of the exact dates. His superiors signed him up for every accelerated promotion course going. He was a rising star."

"I read the file on Sandra Plunkett. She was a Chief Inspector in those days. After the Bramshill sessions, she moved to West Mercia as a Superintendent. They didn't bump into Gardiner then, surely?"

"Never in a million years," said Terry, "that place was well above his pay grade. I'd bet that Ricky was undercover somewhere at that time. Get Neil to chase those bright young things in the Hub to ferret the details of his whereabouts."

"I'll need to carry out any searches myself, Terry. The fewer traces of someone digging into their past, the better. If the shit hits the fan, I don't want Neil or any of my Crime Review Team in the firing line."

"You know you can rely on the three of us to be discreet, guv," said Neil.

"Thanks, Neil," said Gus, "but things could get very nasty. Let me get my head around this. Jump in and correct me if I go astray, Terry. So, it's plausible Culverhouse and Plunkett met for the first time at Bramshill in 2002. Sandra moved to West Mercia in 2003. Culverhouse had recently joined you at the Old Police Station."

"That's right, Phil Hounsell moved to the Serious Crime Agency in London. Dominic Culverhouse took over the reins."

"Since I returned to work, I've learned that you two worked on the Trudi Villiers case in 2003 and the botched investigation into Daphne Tolliver's murder in 2008. Culverhouse left for Portishead in 2013, just before you made a run for sunnier climes."

"That's your interpretation of events, Freeman. I prefer to say I had done enough years in the job to deserve a comfortable and lengthy retirement."

"We must find a joint operation covered by the forces they served with in the months, or years, following their first meeting. Gardiner must have an involvement, too, somehow. Nothing jumps out as being a likely candidate. Can you offer a suggestion, Terry?"

"West Mercia covers Hereford and Worcester," said Neil, "and Avon and Somerset Police are on the other side of the Severn. The two forces are next door to one another. There had to be something they worked on together."

"The timing's wrong, Neil," said Gus.

"Yes, son," said his father, "Culverhouse and I were on the same team until several months before I quit. Sandra Plunkett wasn't with West Mercia in 2013; she moved onward and upward regularly. That's how the real high-flyers do it. They don't stay long enough to make a difference. They only stay long enough to give their superiors the impression they're after their positions, then they get moved on again to become someone else's problem."

"It's a game of pass the parcel, Dad. Is that what you're saying?"

"That's a cynical version of what's happening, Terry," said Gus, "several make a difference with ideas they bring to the top table. I agree that more of them get promoted into a position where they can't do any more harm than they've already inflicted on their colleagues and the public."

"I don't suppose you know where Ms Plunkett was, Freeman?" asked Terry.

"Sandra got promoted to Chief Superintendent within two years of joining West Mercia. The next item might interest you, Terry; you were fortunate to avoid coming into contact with her colleagues. Instead, Sandra went to Hindlip Park, near Worcester, and stayed there until 2011."

"The soft-shoe brigade," said Terry, "as I keep telling you, Freeman, Professional Standards never had a thing on me that stuck. It doesn't surprise me. It's one of the prize spots the high-flyers aim for, that and counter-terrorism. They score heavily with the public when a Chief Constable or Commander gets their name and achievements listed in the media after a major appointment."

Gus allowed himself a brief smile.

"Sandra negotiated her way through the Strategic Command Course in 2009 with flying colours, and when she became an Assistant Chief Constable, it was on her old stamping ground in Staffordshire. She became Head of Counter-Terrorism in June 2011."

"When did she get the top job?" asked Terry.

"Three years later," said Gus, "as Chief Constable for the West Midlands."

"The window is narrowing," said Neil, "if Culverhouse was at Portishead from early 2013, and Plunkett moved eighteen months later, there can't have been many operations where they could have worked together."

"My memory hasn't suffered much damage in the Marbella heat," Terry Davis said. "One thing I know for certain is that Sandra Plunkett and Dominic Culverhouse never came into contact when he and I worked in the same station. He never mentioned her name in my company, and he didn't disappear on an assignment for weeks at a time when I didn't know where he was unless they met up when he flew out to Majorca or the Greek Islands for his summer holidays. Those were the only weeks when we were apart."

"I'm still struggling to place Ricky Gardiner with those two," said Gus, "they seem such an odd group of people. They've got nothing in common."

"Until you find out they have," said Neil.

"If you stay here much longer, your dinner will be in the bin, Neil," said Gus, "I can run you home if you wish. What are your plans, Terry?"

"Don't worry about me, Freeman. I'm out for the duration. I know the decent drinking holes in town. They haven't seen me in five years. I'll enjoy catching up with a few old faces. I won't say which pubs or which faces. One or two of them might have useful information. If you get my drift."

"Kenneth Truelove will find out who your sources are one day," warned Gus, "and they'll not be so keen to lift the phone to contact you after they've had their knuckles rapped."

## About the Author

Ted Tayler is the international bestselling indie author of The Freeman Files and The Phoenix series. Ted lives in the English west country, where his stories are based. He was born in 1945 and has been married to Lynne since 1971. They have three children and four grandchildren.

His thought-provoking mysteries appeal to readers of Sally Rigby, Joy Ellis, Pauline Rowson, and Faith Martin. His action-packed thrillers are a must for fans of Mark Dawson and J. C. Ryan.

Gus Freeman's cold case investigations are carried out with reasoned deduction rather than bursts of frantic action. In each of the twenty-four books, unsolved murder is accompanied by romance, humor, and country life. The core message in the twelve Phoenix novels is that criminals should pay for their crimes. Unfortunately, the current system fails to deliver the correct punishment, so Phoenix helps redress the balance.

# Acknowledgments

The love and support of my family; without them, this would have been impossible.